carly james

A.M. McCoy

COPYRIGHT

contents

CHAPTER 1 – CARLY

His dick grew hard under my ass as I rocked my hips back and forth against it. He groaned and thrust his hips up, grinding against me. I moaned and ran my hands up through my hair, letting it tease his chest, how I knew he liked it.

"That's it, baby." He groaned, fisting his hands along the back of the couch like he was aching to touch me, but wouldn't.

He couldn't.

"You're so hard, Kenny." I purred.

"All for you, Sunny." He said, as I looked over my shoulder and he licked his lips.

I turned around to face him and straddled him, pressing my chest into his face. He buried his face between my breasts and sighed as I ran my fingernails over his scalp. "You turn me on so much," I whispered in his ear as I ran my crotch over his dick again through his pants. I had to admit, he was packing. And part of me could use a good dick like his for a while.

My blood hummed with arousal the way it always did when I was working, but it wasn't as strong tonight. And it had been getting weaker every night for the last few weeks, even as I tried to ignore the nagging feeling in my brain telling me I was burning out.

"Take your top off." He commanded, taking out two-hundred-dollar bills and sliding them into my bikini bottom strap.

I leaned back, put my hands on his knees, and rocked my hips front to back, drawing a moan from his lips. He was attractive for a man in his forties. His dark blonde hair and blue eyes paired well with his clean-shave and clean scent.

He was clean.

Which, in my profession, was a blessing.

"Give me two hundred more and I'll let you take it off for me." I winked at him and twisted around, knowing he'd jump at the chance to strip me.

I felt him slide more bills in the string of my bottoms and then he leaned forward, wrapping his arms around me, and pulling on the tie at my back and then the one at my neck, taking my top off and twirling the strings around his fingers as I turned back to face him.

"Fuck, you've got the sexiest tits in here, Sunny." He said, dropping his hands to my thighs and squeezing before putting them back on the back of the couch. He knew better and he knew he was only allowed to touch me when I told him he could.

That's why he was one of my favorite customers. He was a rule follower, clean, good looking, and a few times I'd allowed him too, he'd gotten me off in the VIP room.

I ground on him, letting him get up close and personal with my bare tits for a few minutes before Shawn, my bouncer, stepped into the room and called for the end of the dance. Kenny's time was up, and even though I liked him, I was anxious to get out of the small dark room.

He handed me a couple more hundred for my time. "See you soon, Kenny." I purred and kissed his cheek before putting my top back on and sliding my white satin kimono back on and walking out.

I stopped in the dressing room and stored my money, locked away in a locker since I no longer trusted anyone after a couple of girls tried to steal from me a few months ago. Then I went back out into the club and straight to the bar for a drink. I looked out over the club, taking in how packed it was for a Wednesday night, when I caught a pair of bottomless black eyes staring at me through the crowd from along the wall in the darkness.

Jed.

I tried and failed to hide the shy smile that crawled up my lips as I saw him staring at me, turning my attention back to the bartender who handed me my vodka soda with a wink. I tipped her and then turned on my seat again and let my eyes slide over the club, landing on the dark and mysterious man in the corner. My best friend's bodyguard was so intimidating and yet tonight he looked so relaxed in the large chair with his ankle over one knee and his fingers running over his lips as he stared at me.

He was a giant, towering over nearly everyone else in the room when he stood, and he was so muscular, there wasn't a shirt he wore that wasn't stretched around his biceps and powerful chest. He was covered in tattoos too, which was one of my biggest weaknesses with men, and his ink downright fascinated me.

His dark hair was cut short on his scalp, and paired with his dark eyes and black ink, he always looked brooding, even when he was smiling and joking with Elora while he worked.

Elora was my best friend, and the Queen of Shadeport, recently married to her soulmate Ryker Lawson. Ryker was known for his ruthless and heavy hand when ruling his city, and Jed was one of his most trusted men, one of the few that he tasked with protecting his wife and his whole world.

I'd known of Jed for years before Elora came back to Ryker and got him as her bodyguard, but I'd never dared get close to him because of how intimidating he was. But over the last few months, I spent countless hours with Ellie at her house, sunbathing and relaxing, and Jed was always near, guarding the Queen.

A couple of months ago, he'd asked me out on a date after he got pulled into a rouse to rile up one of Ryker's men, thanks to Ellie. Frankie, a guy I sometimes hooked up with, had rubbed her wrong, treating her like shit really, and she'd used my obvious attraction to Jed against him.

But we'd never gotten the chance to go out because Ellie had been kidnapped and hurt and since then, Ryker kept her under lock and key, which kept Jed at work. All the time.

But here he sat tonight, without Ellie or Ryker near, staring at me.

I drank a large amount of my drink, fighting to look composed and in charge, and then slid off my stool and slowly strolled across the club towards him.

I stopped and talked to many people on the way, refusing requests for dances left and right, which was stupid because that's what I was here to do. But a part of me didn't want Jed to see me grinding on anyone else right now. My skin burned and tingled as I neared him, like his gaze alone was caressing me on my way to him.

When I was a couple of feet away from him, I looked him straight in the eye and smiled seductively and stopped at his feet. "Well, look who was let out tonight." I joked.

Dropping his fingers away from his lips, he grinned at me seductively, and I licked mine, watching his eyes drop to them before snapping back to my eyes. He was the only man in the world who maintained eye contact with me in the club, even when I was dressed in so little.

He'd seen my bare chest a few times now, seeing as how I always sunbathed topless, and he was always around the pool deck at Ellie's, but he was respectful about it. He never treated me like a stripper.

"I got a night off for once." He said, his deep voice rumbling across the space to me. I pressed my thighs together, trying to act like it didn't affect me. But there was no hiding anything from this man, he was trained to be preceptive and his eyes dilated as he watched my movements.

"And you decided to come to your boss's club in your free time?" I joked, walking around his legs, and sitting down in the chair next to him, crossing my legs and pulling my kimono open to show him my body. But he didn't look down at it, he just kept his eyes on mine.

"I decided to come to *you* in my free time." He said straight. And his bluntness made me blush.

I was a high-paid stripper for fuck's sake, I should not blush like this. I brought my glass up to my lips and took a slow drink and he finally let his eyes drop to my lips, watching the movement.

"Why would you want to do that?"

"Because I owe you a date, and I wanted to ask you to give me another chance to take you out."

I rolled my lips, fighting the smile that pulled them again. "You want to take me out still? I thought that whole thing was just Ellie's ploy to make Frankie jealous."

"That may be how it started, but it's far from the only reason I'd be interested in it." He spun his chair towards me and uncrossed his feet, dropping them both to the floor with a wide stance, leaning forward on his knees. His nearness was overwhelming; I could smell his aftershave, so I closed my eyes, inhaled deeply, and didn't worry about him noticing. He smelled fucking delicious. "Will you go out with me, Carly?" He asked, dropping his voice low, so no one else heard my real name, while also refusing to call me by my stage name.

"I'd love to," I said, uncrossing my own legs and leaning forward until our faces were less than a foot apart. "When?"

"When is your next night off?" He asked, and I loved his confidence. It was dominant and sure without being pushy and suffocating.

"Whenever I want it to be." He raised his eyebrow at me, and I elaborated, "I only work when I want to. I make my own schedule to fit my needs."

He smirked and nodded at me. "How about tomorrow then?"

Now it was my turn to raise my eyebrows at him. "You get two nights off in a row?" I asked, not even trying to hide my surprise. "Is Ryker ever going to let my best friend out of the house again?"

He smirked but I didn't miss the grief that flashed in his eyes at the mention of the fallout of her attack. Ellie had told me Jed took it personally that she was kidnapped, even though he'd been out on a job with Ryker at the time. He was her bodyguard, and he'd failed to guard her, and she'd nearly been killed because of it. I reached forward and put my hand on his inner forearm and tilted my head.

"It's not your fault she was hurt, Jed." My voice was soft and gentle, and his eyes flashed with something else entirely before he covered it up. He put his large, like really fucking large hand over mine on his arm and stared deep into my eyes.

"Regardless, she was hurt, and I should have protected her. Ryker is right to keep her under lock and key to keep her safe."

"Is there any point in being safe if you're miserable?" I asked, challenging him.

"She's miserable?"

"She isn't happy."

He pondered that for a moment and then he leaned back. "I'm here asking you out, and you're talking about another woman."

I chuckled and leaned closer, "Ellie isn't another woman, she's the only woman in the world that I'd never feel jealousy towards for taking my man's time." I said straight and to the point. His eyes flared again, and he caught my point. "She's the only person in the world who genuinely loves me, Jed. She's family, and I love her. Don't ever worry about trying to keep your two world separate for me."

"You're incredible. You do know that don't you?" His features darkened.

"I've been told a time or two," I said, leaning back and reluctantly letting my hand slide from his arm. "Doesn't mean I don't like hearing it now and then though." I winked at him. Trying to lighten the mood again.

He laughed and I was sucked into another world as the dark and dangerous man dropped the usually somber look over his face and smiled at me. His laugh was warm, and he almost looked young and carefree when he did it. "Ryker and Ellie are going away for a week or two to relax. They're going full seclusion, so we're off work for a few days while they're gone."

This was the first time I'd heard of it, but that didn't surprise me, Ryker was always surprising Ellie with things like this to pamper her, especially lately.

"Well then, I'm going to take as much of your free time as you'll give me." I flirted.

"It's yours. All of it." He joked and I once again was speechless at how attractive he was.

"Sunny." A voice called off to the side and I turned to see Theo, the house host, calling me over to him. Which meant he had someone who wanted a private dance in the VIP room for me.

I sighed and felt my shoulders drop slightly before I stiffened my spine and turned back to Jed. He watched me with an intense stare, sensing my hesitation. "Carly–" He started, tilting his head to the side, but I held my hand up, stopping him.

"Don't," I said easily. "Elora is the only one who gets to tell me I'm worth more than this."

"She's right." He said easily. "Why don't you believe her?"

"Because if I believe her, then I'll hate myself for doing this for a living."

He didn't say anything else but stood up and held his hand out for me like a gentleman. I slid my fingers over his rough palm and bit my lip, letting him pull me to my feet close to his large chest. I tilted my head way back to look up at him as he held onto my hand, running his thumb over my knuckles. "Just say the word, Carly, and I'll take you far, far away from this place. Because you *are* worth so much fucking more than this."

I sighed and smiled up at him sadly. Not offering anything else, because I didn't have anything else to say that wouldn't make me sad. I leaned up on my toes and he leaned down so I could press my lips to his cheek. He turned his head slightly and took a deep breath against my ear before his rumbling voice tickled every nerve in my body. "I'll pick you up at your apartment tomorrow at six." He pulled back and stood up to his full height.

"I can't wait," I said honestly and then walked away towards Theo, steeling my body and my mind away from how Jed made me feel and focused on my job.

I loved my job.

I loved my job.

I loved my job.

Chapter 2 – Jed

As soon as I pulled up next to the garage, I could tell something was wrong. It was a sense, something I felt in the air. I walked through the garage and into the security room, where multiple crew members stood. The door into the kitchen was open, and the sound of glass breaking rang out through the room. A couple of the guys were grimacing, and Razz was taking cash from some of them.

"What the fuck is going on?" I snapped. The lower guards flattened themselves against the walls and got out of my way as I walked deeper into the room.

Razz grimaced at me and hid the cash, but I didn't care that he was taking bets from the guys, but I wanted to know what he was taking bets on.

He nodded towards the racket still coming from the kitchen and just said, "He fucked something up. I'm not sure what, but he *fucked* up."

I pushed past the last few guys and walked into the kitchen and ducked as a glass soared past my head and shattered against the wall. Elora stood in the kitchen, in a ruby red satin robe with her dark hair piled high on top of her head and murderous rage in her eyes.

"Did you know?" She screamed at me, pointing her finger at me angrily. "Did you cover for him?"

"Know what?" I asked, trying to keep my rage in check after having a glass thrown at my head.

"That he's running around on me!" She screamed. "We've only been married six months and he's already bored and fucking some slut."

"Stop it. You know that's not true." I ordered her, stepping over the line as her bodyguard and friend and into Ryker's dominating role. I needed to use that power to settle her, and quickly. I only spoke to her like that when she needed to be put in check the way Ry would. And right now, she was out of control with rage, and it wasn't good for her in her condition.

"Fuck you, Jed! You had to have known, you know everything. The least you could have done is told me I'm going to be a single mother!" Her hands dropped to her growing baby bump as her face screwed up in agony.

"You need to calm down right now, Elora. Screaming like that isn't good for you or the baby." I walked towards her, avoiding the numerous glasses shattered around the room.

She held her hand up to stop me from getting closer to her, and it was then that I saw the tears pooling in her eyes. "Don't touch me, Jed. I'll lose my fucking mind if you're nice to me right now." She stopped screaming, but now her voice was calm, which somehow hurt more to listen to.

Razz stepped out of the security room and stood in the doorway, and I turned to him. "Where's Ryker?"

"At Erotiq, with Zeke." He said, not offering any other information as his eyes jumped to Elora and then back to me.

It was almost midnight, and I'd just gotten back from Lux, where I asked Carly out on a date. Ryker was hardly out this late anymore, since marrying Elora and even less since she found out four months ago that she was pregnant.

"Probably fucking his side piece!" Elora sneered and moved to grab another glass. She was irate and not paying attention and stepped directly on a piece of broken glass with her bare foot in her rush to cause more destruction.

"Shit." I cursed.

She gasped, and her leg gave out as she started to fall to the ground. I rushed forward and slid my arms around her, catching her before she fell onto the pile of glass, and picked her up as she started crying.

"Shh." I tried soothing her as I carried her over to the island and set her down on it, turning her so her feet were in the empty prep sink. "Calm down, Elora, think of the baby."

She covered her mouth with her wrist as her eyes closed in anguish. "That's all I'm thinking about, Jed." She cried. Her hand fell to her stomach, and she hissed as I lifted her foot to look at the cut on the bottom.

"What do you need?" Razz asked, walking further into the kitchen, looking a bit green in the gills, knowing Ryker was going to lose his shit when he found out she was hurt. I grabbed my phone out of my pocket and dialed Zeke. "First aid kit," I said to Razz, and he turned and ran to grab the suture kit from the security room. We were used to patching ourselves up after getting hurt but I'd never had to do it for her before.

"What?" Zeke snapped as he answered. "You're supposed to be taking the night off."

"Something happened at the house, Elora is in a rage, and she cut her foot open on broken glass."

"Fuck." He cussed and I heard him talking to someone, and a second later Ryker was on the phone, and I grimaced as his irate voice cut through the phone.

"What happened?" He demanded. "Put her on the phone."

I turned the water on, pinning the phone between my ear and shoulder, and tried to rinse away some of the blood to see the cut. There was a ton of fucking blood.

"She's destroyed the kitchen and cut her foot. She's bleeding badly and I don't know if I can get it to stop. You need to get home." I snapped back at him. Angry that something had happened while I wasn't here setting her off and distressing her this badly.

She cried as the water hit the cut, and he set off a slew of curses in my ear. I held the phone out to her, but she pushed my hand away. "I don't want to talk to him." She cried.

I tucked the phone back to my shoulder, "Oh yeah, and she's convinced you're fucking around on her and that she's going to be a single mom. That's what started this all."

"Fucking hell." He groaned, "I'll be home in two minutes." And hung up.

I threw my phone down on the counter and looked over at her face. She was pale, and tears stained her cheeks. "Lay back before you pass out," I said, but she ignored me.

Margaret, the housekeeper, came up the stairs from her apartment, wrapping a heavy robe over her body, and saw the chaos and ran forward. "Oh my God, Mrs. Lawson." She cried. "What happened?"

"Get her to lay down, she's going to faint." I snapped, and Margaret grabbed Ellie's shoulders and pulled her down to the counter and used her arm to cushion her head.

I finally got the spray in the right direction and could see the cut, the problem was, there was a giant piece of glass in the bottom of her foot still. Her pained expression met my gaze as I looked at her. "There's a piece of glass in there that I have to get out so I can get it to stop bleeding." Her face paled even more, and she closed her eyes. "It's going to hurt like hell, Ellie." I said, softening my voice, trying to comfort her.

She set her face and swallowed down her fear. "Just do it." She said, gritting her teeth and taking a deep breath.

Razz ran back in with the kit and opened it up, looking at her foot. "Fuck, that's a big piece of glass." He said, and Ellie groaned.

"Shut up, idiot." I snapped. "Give me the clamps. And get a lot of gauze and a pressure dressing ready." I ordered, and he did exactly as I said.

Margaret grabbed some towels from the drawer and put them under Ellie's head and then took her hand tight between both of hers. "What can I do to help?" She asked.

I shrugged, grabbing for the clamps, and looked back at Ellie. "Hold her down and keep her from falling off the counter." Margaret nodded and placed herself next to me at Ellie's side, using her body to keep Ellie from falling to the floor if need be. I kept my eyes on Ellie as Razz laid everything out. "I can wait for Ryker if you want." I knew she was mad at him, obviously, but I also knew she was in pain and scared.

Just then the front door slammed open, and Ryker yelled out, "Ellie!"

"Kitchen!" I yelled back, and a second later, Ry and Zeke barreled into the kitchen. His face screwed up when he saw her lying on the counter with my hands covered in blood. Zeke looked around the kitchen, shaking his head.

"What the fuck happened?" Zeke snapped, but I shrugged my shoulders, still unsure.

"I have to pull the glass out," I said to Ryker as he came to stand next to me as he grabbed Ellie's hand, and kissed her forehead. Which caused her to cry harder. He looked down at her foot and cursed.

"Go ahead. I got her."

Turning my attention to her foot, I knew he would control her from thrashing around and hurting herself anymore. I took the clamps and carefully grabbed onto the glass and made sure I had a good grip and pulled it out as straight and as quickly as I could, hating the cries that tore from her lips as I did. When it was out, I threw it down on the counter and ran the water over the cut, which was bleeding even harder now, to see if there was any more glass in there.

It looked clear, and I was praying to god I hadn't missed any before I had to wrap her up to stop the blood flow. "Gauze," I said, and Razz handed me the gauze he already had laid out, and I pressed it to the bottom of her foot, drawing another cry from her. I took the roll of dressing and started wrapping it tightly around her foot to stop the bleeding.

When I was confident it was tight enough; I tied it off and lifted her foot into the air higher, using gravity to help stop the bleeding, and took a deep breath for the first time since I got out of my car.

"Doc's on her way," Zeke said, nodding to Ryker, who slid his hands under Elora's body and lifted her off the counter. She dashed at her eyes and curled into him. I let her foot go and he carried her out of the kitchen and upstairs to their bedroom.

I hit the handle on the sink and rinsed the blood off my hands and arms and cursed under my breath at the whole situation. I hated seeing either Elora or Ryker in pain, but I hated even more not knowing what started it all to begin with.

Zeke leaned next to me as I cleaned up the sink while I barely contained my rage. "Why didn't you call me before you left?" I snapped at him.

He raised his eyebrows at me briefly as I scrubbed her blood away. "Because Razz had it handled."

I exploded, "You call this handled?" I threw the rags in the trash and turned on him. "If you and Ryker leave, I'm on her. You fucking know that! I should have been here; I could have avoided all of this!" I flung my arms out at the destroyed kitchen. He watched me struggle to keep it together but remained silent. "I should have been here," I said again, quieter this time.

"You can't be here all the time, Jed." He said with his calm authority, and I shook my head, not buying it. "Why did she go berserk?"

"I don't have a fucking clue! I walked in on the guards cowering in the security room and Razz taking cash for bets as she unleashed her fury on the glasses cabinet. The second I walked into the kitchen, she chucked a glass at me and accused me of knowing Ryker was fucking around on her and not telling her; covering for him, she said."

His scowl darkened. "He's not cheating on her."

Throwing my arms out in frustration I replied, "I know that! I told her that, but she was so enraged she wasn't hearing logic, and then the next second she stepped on the glass, and it didn't matter anymore."

"I'll find out what happened to make her think that, if someone is spinning lies and rumors and upset her, he'll want them to burn for it."

"Him and I both," I said, leaning on the counter and rubbing my hand over my face. A long silence filled the room until he broke it.

"So—" He said, eyeing me with a bit of a smirk on his face. "How'd your night go, what did she say?"

I groaned and blew a giant breath out, crossing my arms over my chest, regretting telling him anything about my plans for tonight. "She said yes. We were going to try again tomorrow night but—" I paused and shrugged. "They're obviously not going to Cabo now."

"Don't you dare cancel on that girl twice," Zeke said, shaking his head. "We don't know if they're going or not, and even if they stay here, we can manage without you."

"What's the point?" I asked, getting frustrated at the feeling of being split in two directions. "Even if you cover for me tomorrow, chances are something else will come up the next time and the time after that, and it's not fair to Carly to give her only what little is left of me outside of this place."

"So, you're going to what? Stay single and fuck your way through casual one-night stands for the rest of forever?"

I smirked and looked at him. "It's working pretty well for you, isn't it?"

He punched me in the arm and stood up off the counter. "We're different Jed, I'm okay being alone. You long to be with someone. And there's nothing wrong with that. So go out on your date tomorrow night and don't stress about anything after that." He started walking out but turned back to me, "Besides, I have the feeling that girl is the perfect one for you to have in your life while you balance these two worlds."

With that, he left the kitchen and I heard him escorting the doctor upstairs a couple of minutes later.

I checked on the guards who were actually on duty and then headed back out of the house to the barracks between the house and the shop and went straight to my room. Living on the property never bothered me before. It kept me close and available twenty-four seven, which was a luxury because Ryker only allowed his most trusted crew members to live on his property and it had helped me climb quickly through the ranks. But standing inside my little studio apartment in a giant concrete building behind his mansion left me feeling lacking for the first time since I joined his crew when I was sixteen.

I'd been a scraggly foster kid who didn't have shit going for me when I got busted stealing food from a corner shop in the Shadeport territory. Ryker and Gavin weren't kings of the land yet at that point, but they were climbing the ranks under the old king, Tate Benson.

Tate was calm compared to Ryker, but he was still known to rule with an iron fist and the orders had been clear.

Make an example out of me for stealing like some medieval jester court show, and Gavin had shown up to do it with Ryker in tow. I remember seeing them come for me, with a calm sort of temperament, and instead of fearing them, I envied them.

They were only six years older than me, and instead of running around the streets eating out of dumpsters and fighting off old homeless douchebags who constantly tried to get the upper hand on me, they ran this shit. Because they belonged to something.

Ryker had been there for blood, the task at hand was simple to him. But Gavin had seen something inside of my eyes, that he said called to him. He told me he could tell I was loyal and fearless, even staring into the eyes of Tate Benson's most feared up-and-coming enforcers. So, he gave me a chance.

One shot.

Fuck it up and pay the ultimate price for two wrongs.

Get it right and earn a spot on the Shadeport Crew and in a family. And I'd clawed my way out of the streets and into something I was proud of every single day since then.

But now, this family didn't seem to hold everything I'd ever wanted anymore. Something was missing and I'd been longing to fill that void for a while now but wasn't sure what it was. Until I met Carly.

And now I was all sorts of fucked up in the head over my duty to the family that saved my life, and my desires and needs to have something more.

I stripped my shirt off over my head and walked into my bathroom. It was small and simple, but it was mine.

I'd earned it.

Zeke and I were the only ones who lived in the barracks full-time. There were a few bunk houses on the property that men would sleep in when they were on a job or unable to make it home for whatever reason, but none of them lived here.

I shook the melancholy feeling from my gut and turned on the shower. Stripping down and stepping under the hot spray as I let the steam work on the tense muscles in my shoulders. As I stood there, I thought about my date tomorrow night with Carly and what I was going to do with her, and my body started stirring as the memories of how sexy she looked tonight invaded my brain.

She was wearing that long white robe that made her look angelic with her light blonde hair and glowing blue eyes. But the white set she wore underneath it, stole the show.

I'd seen her topless a handful of times both at the club and here at the house, when she'd come hang out with Elora. And the more times I saw her, either dressed or undressed, the harder it got for me to keep my eyes locked on hers and my hands to myself.

And it was even harder because I knew she was attracted to me; she was one of those girls that was unable to hide much from their faces when they weren't on guard. And more than once I'd caught her biting her lip or running her hands up and down her thighs as she watched me from her lounger at the pool.

Then there was that time at Lux when I'd got sucked in by Elora to stay and enjoy the services the club provided.

Elora had felt empowered in her new role as Queen of Shadeport and had begged me to let her stay at the strip club after talking with Carly. And I'd allowed it because, for the most part, I could control what went on there, being that it was Ryker's club to begin with.

But what I couldn't control was how fucking sexy Carly had looked in a similar white piece of lingerie as she climbed up on Ellie's lap and gave her a lap dance. Or the way she's taken her top off and placed my hand on her bare breast, squeezing her flesh with my hand as she teased Ellie's shyness.

I couldn't control how fucking hard I'd gotten as she rocked her hips back and forth while she watched me. The girl who had been dancing on me knew my body wasn't reacting to her and instead was reacting to the show Carly was putting on next to us. But she'd been a good sport about it and was more than happy to let me watch Carly while she rubbed me off.

My cock continued to grow under the warm water as I remembered the feel of her breast in my hand and the way her pupils dilated as she rode Elora but watched me.

"Fucking hell." I groaned and soaped up my palm and pumped my cock, leaning forward and resting my forearm on the wall as I spread my legs wide and jerked off thinking of the sexy blonde that seemed to keep my attention regardless of who else was around.

She smelled like vanilla tonight when she leaned forward and challenged me with her sexy legs crossed and robe open, showing me everything I wanted to see but wouldn't let myself look at.

Well, almost everything I wanted to see. I wanted to see her naked and laid out in my bed, legs spread with her blonde hair fanned out over my pillow as I fucked her into orgasm after orgasm. I wanted to worship her body and give her back even an ounce of the pleasure she gave to everyone else.

My balls were tight, and the base of my spine tingled as I pushed myself closer to my orgasm, fantasizing about what she would sound like when she was underneath me. She was tiny, hardly over five feet tall without her heels on, and yet I knew she'd match me thrust for thrust when I made her mine.

"Yes." I hissed as I imagined sliding into her body for the first time, stretching her out around my cock as she looked up at me. Her pretty lips would part as she gasped and moaned my name while I kissed her neck and held her hands above her head, holding her in place to take everything I had to give to her.

"Fuck." I growled as I started coming, shooting rope after rope of come out of my cock and onto the floor of my shower as my skin tingled and my muscles cramped.

Jesus Christ that was a giant orgasm.

If that was any indication of what it would feel like to have her, I was going to need to up my dick game, or I'd embarrass myself.

CHAPTER 3 – Carly

I t was an ungodly hour in the morning, and my phone was ringing off the hook. I groaned, rolling over and slapping the end table where my phone sat charging, trying to get it to shut up. The ringing stopped, and I sank back down into my bed and pulled the covers over my head, shutting out the light. I hadn't gotten home until three am and judging by the light coming in around my black-out curtains; it was still too fucking early for me to function.

The ringing started again, and I threw my blankets off my face and grabbed my phone, bringing it to my ear without looking at it. "If you're calling to tell me about my car's extended warranty, I'm going to find you and murder you with a spoon and a wineglass."

My best friend's chuckle sounded through the phone, "What's the wine glass for?"

"To catch all of your blood so I can drink it when you're dead." I deadpanned.

"You're such a weirdo." Ellie cackled. "I was just calling to tell you we're going to Cabo for a week or two in a couple of hours, and I won't be around. Unless of course, Ryker is just using this all as a ploy to take me somewhere and kill me for being bat shit fucking crazy because of all of these pregnancy hormones that are making me a walking lunatic. In that case, it was nice knowing you, and I left all of my Prada and Louis to you in my Will."

Elora's dark, dry humor was always my favorite part of her, even if it was way too early in the morning for me to follow her train of thought. "Can I have the crown too?" I asked, and she scoffed, like that was the most offensive part of this conversation. "Cabo? That sounds amazing. You could have told me yesterday when we videoed. But anyway, what did my baby nephew make you do this time?"

She didn't know if it was a boy or a girl yet, but I was putting my bet on a boy because she was glowing and completely perfect other than crazy emotions. I'd read somewhere that girl's made you break out and puke for months.

"Uh well, you know, nothing out of the ordinary for the last few months. Except I got a phone call from a woman confirming a hotel room for this trip and my pregnancy ears didn't hear the words Cabo and resort, and instead just heard that he was booked for a massage with a woman named Magdalena at a place called Lovers Paradise." I groaned, knowing exactly what conclusions she had come to from that. "And then I went completely crazy, breaking glasses all over the kitchen and cutting my foot to pieces and nearly bled to death in my kitchen sink before he got home cand explained."

I bolted upright, "Elora!" I snapped. "Are you okay? Why didn't you call me? When did this happen?"

I swung my feet over the side of my bed and put my phone on speaker as I started getting dressed.

"I'm fine." She sighed, and I could hear the embarrassment in her voice and felt for her. This pregnancy was waging war on her emotions and feelings, and she had called me crying nearly every single day during the first few months, but it had started leveling out recently. "I can't walk which is going to make Cabo interesting, but let's be honest, Ryker wasn't surprising me with a trip to paradise so I could walk around on the beach all day."

I snorted as I slid a sundress on with a pair of panties and clipped my hair up in a tortoise clip and grabbed my phone, heading for my front door. "No, he's planning on keeping you completely horizontal the entire week."

"Exactly." She said, and I could hear the lightness coming back to her voice. "I think Jed hates me too. I've been avoiding him all morning."

"Why would he hate you?" I asked, grabbing a bottle of water and a granola bar on my way out my front door.

"Because I may or may not have thrown a glass at his face when he walked in the door last night in the middle of my rage-induced rampage to redecorate the kitchen. And then I blamed him for not telling me about Ryker's lover and all sorts of other cringy things."

I chuckled riding the elevator down, listening to her go on and on about how she was so sure Ryker was cheating on her because of her changing body and crazy emotions. But I knew he'd never dare, he worshipped her in a way that made me green with envy.

I hailed a taxi and muted the phone as I told them the address and then went back to my conversation. "Ellie, Ryker loves you more than this entire world. He'd burn the whole thing to the ground for you; there's no way he'd step out. And I know the logical part of your brain knew that, even at the height of your rage. Why didn't you just calm down and think about it?"

"I don't know, I guess I'm still just waiting for the other shoe to fall. Always waiting for someone to rip this fantasy world away from me and say 'gotcha!' before I go back to being a waitress at a burlesque bar trying to decide between buying tampons and eating."

I groaned as I remembered how hard Ellie's life had been a year ago. She struggled, forcing herself to live through so much pain because she was sure she was going to die before she ever got to her golden years. I offered left and right to help her with money and food and a place to live over the years of our friendship, but she had always refused. She was confident that nothing good ever happened to her, and that anyone associated with her was going to be affected negatively by just being near her. So, she'd kept herself at arm's reach from everyone in her life, struggling through miserably.

My heart ached for her; I knew how much this lack of control over her feelings was weighing on her.

"You'd never go back to worrying about that, I'd take care of you," I said confidently.

"Yeah, and I'd have no choice but to come work with you at Lux, big flappy stretched-out belly sagging in everyone's face as I fell off the stage in my heels." She snorted, but I couldn't muster the energy to laugh at it. My recent disdain for dancing had become stronger in the daylight lately, and right now I almost loathed my profession. "Hey, where'd you go all of a sudden?" She asked quietly, sensing my mood.

We pulled up outside the gates of East Valley and I gave the guard my name, and he passed us through. "Nowhere. Can I call you back in a minute?" I asked.

"Sure." She said softly, "No problem." I imagined her fear of rejection blooming even more as I hurried to get off the phone with her, but that was why I was pulling up at her house as I did it.

"I'll talk to you in a few minutes, I promise," I said confidently, and she sighed and hung up.

I paid for the cab and got out at the front door of Ryker and Elora's mansion, and before I could even knock on the door, Zeke Evans opened it and eyed me. "Good morning, Ms. James." He said speculatively. "Are you here to see Elora or Jed?" His lips turned up a bit on the edges as I cocked my head and rolled my eyes.

"Why didn't anyone call me last night?" I got right to business and walked in, stepping around his large and intimidating body. He wasn't as big as Jed, but somehow, he was even scarier because I wasn't attracted to him like I was to Jed. Over the last year of Ellie living here, I'd gotten over my fear of the man, but he still liked to try to intimidate me for fun.

"Because we had it handled."

I rolled my eyes at him and went to ask where Ellie was when Jed walked down the hallway from the offices and anything I was about to say dried up on my tongue.

God, the man was incredible to look at.

He wore his usual black dress slacks, but instead of a suit jacket to match it, he wore a tight white t-shirt that hugged every single ridge and bump on his body. His eyebrows dropped low over his eyes as he saw me and walked towards me. "What are you doing here, Carly?" He asked, and the ice in his voice caught me off guard.

"Uh—" I started and licked my dry lips as I tried to ignore the way his tone and look on his face made me feel small and unwanted. "Ellie called me. I wanted to check on her."

"She's fine." He said aggressively, and I stepped back away from him, involuntarily.

"Okay, well she told me she's avoiding you so let's be honest, you have no actual idea how she is right now and I'm going to check on her regardless of what you think," I said back, trying to keep the bite back out of it, but failed.

I turned to Zeke, "Where is she?"

He eyed me but turned his brutal gaze over my shoulder to Jed and nodded to the stairs, "In her room. Go on up."

"Thanks," I said, putting my hand on his arm as I passed. I was on the bottom step when Jed called my name.

"Carly." His tone was lighter and almost tired sounding as I slowly turned back to him. He walked forward until he stood in front of me, and Zeke walked away down the hallway as I looked up into his eyes, "I'm sorry. I'm on edge, and it wasn't fair of me to speak to you that way."

"Why are you on edge?" I asked, leaning against the banister as I tried to crack the code to get into his head.

He held my gaze for a long time and then sighed. "Because I should have been here, she wouldn't have hurt herself if I'd been here to calm her down."

I watched the grief in his eyes, and it matched the look that passed in his eyes last night at Lux when we talked about her kidnapping. "You care for her," I said softly.

He dropped my gaze and clenched his jaw. "Not romantically. I just—she trusts me." He paused. "She doesn't let anyone take care of her, you know that, but for some reason, she lets me. Just like she lets you. And I hate when I can't do that." He sighed again, "And now you probably think I'm incapable of giving you my attention because of her." He looked pained.

I wasn't jealous, though a part of me knew if it were any other woman in the world, I would be. I looked around the empty foyer quickly and then gently put my hand on the side of his face, drawing his eyes back to mine.

For the first time since I walked into the house this morning, a fire burned in his eyes as he looked at me. He stepped closer to me as I slid my fingers around the back of his neck and pulled his head down to mine. I paused with his face an inch away from mine.

"I love Elora, and I feel only relief that you care for her as much as I do. She deserves to be cared for, Jed. What I worry about is that you won't allow yourself to give me or any other woman your attention romantically because of your sense of duty to her and Ryker."

"I want to." He said softly. "I like you."

I smiled and took a deep breath of his scent and leaned even closer. "I like you too. And I'm willing to be patient with you while you figure it all out."

"Jed." Ryker bellowed from somewhere deep in the house, and he groaned. He turned his face until his lips touched the inside of my wrist and he kissed my sensitive skin there.

"Until later." He said softly and then pulled away, walking towards the back of the house, leaving me panting and breathless.

"Holy fuck." A voice hissed from above me. I snapped my head around to look at the top of the stairs to where Ellie leaned against the wall, hidden for the most part but visible to me now that I'd heard her. "Lucy, you've got some explaining to do." She said in an impersonation of Ricky Riccardo as I ran up the stairs to her, unable to wipe the stupid grin on my face.

At least I hadn't been able to until I saw her leaning on the wall for support with her foot bandaged and her cute little bump stretching out her tight shirt.

"Jesus! Did you cut your entire foot off?" I asked, taking in the bandage from her toes to her ankle.

She rolled her eyes at me and held her arms open, and I walked straight into them and hugged her tight. "I didn't call you, so you'd come right over, Carly. I just wanted to tell you about Cabo."

"I know, and I just wanted to give you a hug and make sure you were okay."

She pulled back and limped back towards her bedroom as I put her arm over my shoulder and helped her. "I'm fine. My ego and pride are hurt way more than my foot is." When we got into her room, she shut the door behind us and turned on me. "But enough about me, what the fuck was that with Jed on the stairs?"

She nearly vibrated with excitement as she threw herself down on the bed and pulled me in next to her. I laid my head back against the headboard and held her hand as I replayed how it felt to be so close to him.

"I have a date with him tonight."

She gasped, "What! When did that happen?"

"Last night. He came to Lux and asked me on a date. A redo of the one we'd kind of planned before but never got around to doing."

"The one from before I was—" She trailed off as darkness clouded her eyes. "Well," She shook her head and snapped out of it. "What are you doing? Where are you going?"

"I don't know, he didn't say. He just told me he'd pick me up at my place tonight at six."

"What was all that you said about me and you and attention, then?"

I didn't know what to say to her, not wanting to betray him but at the same point, we didn't keep secrets between us. I held her hand and leaned my head on her shoulder. "He feels a lot of guilt still about your kidnapping. About not being here to protect you."

"What? That's absurd, he didn't do anything wrong." She snapped, turning to face me as anger crossed her features. "I thought he was getting past that."

"I know. But that's what he feels, and then last night, he was with me when you got upset and he's feeling even guiltier now. I think a part of him is trying to figure out how he's going to balance his work life here with you guys and personal life, whether that's with me or someone else."

"Oh my God, I'm such a cunt." She cursed and threw herself backward onto the bed.

"Why?"

"Because I monopolize *ALL* of his time! He'd always been so dedicated before I even moved in here, so I didn't think he wanted anything else outside of the crew. But now I see it clear as fucking day, and I'm getting in the way of it all."

"Stop it," I command her quickly, silencing her self-deprecating rant. "You're not in the way of it, but he does need to work on balancing it all. And I get it. Obviously, he knows I'm a dancer, but I can't stop thinking that he's not going to want to date a stripper who's rubbing on every guy he knows every night. You know?"

"Oh, babe." she said, eyeing me sadly. "What are you two going to do? You can't both work your lives away for the rest of your lives."

"I know. You know I love my life, I've never regretted it, not once. But lately," I paused looking up at the ceiling. "I can't help feeling that I need something more in my life, away from this lifestyle."

"And so does Jed, I bet."

"Yeah, I think so too."

She sat up, her dark hair flying out in her rush, "I've got it."

"You've got what?"

"How to help you balance it all. Both of you."

I raised my eyebrows at her, waiting for her to let me in on her plan. But she bit her lips shut and shook her head. "I have to talk to Ry first. You know I never keep things from you, but I need his blessing on this before I start the wheels spinning into motion."

"How about you let me know what you're thinking before you start spinning my life around for me?"

She laughed, "I'll tell you before I do anything, I promise. I just have to talk to Ryker first." I watched the happiness that filled her eyes as she thought about her plan and tried to just trust her. It made me happy to see something besides manic emotions in her eyes for once and trusted her enough to just let her work it out in her way.

We lay in her bed for a while longer and then I helped her pack her clothes. Apparently, Ryker had told her he packed for her given her injury, and I laughed loudly when I opened her suitcase and saw it filled with only bikinis and lingerie as she looked on in horror from the bed.

"Men." She cursed and ordered me to take it all out. I of course refused, but I did add a few summer dresses, wraps, and some lounge clothes for her to be comfortable in that weren't going to be tight on her belly. I also threw some of her new comfy maternity panties in as well because no woman should be forced to wear a thong while pregnant if they didn't want to.

"I'm going to miss you," I said as I hugged her an hour later when Ryker came up to get her to go to the airport. They were flying in his private jet and could make their schedule, but they still needed to get going to get to Cabo on time.

Ryker hugged me, thanking me for coming as soon as she called me, before scooping her up in his arms and carrying her down to the car. She waved over his shoulder to me and winked. "I'll call you tomorrow." She said and I laughed at the way her doting husband rolled his eyes at her need to talk to me every single day, but I knew he loved that she had someone she could rely on in her life.

"Jed, drive Carly home, please," Ryker called out as he sat her down in the seat of his Audi and snorted at the ridiculous eyebrow wiggle, she gave me around his arm. I felt Jed's presence behind me without looking over my shoulder to see him where I stood on the front step.

I waved goodbye to them, and Jed leaned down to speak directly into my ear. "What was her little eyebrow wiggle about?"

I smirked and licked my lips as shivers ran down my spine. I turned my head to face him and stared directly into his eyes. "She told me I should keep you entertained and busy while they're gone. I guess she was hoping I'd read between her lines."

He swallowed and licked his lips as fire lit his eyes, "You guys talked about us?"

"Us? I wasn't aware there was an us." I said sarcastically and smiled at the challenge in his stare. "She heard us talking on the stairs when I got here, and she thinks she has the magic fix to give us both the time to date."

"Does she?" He stood up to his full height and towered over me again. "Hmm."

"She's probably going to fire you," I said, flipping my hair over my shoulder. "Unemployed Jed will have all the time in the world for me."

He laughed boisterously and I stared in wonder at him. He took my hand and pulled me up the step to be on the landing next to him and stared down at me. "Unemployed Jed would have far too much time on his hands and would need something to fill them up with."

I bit my lip and leaned into him a bit. "Unemployed Jed sounds fun."

"Be careful what you wish for, darling." He still had a hold of my hand and was rubbing his thumb over my knuckles in a way that was driving me mad. I was a stripper, for crying out loud, how did one thumb on the back of my hand have me shivering more than an entire lap dance on a good-looking man?

"I'd better get going," I said reluctantly. "I have a date to get ready for."

He smiled and nodded his head, "Oh, believe me, I know. I'm counting down the minutes."

"Are you?" I asked, surprised.

"Hmm. I've been waiting for months to get you alone. Don't think I'm taking this lightly."

"Care to share with me what we're doing so I know how to dress."

He tilted his head back and tapped his chin like he was contemplating it. "Dress warm."

"Warm?" I asked, more confused now than I was earlier.

"Yes, warm. Dress in layers."

"I'm—I'm so confused," I said, shaking my head, and he laughed again, pulling me down the steps and holding my hand as we walked around the house towards the garage.

"Good. We're doing something outdoors, and it gets cold at night. That's all I'm telling you."

I laughed and conceded. "Okay, fine you win. My unicorn onesie with my fuzzy frog slippers it is."

"Oh my god, yes! Please wear a unicorn onesie on our first date, I'm begging you." He said overdramatically.

He walked over to the classic Dodge Charger parked next to the garage and opened the passenger door, holding it open for me and I raised my eyebrows at him and smirked. "Sexy car."

"Wait until you feel her purr between your legs, baby." He said, his voice deep with grit and it was one of the first times he'd openly been seductive with me, and I nearly melted at his feet.

"Dear lord." I sighed and slid into the car and felt his chuckle vibrate through me as he shut the door and walked around, sliding in behind the steering wheel. "For a tall guy, you fit pretty well in this car."

"I do a lot of things pretty well for a tall guy, Carly."

I panted again, smacking his arm. "Are you just full of one liner's packed full of sexual innuendos?"

He laughed, started the car, and watched me as he revved the engine. I pressed my thighs together and ran my hands up my bare legs, pushing my head back into the headrest as he watched, knowing he was enjoying the show.

"Only around you, apparently." He winked at me and then slammed the car into gear and tore down the black-topped driveway. I screeched and closed my eyes, laughing, holding onto the seatbelt as he drove through the gate at the end of the driveway before it even opened the whole way without an inch to spare.

I sat back in my seat and watched him drive, and it was the sexiest thing I'd ever seen before. His strong arms drove me wild, his muscles bunching and moving under the skin as he gripped the wheel and the shifter, changing gears, feathering the clutch, and commanding a car that was so full of power like it was kitten under his hand.

"Who needs foreplay when they can watch you drive?" I mused, licking my lips when he looked over at me as he passed in and out of cars without looking.

All too soon we were pulling up outside my apartment building, and I was sad for the ride to come to an end, even though I knew I'd get another one in a couple of hours.

He parked in front of the main doors, and the doorman came running out to get my door, knowing who was driving. But Jed was fast for his large size, and he beat him there, holding his hand out for me and helping me step from the car. He didn't step back as I did though and my chest pressed against his stomach as he looked down at me with a seriously sexy, smoldering look in his eyes. "I'll be back at six." He said in his deep voice that did naughty things to me. "Wait for me in your apartment, I'll come up. I don't want you waiting out here for me, okay?"

Swoon.

"Okay."

He leaned down and kissed my cheek, just like I did last night at Lux on his cheek, and then pulled away and stepped back, letting me pass him on my way to the front door. As the doorman held it open for me, Jed called my name again, and I turned to find him standing in the same spot watching me. "I forgot to tell you earlier, but you look beautiful today."

A stupid smile pulled my lips up, and I blushed like a fucking teenager. "Thank you."

"See you soon." He walked around the front of his car and got back in, driving off, after watching to see that I got inside the lobby first.

Holy fucking shit tits.

I practically ran to my apartment and slammed the door, locking it on my way to the bathroom as I pulled my phone out and texted El.

> *Me: Holy fuck, that man can drive a car.*

I added the drooling emoji to the end and hit send. Knowing she was probably in the air or close to it, I didn't expect a reply right away but a second later my phone pinged, and I read her reply.

> **Elora: Tell me he took you in his car. Oh please tell me he rode you all fast and furious style. I mean drove... drove you all fast and furious style.**

> *Me: Very fast, very sexy, I need to go take a cold shower.*

> **Elora: GAH! That's so hot! Okay, we're almost wheels up, and now I need to go ride my husband like a rodeo bull because you have me all worked up. I'm sure he'll appreciate it. I want to know every single thing that happens tonight! EVERY SINGLE THING! Love you, bye!**

I laughed and tossed my phone down on the counter and took my dress off and turned the shower on. As I was about to step in though, my front door opened and slammed shut.

Fear ran up my spine as I turned the water to the shower off and grabbed my towel to wrap around my naked body quickly as footsteps came down my hallway. I grabbed my phone and had the emergency call number dialed and my finger over the call button as Frankie walked around the corner into my bedroom.

I deflated and tossed my phone down onto the counter as he looked me over. "Morning babe."

"Frankie. What are you doing here?" I asked, tightening my towel around my chest, and walking past him into my bedroom to grab clothes. He was wearing dark jeans and black combat boots with a white tank top and a thick gold cross hanging around his neck. His dark hair was curly on top of his scalp and sparse facial hair dusted his jaw. I'd never been super attracted to him before but slept with him strictly because he was someone in my life that I trusted and could relax with. But now, standing in my bedroom, undressed, while getting ready for my date with Jed, I got an icky feeling on my skin.

"Was that Jed dropping you off?" He asked, a seriousness in his eyes as he chewed on a toothpick.

I contemplated my answer for half a second as I grabbed clothes from the dresser but knew this was the thing needed to sever this fucked-up situationship. "Do you know of any other seven-foot giants?" I kept grabbing clothes and then turned, finally looking up into his glowing eyes.

He was angry.

"So what? You're fucking him now too?" he asked, grabbing the toothpick, and rolling it between his fingers.

"I'm dating him, Frankie; I'm not just fucking him." I kept my voice calm and steady but strong. I hated that I was backed into a corner with him standing between me and the doorway.

"Years of being my girl and you're just going to walk away? Just like that?" He snapped, pointing at me with his toothpick.

"We're friends Frankie, we fuck because neither of us had any interest in dating anyone else and it was convenient. But we weren't in a relationship, and you know it. I know you fuck around with other girls all the time, so why are you acting like this is a big deal?"

"Because I'm not out there dating any of them."

"Frankie." I tried, but I could tell he was past the point of reasoning. "I think you should go and calm down, and then we can talk another time."

"Another time." he said, nodding his head as he leaned up off the door. "No." He said, moving towards me as quick as a bolt of lightning flashing through a midnight sky. "You think you're going to just move from my bed to his like there's no fallout from it?" He grabbed me and slammed me into the wall, my head bounced off the drywall, rattling my teeth. "You're a fucking stripper! You're nothing! Just a wet hole for us to shove our dicks into." He wrapped his hand around my throat as he sneered at me. I let go of my towel and tried to push him off of me as he squeezed my throat tighter, making it harder to breathe.

He ripped my towel off of my body, but I kept my eyes on him as he clenched his teeth looking down at me. All of a sudden his anger snapped, and he spat in my face and pushed away from me.

I stayed with my back against the wall, knowing I'd lose in an all-out fight if I tried to challenge him. He backed up, looking over my naked body again. "This conversation isn't over Carly. I'm going to calm down, and when I come back, we'll talk like adults. And you'd better fucking be here when I get back."

I stayed silent as he walked back down my hallway but cringed and shook when I heard him slamming things around in the kitchen, breaking them. As soon as the front door shut, I ran out and slid the chain in the lock, which I never used because the lock and deadbolt were always enough, but Frankie had a key and now a steel vault door wouldn't be enough to keep him out.

I leaned against the door and caught my breath, forcing the tears that pooled in my eyes to dry, unwilling to let them fall for him.

I wasn't nothing.

I deserved happiness.

Jed could give me happiness.

Frankie would only give me pain.

I took the house phone by the door and called down to the front desk, telling them I needed my locks changed immediately due to a security breach and that Frankie wasn't allowed to visit me. It was one of the perks of living in a nice building. It was expensive as hell, but given my profession, I liked knowing there was someone always here to watch over me.

When I hung up with them, I went back to the bathroom and forced myself to get in the shower, although I shook the entire time as adrenaline and shock roared through my veins and then faded, leaving me weak and tired.

When I got out of the shower, I blow-dried my hair and stared at my phone, contemplating texting Elora and asking for Jed's number to cancel tonight. But she would know something was up the second I asked, and it wouldn't take much pressure from her before I cracked and told her that Frankie had assaulted me. And that would ruin her trip because she would demand that Ryker fly her home immediately, and she would hunt Frankie down and have his head on a silver platter by sundown.

And don't even get me started on how Jed would react if she called him with this.

And while in theory that sounded good, I just wanted Frankie to leave me alone. I lay in bed and covered myself up with all of my blankets and set an alarm so I could get a few hours of sleep to recover from last night and whatever happened just now.

But every time I closed my eyes, I heard things in my apartment and ripped my eyes open expecting to see Frankie standing at the end of my bed. Exhaustion eventually won out, and I fell asleep, only to be woken up an hour later by my alarm.

I forced myself out of my bed, groggy and miserable, and tried to muster the excitement I'd felt earlier in the day for my date tonight. I cracked a bottle of wine and smoked a joint to relax as I started getting ready and blared some music and before long, my party-girl mentality had me vibing and pumped for my night.

In my closet, I eyed my choices, searching for something sexy and warm, remembering Jed's words. I sifted through a pile of clothes; the textures a mix of rough denim and soft lace, before deciding on black ripped skinny jeans and heeled boots with a black lacy bralette under a burgundy V-neck top that cinched my waist with its tie.

I added a layered gold necklace and a couple of rings to my fingers and threw on a white leather jacket with gold zippers to finish off the look. My hair was down and wavy, and my makeup was dark black around my eyes, and I was swiping on a wine-colored lip stain when my doorbell rang.

I looked at myself in the mirror and tried to calm my racing heart as I walked towards the door. I looked through the peephole and saw only a large, imposing chest and laughed to myself.

Jed didn't even fit into the peephole view; he was so big. I slid the chain back and unlocked the locks and opened my door, leaning on the jamb and looking him over.

"Damn." He said, letting his eyes drop over my body as I looked him over as well. He had a long sleeve black Henley shirt on that was unbuttoned at his throat, and his dark hair was messy on top of his head in a way that looked like he ran his fingers through it often. He wore a pair of light blue distressed jeans that I could tell were distressed from actual wear and tear and not made that way in the store. They looked soft and my fingers ached to touch them over his powerful thighs. On his feet, he wore a light tan pair of Timberlands and he looked good enough to eat.

And God, he smelled so fucking good.

"Hi," I said shyly. Having let my eyes rove over his body for far too long.

"Hi." He said back. "You look beautiful." He pressed his hand against the door to hold it for me as I turned to grab my purse, and I cringed when his eyes looked over my head to the mess that Frankie had made earlier. I'd forgotten to clean it up before I fell asleep, and then after, I hadn't had time. "What happened?" he asked, with eyes dark and serious.

"Oh, nothing," I said, shrugging him off and walking out the door he held open and pulling it shut behind me, locking it and then smiling up at him, trying to distract him from it. "Ready?"

He raised his brow at me but turned to walk with me down the hallway with his hand against the small of my back. When we got into the elevator, I took a couple of deep breaths as he leaned against the bar on the side opposite me and watched me closely.

He was serious and honestly scary, and I wanted the fun, carefree, sexy Jed back that had driven me home earlier.

The elevator doors opened, and we walked out to the lobby and towards the front door. His car sat out in the fire lane waiting for us, and a rush of excitement ran through my veins as I thought about riding in it again.

"Ms. James!" The front desk attendant called for me as we neared the door, and I smiled up at Jed.

"Hold on," I said and turned, walking over to the attendant, hoping that Jed stayed by the door, but he was right behind me as the man handed me a new key.

"Maintenance is on their way up in a few minutes to change your locks and that will be the new key for your knob and deadbolt." I took the key from him silently and took the old key from my ring and handed it to him.

"Thank you," I said, turning away from him and straight into Jed's large chest.

"Why are you changing your locks?"

"It's a long story," I said flippantly and tried to walk around him, but he put his hand on my hip and held me in front of him, looking down at me seriously before looking over my head at the employee.

"Why is she changing her locks?" He asked the man, who quickly answered him, no doubt aware of who he worked for.

"Uh, there was an incident this afternoon. Some sort of disturbance inside the apartment. Ms. James asked that we change her locks immediately and add Mr. Rivera to the trespass list."

"Rivera?" Jed asked, looking down at me with fire in his eyes. "As in Frankie Rivera?"

"Jed," I whispered, imploring him with my eyes to drop it.

"Yes, Mr. Manning, Frankie Rivera."

"Make a note that if Frankie Rivera shows his face at this building ever again, you call me immediately." He said, writing his number down on a piece of paper behind me without ever moving me, keeping me pinned between him and the counter. I laid my forehead against his chest as he did it and breathed him in. That was not how I wanted the night to start.

"Of course, Mr. Manning." The employee replied, and then Jed took my hand and pulled me from the lobby towards his waiting car. His body was nearly vibrating as he opened the passenger door for me and nodded for me to get in, but I dug my heels in and looked up at him.

"Please don't be mad at me right now," I whispered, and his eyes softened for the first time since he saw the mess in my apartment. "I didn't want to ruin tonight."

"You didn't. And I'm not mad at you, Carly." He said, leaning forward and pressing his lips to my forehead briefly before sliding his hand over the small of my back again, guiding me towards his car. "Get in, baby."

I sat down on the seat, and he shut the door, walked around the front of the car, and got in, keeping his head on a swivel the entire time, looking over the parking lot and the road.

He turned the car on, and she rumbled under my legs in a way I loved, and he pulled out onto the road, heading away from Shadeport and towards the rural outskirts of town.

"Tell me what happened." He said after a minute, slamming the car into the next gear and racing off into the setting sun.

"Please don't let it ruin tonight, I wanted this night to go perfectly," I begged him, hating that we were already having issues.

"Just tell me what happened, and then we can have the date you deserve." He looked over at me "But I need to know what happened, Carly, because my mind is making up all sorts of worst-case scenarios, and I'll go crazy if I keep that up."

I sighed and played with the zipper on my jacket sadly. He pulled the car over on the side of the road and slid his fingers under my chin, turning my head to face him as he leaned over the center console. "Tell me what you need from me right now, Carly."

"A promise that you won't do anything rash to ruin the night or Elora's vacation."

His brows dropped over his eyes as he stared at me, and then he nodded. "I promise I won't do anything rash. I won't ruin this for us, Carly, and I wouldn't ruin her vacation either."

I searched for something that said he was lying on his face, but I didn't see it. "Frankie and I have hooked up for years, never anything serious, but it was convenient, so we did it."

"I know that already." He said plainly.

"Apparently, he saw you drop me off and went on a rampage in my apartment after I got home. He left and said he'd come back later to talk when he calmed down."

"He had a key to your place?"

"Yeah, I gave him one after I locked myself out one night."

"He tore your apartment up. That mess in your kitchen, it was from him."

"Yeah," I said again. "On his way out, he did it."

"Did he touch you?" He asked, and I saw the barely restrained fury in his dark eyes. I looked away, but he pulled my face back up to look at him. "Tell me right now, Carly." He demanded, and I submitted to him, feeling the alpha in him call to something in me.

"Yes. He shoved me into the wall and held me there with his hand around my throat," I whispered. "But I'm fine. I'm tougher than he is."

He dropped his forehead to mine and took a deep breath in as he tangled his fingers in my hair and pulled me closer to him. "I'm going to make him pay."

"No!" I gasped. "You promised–"

"Not right now. Not tonight. But I promise you, he'll pay for touching you and scaring you."

"I never said I was scared," I said softly.

He chuckled and shook his head back and forth, rubbing his nose against mine, "You didn't have to say it, Carly. I can feel it."

I shuddered and he groaned. "I'm scared of what you'll do to him." He pulled back and looked into my eyes. "I've seen what men like you can do with your power and influence, and I can feel your rage."

"Are you afraid of me? Are you afraid that I'll hurt you?" He asked as though it pained him.

"No!" I answered instantly. "I know you won't hurt me. I know you're not like that." I said putting my hand on his chest and holding it over his racing heart.

"I'd never hurt you, but I am going to hurt him." He said, "That's who I am. It's what I do."

"I know," I whispered.

He pulled my hand off of his chest and kissed my palm and then kissed my forehead and leaned back, letting his fingers fall from my hair. "Let's get on with our date then, now that we have that settled." He gave me a small smile, and I watched him closely as he put the car in gear and pulled back out onto the road. He picked my hand up off my lap and put it on top of his on the shifter between us, keeping me touching him as he went through the gears and I settled back into my seat, watching him closely.

"You're really hot driving this car; you know that, right?" I asked, lightening the mood.

He winked at me and kissed my hand again before putting it back on the shifter.

CHAPTER 4 – JED

My god, she was beautiful. I drove through the winding hills that took us away from Shadeport and the chaos of the city and watched her from the corner of my eye. Having her here in my car was surreal, and the fact that I'd been touching her non-stop since I picked her up was making my heart race.

Her bright blue eyes were on fire in the warm sunset light, and her hair blew in the wind from the windows. "Are you going to tell me where we're going yet?" She asked, pushing her hair behind her ear, and looking at me.

"No," I said simply and smirked when she rolled her eyes at me.

The sun was setting over the horizon as we finally pulled into the driveway of the land I owned in the hills. Her eyes scanned the empty land questioningly before looking over at me as I turned the car off. "Just so you know, Ellie knows I'm with you, and if you brought me here to kill me, she'll kill you."

I chuckled and shook my head. "Is that so?" I asked, leaning over the center console towards her and invading her space. Her eyes widened and she bit her lip but didn't back up.

"Yes, that's so." She said in a whisper.

"Good to know," I said, and then backed away to my seat again and opened my door. "Let's go or we'll miss the show."

Her brows dropped over her eyes, and she looked utterly confused. "The show? We're in the middle of nowhere."

"Come on pretty girl," I said, getting out and walking around to her side and holding my hand out for her. She took it and got out of the car and looked around again as I grabbed my jacket from the back seat and held my hand out for her to take again. We walked down the worn path deeper into the wilderness.

"It's beautiful up here." She said, leaning into my arm as we walked the path through the trees.

"It's probably my favorite spot in the whole world."

"Is it yours?" She asked.

"Yeah, I bought this property a few years ago. It's my getaway from the city when I need to clear my head."

"Is there a house up here? Or camp or something?" She asked.

"Yeah, there's a cabin back here a bit. It's rough but it's got water and electricity and that's all I need when I want to get away."

We pushed through the last of the trees and she stopped walking when we got to the clearing. The cabin sat off to our left, facing the valley below where the city sat. It was a small a-frame with a large porch on the valley side and a wall of windows. The sunset shone brightly as it bloomed on the horizon, moments from dropping over the hill and it lit up the interior of the cabin. There was a large pond in the center of the clearing, surrounded by trees and the cabin, leaving it completely secluded with a long dock jutting out into the water.

But her attention was trapped on the large, stationary dock in the very center of the pond, which was our destination for the evening. It was a ten-foot by ten-foot swimming platform that I'd set up for us with a million blankets and pillows, and I hung string bulb lights from the four posts on each corner of the platform.

"Oh my god, Jed." She gasped and turned to me with a giant smile on her face. "Is that what we're doing?" She hopped from foot to foot as she looked back out over the glass like water.

"Yeah, I thought you might like to watch a meteor shower away from the city lights tonight."

"This is the most romantic thing in the world." She said softly, and I leaned down, kissed the top of her hair, unable to keep my lips from her for long.

"Wait until we get out there and see what else I have in store for you."

She shrieked excitedly and followed me as I walked down the dock to the large rowboat that was tied to the last pier. I threw my jacket down into the boat and stepped down, waiting for it to settle before turning around and holding my hands out for her.

She bit her lip but leaned into my waiting hands, and I wrapped them around her waist and lowered her gently into the boat with me. She sat down across from me, and I untied the rope and pushed us away from the dock and out onto the water. I used the oars, gently pushing us across the surface towards the middle as she looked around with pure glee on her face. "It's so beautiful up here, Jed."

"I'll take your word for it because I can't see anything past your beauty right now," I said honestly and she blushed, dropping her face to look at her boots briefly before raising her eyes and looking at me through her eyelashes.

"I don't blush, ever." She said, shaking her head and rippling her hair around her face. "Yet, with you, I can't seem to stop."

"I like it."

She smiled at me and took a deep breath as I rowed the last few yards to the platform and tied the boat off. She looked up onto the platform and squealed with mirth as I stood up and helped her stand. There were cushions over the whole surface and a small low-top table in the center with candles and plates on top.

I lifted her onto the platform, loving the way her body fit in my hands, and then hauled myself up onto it next to her. She shook her head back and forth and turned to look up at me, leaning against my chest. "No one has ever done anything like this for me before Jed. I had no idea you were such a romantic."

I laughed and kneeled to help her take her boots off and tossed them into the boat before taking my own off, and then we walked onto the cushions and sat down on each side of the small rectangle table. "You can't tell anyone I'm a softie," I said, leveling her with an intense stare, and she bit her lip to hide her smile. "I have a reputation to protect."

She held up three fingers and let her smile free. "Scouts honor. Your secret is safe with me."

I opened the cooler and took out the hot food I'd prepared earlier and laid it all out on the table and then grabbed a couple of beers and a bottle of wine from another one.

"You've thought of everything, haven't you?" she asked, helping me arrange the items on the table.

"Maybe. Only time will tell if I've forgotten something." We sat back and watched nature around us as we ate our dinner of grilled chicken, veggies, and rice. I brought a bunch of snacks for later and held off on dessert for now. As it got dark, the string lights over us cast a warm glow as the air started to cool down. "Let me move the table and then we can lay back and watch the show." Scootching the table to the edge, she helped me arrange the cushions and pillows into one big bed. When she eagerly laid down in the center, patting the space next to her, I fought the knee jerk reaction of longing that was building in my chest. In just a few hours, we'd gone past the platonic yet flirty friendship we had built the last few months, and I was falling head first into a lust filled need for her.

If I wasn't careful, I'd embarrass myself with the world's most beautiful woman and every hang out session at the mansion would be awkward as hell.

Hitting the switch for the lights, I crawled in next to her, pulling the blankets up over us and after a few minutes, our eyes adjusted enough to see the stars above.

I turned to watch the way her eyes widened as she took in the vast sky overhead and found myself unable to even watch the show once the stars started flying. She reached between our bodies and grabbed my hand, bringing it over to lay on her stomach, wrapped between both of her hands as she watched in awe. I turned to my side and didn't try hiding the way I was looking at her as she experienced this because she was far more magical than space.

Watching the awe play out across her face, was like watching the stars align and destiny fall into place.

A tear fell from her eye and rolled down the side of her temple, into her hair, and I leaned forward, using my thumb to wipe it away. "Why are you crying?"

She took a shuddering breath and turned her head to look at me, holding my hand tightly against her stomach, which quivered with her emotions. "Because I'm unworthy of you," She swallowed, "Of all of this, and I wish that maybe we'd met in a different life when I could have been."

I leaned up on my elbow, taking my hand from her stomach and threading it into her hair as she closed her eyes, more tears falling from her lashes, and pressed my forehead to hers.

"I've never met someone like you, Carly. Your heart is pure."

"But my body isn't."

"It is," I said back firmly, tightening my fingers in her hair and holding her tighter. "Just because you dance doesn't mean you're bad. You've chosen to give your body freely over the years, that doesn't make you a bad person; it makes you adaptable and brave. You've done what you needed to survive, and I know you've enjoyed it along the way. Don't feel bad about that. I knew exactly who you were, and what you do at work, and parties on the side and I'm still painfully attracted to you." She threaded her fingers through mine at the side of her face and searched my eyes. "I'm so fucking attracted to you, Carly. And not just your body. I'm attracted to your heart and your mind. The way you protected and provided for Ellie all these years and took care of her shows exactly how big your heart is." I sighed, rubbing my nose against hers and breathing her in. "If either of us is unworthy, it's me. I'm a thug and a menace. I use my power and my strength to do my job, and I've hurt a lot of people along the way to get it done."

"You're incredible." She whispered. "The power inside of you, it doesn't define you. I've watched you. I've seen how you use it for good, and that speaks so loudly of your character. You are far from unworthy of anything."

I leaned forward the last inch and kissed her, pressing my lips against hers hungrily. She leaned up into me and clung to me as I pulled her bottom lip between my teeth and then teased it with my tongue. She moaned into the kiss, turning on her side and pressing her body against mine as I deepened it.

Carly opened to my urgings and tangled her tongue with mine as her hands gripped the front of my shirt, pulling me closer.

"Jed." She moaned, biting my lip, and sucking it into her mouth. I rolled, so she was on her back, and I leaned over her and deepened the kiss even more, consumed with fire. She hooked her foot behind my leg and tried to pull my body on top of hers completely.

I hesitated and pulled back, pressing my forehead to hers to take a couple of deep breaths to calm down. "I'm sorry." I panted. "I got carried away."

"I'm not complaining." She smiled against my lips.

I laughed softly and untangled my fingers from her hair and ran my fingertips down her cheek. "I didn't bring you out here like this, so you'd sleep with me, Carly. Please don't think I'd cheapen our date like that."

"I don't think that was your intention, Jed. But I'd be lying if I said I wasn't hoping it ended there either way." She wasn't shy about sex, and I loved that. I loved that she knew what she wanted and wasn't afraid to just say it.

I groaned and kissed her again, and this time when she pulled me closer, I went willingly. She spread her legs, and I laid between them, keeping my weight off her tiny frame with my forearms as we kissed on and on. I trailed my lips from her mouth down to her ear and felt the shivers cover her body as I sucked on the lobe and then bit it.

I moaned when her cold fingers slid under the bottom of my shirt and her hands pressed flat against my abs before her nails teased the skin up and down from my belt to my chest and back. My hips jerked forward, and she moaned as my hard-on ground against her core.

"I need you, Jed." She panted as she grabbed my ass and pulled me closer.

"Fuck Carly, you're killing me here," I growled, kissing down her neck to the top of her cleavage.

"Let me take away the pain then." She said with a laugh and untied her shirt and opened it up, revealing her sexy as fuck tits in a black lace bra that was nearly see-through. I groaned and dropped my lips to them, pulling the lace away, unable to stop until my tongue flicked over her pink nipple as it hardened. "Oh, God." She moaned and dug her nails into the hair at my scalp and held me to her. "Yes." The moonlight cast a cool glow over her beautiful body as I played with her.

I used my fingers to roll the nipple I'd just sucked on and moved to the other one, fighting with the lace to bare it to my hungry mouth. "Fuck." I grunted, sitting up, so I was kneeling between her spread thighs. "Take it off. All of it." I nodded towards her jacket and shirt too.

She bit her lip, sitting up and shucked off her jacket and shirt and then I pulled the bra up and over her head and added it to the pile. I leaned forward to lay her back down and cover her up with my warm body, but she put her hand out against my chest.

"I showed you mine, you show me yours." She said, nodding to my chest with a sexy as fuck smile on her face. I leaned back and grabbed the back of my collar and pulled my shirt off over my head, and her eyes fell from mine and scanned my chest and abs. "Holy shit." She said, playing with her bottom lip with her fingers before she reached forward and ran her hands over my pecks and down to my belt. "You're so sexy, Jed."

I grabbed her hips and slid her down again until she lay flat on her back with her light blonde hair spilled over the pillows, looking up at me with a come-hither look in her eye. "Sexy doesn't even begin to describe how beautiful you are, babe," I said as I covered her body with mine, noting how her chest was cool pressed against mine. "Are you cold?"

"Not when you're touching me. You're so warm."

"Hmm." I hummed and lowered my face into her neck and covered one of her breasts with my hand and worked on her nipple again. She rocked her body underneath mine and arched her back, pressing her chest into my hand more. I dropped my lips to her perfect chest again and pinned her hands next to her head, threading my fingers through hers as I feasted on her nipples.

She was begging and pleading for more as I worked us both into a frenzy. "I need you, Jed. I can't take the teasing anymore."

I chuckled, "I'm not teasing baby, it's foreplay."

"I don't need foreplay, Jed. I need you devouring me."

Growling at her confidence, I moved back up her body. "You're tiny, Carly," I said forcing her gaze to lock onto mine. "And I'm—not." I demonstrated, rocking my hips against her, rubbing my cock from base to tip and back. "I'm getting your body wet and relaxed to take me."

Her eyes widened, and her lips parted before she moaned, and her eyes fluttered closed. "Oh, sweet Jesus." She whispered, clawing into my back. "Show me."

Now it was my turn to moan. I took the gun out of the waistband of my jeans in the small of my back and put it safely away from us while still keeping it close if I needed it. I was never without a gun, even in the middle of a pond on my property.

I rolled over onto my back, and undid my jeans, watching her eyes intently the whole time as I pulled the zipper down and lifted my hips, pushing down my pants and black boxer briefs to my knees and then pushed them to my feet and kicked them off. When I looked over at her, she was staring at my cock where it rested on my stomach.

"There's no way that's going to fit inside me." She whispered in awe and fear.

I rolled towards her and captured her mouth with mine, kissing her powerfully and passionately until she was clawing at me and climbing me like a tree. She needed to be aroused and out of her head for this to work.

Because she was right, I was fucking huge, and it wasn't going to fit if we didn't work at it first.

Carly took my hand and put it on the button at the top of her jeans and bit my lip. "Take them off." She demanded. I flicked the button open and pulled her zipper down, rolling us over so she was once again on her back and then I kneeled between her spread legs like I had earlier. She lifted her hips and shimmied the tight jeans down, and I tore them off, adding them to the pile of clothes at our feet. She was wearing a high-cut black thong and I leaned down and kissed my way down her body until my teeth bit the fabric of her panties, and I pulled them down her long legs. When I tossed them aside, I put my hands on the insides of her knees and pushed her legs wide, opening her pussy for me to see.

"Hold on," I said, leaning over her body to plug the lights back in so we were bathed in the warm glow once again.

"Why did you do that?" She asked, closing her legs a bit before I pushed them wide again.

"Because I want you to be able to see me the first time I take you. Because it's going to be the last time you ever feel a man move within you for the first time again. The first time I slide into your tight body, you'll be mine."

She pushed her head back into the pillows and palmed her heavy breasts as my words hit her exactly where she needed them. She needed to be owned and taken care of. And I was going to be the lucky bastard that got to claim her.

I fell to my elbows between her legs and kissed the inside of her thigh before lowering my face to her soaked pussy. "Mmh." I hummed as I took a deep breath and smelled her arousal.

"Fuck." She moaned, lifting her hips aching for more. "Do it."

"Say the words, Carly." I countered.

"Taste me. Lick my pussy. Suck my clit. Tongue me. Finger me. Fuck me!" She bit between clenched teeth. "Please, Jed, for the love of God, make me orgasm and make me yours. I'm desperate for you."

"Well, because you asked so nicely." I lowered my mouth onto her pussy and sucked hard, bringing her swollen clit between my teeth, and flicking my tongue over it as she flailed under me. She moaned and howled into the open air around us as I tortured her. I pushed my tongue into her pussy and growled at how fucking tight she was. Rolling my face back and forth over her sensitive skin, using my whiskers to stimulate every inch of her.

She curled forward, holding onto my head as she rode my face and rolled her hips. "Please! Please! Please!" She begged, and I pushed two fingers deep into her in a fast, rough thrust, and her knees fell wide, and her entire body snapped like a rubber band.

I watched her body as she reached her climax, her eyes rolling back, her skin turning red as her nipples became even more erect, and her grip on my fingers tightened. All the while I kept flicking her clit and scraping my whiskers across the swollen nub and fucking her with my fingers. She screamed into the expansive wilderness, and wild animals answered with their calls as she shattered around me.

It was single-handedly the most beautiful thing I've ever seen before, and it tasted even fucking better.

CHAPTER 5 – CARLY

I came apart. My soul no longer lived inside of my body in a painful, cataclysmic way that left me panting, raw, and tingling all over.

And forever addicted to Jed Manning.

I fell back onto the pillows as my aching lungs gasped for air and he still kept his unrelenting tongue and fingers working over me. He lessened the pressure of both and then softly kissed my oversensitive flesh over and over again.

"That was the most beautiful thing I've ever seen." He said softly to me, as he kissed his way up my body and laid his giant baseball bat cock against my stomach as he lay between my legs.

Chuckling, I grabbed two handfuls of his hair and pulled his lips to mine and kissed him with everything I had until we were both breathless and desperate for each other. "I've never been with anyone that made me feel that good before, Jed. I've never felt so good."

"I've never wanted anyone as badly as I want you." He replied. "I need to be inside you now though."

"I'm ready for you." He chuckled and his white teeth glowed in the lights. He pulled back and grabbed his pants and took a condom from the pocket. "Not expecting anything, huh?" I asked with a wide grin on my face as he tore it open. And then I was quiet as I watched him work the magnum onto his glorious cock and started worrying about it fitting again. I'd taken some big dicks in the past, but Jed was in a whole other class of human compared.

"Eyes on me." He said, drawing my attention away from his cock and onto his eyes. "Good girl. Are you sure you still want this?" He was so serious and not at all condescending. I knew without a doubt if I told him I'd changed my mind, he'd treat me the same as he had before our clothes started coming off, even with a case of blue balls.

"I'm positive," I said, resting my head back on the pillows and offering my lips to him. He took them hungrily and lowered his pelvis to mine. I kissed him deeply as he ran the head of his cock back and forth through my wetness, coating the head with my arousal, and then pushed forward. It was so sexy watching his tattooed hands holding onto his massive cock, rubbing himself against me, and then entering me.

"Jesus fuck." He groaned as I held my breath and tried not to tense. He pulled out and then pushed back again, going deeper and the burn was magnificent.

It was intense, and it was painful, but on the edge of that pain was the blinding light of pleasure from every other thing he was doing to me. His tongue and lips kept me busy while his hands never stopped moving over my body, teasing and pleasing my nipples and my clit, gripping my ass and holding my legs around him. He was a talented lover, and before I knew it, his pelvis was rubbing against my clit as he growled in my ear.

"You are fucking perfect." He praised. "So perfect for me."

"Yes." I moaned, rolling my hips to move on him where he stayed still buried inside of me. "I need you to fuck me, baby. I want all of you."

He thrust his hips slowly, pulling and pushing until I stopped tensing each time and started meeting him thrust for thrust. "That's it, Carly." He hissed and slammed into me, making my eyes roll back and my lips part in a silent scream. "Take me, take every inch of me."

"Harder Jed, more," I begged and clawed at his back as he found a rhythm of pounding punishing thrusts and rolling hips to stimulate my g-spot and my clit at the same time and within seconds I was panting, scratching, and screaming as my second orgasm ripped through my body. It was primal and animalistic as he continued fucking me through it, never letting up on his thrusts or magic hips, and I clung to him as it rolled on and on through me.

"I'm going to come so deep inside of you, Carly. I can't hold it back, baby."

"Don't hold back. Come for me. Chase euphoria with me."

"Yes!" He roared, throwing his head back and pounding into me over and over again. The muscles and tendons in his neck bulged, and the veins in his arms swelled as his orgasm took over his entire body. I lay under him and watched in sexual haze and fascination as he transformed from the dark and calculated man to an animal unhinged, chasing pleasure that he was taking from my body with the stars on fire above him. It was all too much. It was too powerful and beautiful, and I fell over the edge of another orgasm, clamping down on his cock again, pulling curses and moans from both of our lips as he leisurely fucked me through it with his cock that already came but refused to soften.

When I released my nails from the back of his neck, he rolled us quickly, so I was on top of him as he lay flat on the bed. I laid my head on his chest, and he wrapped both arms around my back, covering my sweat glistened body with his to keep the chill away.

"Oh, my god." I whispered into his chest and feathered kisses across the strong muscles there. "Tell me it's like that for everyone with you and that I didn't just have the best sexual experience of my life like a total amateur."

His chest rumbled underneath me, and his chest hair tickled my nose in the best way possible. I'd never slept with a man who was so sexy inside and out and hung. It was usually one of the three, but never them all.

Perfect trifecta.

"I've never had a woman complain before, but I've never had one draw blood in as many places as you did either." he said with a smirk. I put my hands on his chest and sat up, straddling his still-hard cock inside of me.

"Did I hurt you?" I asked, pulling his arm up to see the back of it, and sure enough there were claw marks up the back to his shoulder, and I could see the broken skin starting before it disappeared into the cushions. "Oh my god Jed, I'm so sorry." I gasped.

"Don't you dare." He said strongly, sitting up until we were nose to nose. "That's the biggest fucking compliment, Carly. You losing control with me buried inside of your pussy was the sexiest thing in the entire world. I swear to God, you are breathtaking when you orgasm."

I groaned and buried my face in his neck, "I'm so sorry."

"I'm not." He wrapped his arms around me and pulled the blanket around me like a cape and I wrapped it around his back, cocooning us in it. "My kitten has claws, I'll be sure to remember that."

The movement rocked me on his cock, and my eyes fluttered, and a moan slid from my lips at the sensation of still being filled by him.

"Can we do that again?" I asked, biting his lip, and sucking on his tongue when he pushed it into my mouth.

"Let me take the condom off and put a new one on, and you can ride me until dawn if you want, baby."

I hummed my agreement and lifted myself until he came free from my body and then groaned at the tenderness I felt when I was empty. I sat back on his thighs and watched with rapture as he slid the condom off, impressed with how much come was inside of it as he tied it off and threw it in the trash bag from dinner, and fished another condom from his pocket.

"How many of those did you bring?" I asked, palming my tits, and loving the way his eyes struggled to stay locked on mine until I took his hand and put it on my breast in place of mine.

He let his stare fall to them then, and he watched as he pinched and pulled on my nipples before leaning forward and sucking on them. "Two more."

"Hmm. Good." I said as he leaned back and started to open the next one. "Wait," I said, putting my hands over his, smiling seductively at him as I pushed him back to lay on his back. "I want to taste you first." I purred and scooted my hips back and dropped down on my elbows to kiss his hips on each side of the deep V above his cock.

"I've died and gone to heaven." He rasped with grit in his voice as he gathered my hair in his hand and held it to the side so he could see me. "You're breathtaking, Carly."

I smiled as I fisted his cock for the first time and purred deep in my throat at how my hand didn't even wrap around him completely. "You're destroying me for any other man. I'll never be the same." I said, licking up the side of him and moaning as I tasted his orgasm on his skin. "God, you taste so good." I swirled my tongue over the head of his cock as I kept my eyes on his and then spit on it, rubbing it in with my hands down his shaft. I knew I didn't stand a chance of deep-throating him, considering he was almost as long as my entire arm from elbow to shoulder and just as thick, but I wanted to make him feel good.

I started sucking on him and felt empowered as he threw his head back and flexed his hips, moaning as I pleased him. Watching such a powerful man come undone at my fingertips was so incredible.

He put his inked arm behind his head and watched me, keeping a tight grip on my hair as he licked his lips and grunted. "I need to be inside you again, Carly." He implored. My lips curved into a smile as I planted a soft kiss on the tip, then climbed back up his body. I took the condom from him and gently rolled it onto him and marveled again for the dozenth time how impressive it was. "Ride me. I want to watch your magnificent body."

"Yes, Sir." I purred and put my feet on the floor and squatted above him as he fisted his cock, holding it upright for me to sit on. I slowly lowered myself onto him, feeling the delicious burn and bite of the stretch as I took him in one slow thrust until my ass sat on his thighs. My feet were still on the floor and my legs were spread wide as I rose back up and then down again, and it was as if I was spinning gold with my pussy because he was entranced, watching me take his cock.

My consistent squats in my workout routine as a dancer helped so I could sustain this position for quite a while, and I hoped he was relishing the spectacle. I put my hands on my thighs and arched my back as I rose and fell on his cock, and his eyes flashed with fire as he watched.

"You're so sexy, baby." He growled, putting his hands on each side of my thighs, and squeezing the muscles there.

I ran my hands up to my breasts and played with my nipples, pinching and pulling them as he watched and then licked my lips and put two fingers in my mouth, sucking on them and getting them wet. As I slid my fingers down to my clit and started rubbing it as I bounced on him, he lost his restraint.

He grabbed the back of my neck and pulled me forward until I switched to my knees and pressed my chest against his, and then he wrapped his hand around my throat and held my face against his as he started thrusting powerfully under me. "Yes." I hissed as his large hand squeezed my throat, restricting blood flow to my brain as he fucked me like a man possessed.

"I can't get enough of you. You're the sexiest woman I've ever seen. I need your next orgasm like I need my next breath." He urged against my lips as he held me how he wanted. I put my hands on his hard chest and held on.

"Please Jed, just like that. Don't stop, you feel so good, baby." I purred, and his hand tightened on my throat as he tightened a hand in my hair and the two, matched with his punishing thrusts, pushed me over into ecstasy. "Yes!"

He grunted, and his lips parted as he stopped breathing completely under me as he chased his orgasm, and then he roared as he came, deep inside of me. His cock jerked and spasmed as my insides gripped him tight while we both moaned and panted.

"Holy fuck." He mused, laying his head back flat on the pillows and holding onto me. After a while, I pulled off of him and slid onto the cushions next to him while he got rid of the condom, unplugged the lights once again, and then pulled me against his side with my head on his chest.

The stars were still flying across the sky as we lay there under the heavy blankets watching the show in bliss. My eyes were heavy, and my muscles fatigued and relaxed as the steady drumming of his heart lulled me into sleep.

I knew I should stay awake and have him take me home. But I didn't want to leave his arms. I didn't want to leave his presence and space because he made me feel so beautiful and cherished with his words and touches.

"Go to sleep." He whispered against my forehead before he feathered soft kisses there. "I'm in no rush for you to get rid of me."

I chuckled against his chest as he rolled over and pulled me flush to his body. Burying my face in his neck and my leg over his hip, I quickly fell asleep on his arm.

I woke up with the purple glow of dawn just barely touching the skyline. I looked around and was in awe of how beautiful Jed's property was and how perfect our little cozy den of comfort and pleasure had been all night long. Twice more overnight, Jed had awakened me with pleasure, taking me silently and passionately. The last time, we'd been out of condoms, so we used our mouths on each other again and fell asleep spooning with his large body wrapped around my back. And this time when I woke up, he was in the same spot, and I couldn't bear to move out of his embrace.

"Good morning." He whispered against my back. The air was cold, but we were cuddled together with the blanket up to our ears, and his body was so warm.

"Good morning," I said back with a smile as I kissed his arm under my cheek. "Can we do this every morning?" I asked, sighing as I watched the sun start to burn off the fog and dew of the morning.

"I can't imagine a better way to wake up than with you in my arms like this."

"This was a perfect first date, Jed. I had no idea you were so romantic."

"Me either. I just tried to think of a way to woo you."

"I am thoroughly wooed." My stomach growled and rumbled under his hand, and he chuckled against my neck. "And hungry."

"Me too. Want to go to breakfast with me?" He asked, and I couldn't help but feel giddy that he wanted to spend even more time with me today and wasn't eager to part ways. But I also was trying not to get too attached too quickly. Men like Jed never settled down, and I knew that. He was married to his work and that was his number one priority, part of me hated that, and part of me loved that because his work was my very best friend, and she deserved to have someone's commitment like that.

I just wished I could have his commitment too.

"I'd love to," I said and rolled over in his arms, laughing when his cock poked my belly. "Be honest, does that thing ever get soft?"

He laughed and kissed me softly, "Not around you, apparently."

"I'm not mad about that."

We got dressed and loaded up the rowboat with the things from the dock and made our way back to land. I grabbed the cooler and a few blankets, but Jed pulled them from my arms. "I've got this, Kitten." He said impressively, picked up every single thing in his big arms, and carried them all to the car.

While he loaded the trunk, I got in the front seat and pulled the mirror down and groaned at my appearance. My eye makeup was smudged, and my hair looked like a giant had run his hands through it all night long.

Because one had.

I smiled to myself as I remembered the way Jed held handfuls of my hair when he was inside of my mouth or my pussy multiple times last night as I ran my fingers through it to smooth it out. I licked my fingers and fixed my eyes and applied a new layer of lipstick, feeling pretty impressed with my looks after sleeping outside all night, although I did feel grimy.

Jed got into the car and leaned over the center console and kissed me deeply, pulling me against him and nibbling at my lips. "I'm tempted to take you home and skip breakfast altogether." He said, but then pulled back. "But I need to feed your belly first at least."

"First for sure." I smiled and sat back in my seat as his car roared to life. I pulled my phone from my pocket and groaned when I saw it was dead, but a part of me didn't care that no one could get in contact with me. Except for Ellie. I hated not having that line of contact open in case something went wrong. "Did you hear whether Ry and Ellie made it safe?" I asked.

"Let me check." He pulled his phone out and scrolled through some messages, and I tried hard not to look at his screen where he held it on the gearshift between us, but I failed.

I noticed a few women's names with generic *'What are you doing?'* texts from last night and a few from Zeke and Razz. Forcing my body, I looked out the window, giving him some privacy that he didn't exactly seem to want as he didn't try to hide anything. "They landed and got to their house safely."

"Thank you." I turned back and smiled.

"Is your phone dead?" He said, looking over at my black screen and holding out the end of a charger for me.

"Look at you, always prepared." I joked and plugged my phone in, giving it a second before turning it on.

"Always prepared, yet somehow I still ran out of condoms sooner than I thought I would."

I laughed, "Did you think we'd have sex more than three times? Because I wouldn't have thought so. And I'm deliciously sore this morning because of it."

He leaned over the console again and slid his hand over my jaw, turning my head towards his to kiss me. "I didn't think we'd have sex at all, and I sure as fuck didn't think I'd be so lucky as to have you so many times. But I'm not complaining one single bit. It was the best night I think I've ever had."

I melted into a puddle, going soft in his arms as I kissed him back, getting lost in his touch. But then my phone started pinging obsessively with texts, missed calls, and voicemails. Panic rose in my heart, worrying about Ellie, even though Jed just told me they made it safe, so I tore away from his lips to look at my screen.

But it wasn't Ellie who had blown my phone up.

It was Frankie.

302 texts.

71 missed calls.

42 voicemails.

"Jesus Christ," I muttered, cringing at the screen, not even wanting to see what they said.

"Give me that," Jed said, taking my phone from me without waiting for my permission. He scrolled quickly through the messages, and his face darkened the further he got through them. "Do you want to see these?" He asked.

I shook my head and turned to look out the window. "I can imagine what they say."

"Then I'm deleting them all, and I'm blocking his number. You good with that?"

"Yes," I said confidently. I couldn't deal with his bullshit if he was going to be so neurotic about this thing between me and Jed. As far as he knew, it was just a date, and he was already freaking out. "I don't understand why he's so psychotic suddenly," I said quietly. "I've gone out on dates with other people before, I've slept with other people and so has he. But this time he snapped."

"Have you ever dated anyone else from the crew before?"

"No." I shook my head. "The Shadeport crew intimidates me, to be honest with you."

A ghost of a smile pulled at his lips as he turned to me. "Then what are you doing with the third in command?"

I bit my lip as I stared at him for a long pause, "I'll let you know when I figure it out."

He laughed softly, and his features relaxed until my phone started ringing in his hand again, and both of our eyes went to the screen.

Frankie.

"I'm going to handle this," Jed said before hitting accept on the call and placing it against his ear. "Frankie." His deep voice growled into the phone. "You're treading on thin fucking ice, my guy."

I couldn't hear his reply, but I could hear his angry voice through the phone, and whatever he said made Jed's hand tighten around the wheel.

"Consider this your only warning, if you go near Carly ever again, I'll fucking disembowel you in the middle of the fucking street, and then I'll throw your body out in the hills like the fucking trash you are." He hung up the phone instantly and blocked his number and then took his phone out, handing mine back to me.

"Zeke." He said when the call went through. He was barely containing his rage, and this was the side of him I'd heard about but never saw firsthand. "Do me a favor, find Frankie Rivera, and take him to the shop." He paused, listening to whatever Zeke said. "He put his hands on Carly and messed her apartment up for going out with me." Whatever Zeke said was angered and loud. "Hold him there and call me, and I'll head over. Thanks."

He hung his phone up again and took a deep breath, but it didn't do much to calm him down. "I'm sorry," I whispered. Hating that he was dealing with this because of me.

His eyes snapped over to mine as he tossed his phone down in the center console and pulled me to him. "This. Is. Not. Your. Fault." He commanded. "This is a power thing because of the crew. I'm sorry that he got to you yesterday before I knew he was this fucked up. He could have seriously hurt you, and it would have been because of me, Carly, not you. But don't worry, because he's not going to touch you, ever again."

I leaned forward and kissed him, deepening it, and told him how much his protection meant to me, and he reciprocated in his way.

When we finally pulled away, he put the car in gear and winked at me, tearing off through the gravel drive and then onto the road, taking us back towards town. I leaned back in my seat and watched the terrain change as we got down into the valley and the city. Jed drove us to a diner I'd been to a few times in the heart of Shadeport and held my hand as we walked across the street and into the front door.

Eyes fell on us as we passed full tables and found an empty one in the back. Men nodded to Jed or stood up and shook his hand as we walked through, I recognized a few of them from the club and hated the way my skin burned knowing a few of them had seen me naked and I was on the arm of one of their bosses. I slid into a booth, and instead of sitting across from me, Jed sat next to me, warming the side of my body with his and kissing my temple. "What's wrong?" He asked so in tune with my feelings and body language.

"I recognize a few men here, that's all."

He rested his elbows on the table and looked down at me over his arm. "Does that bother you?"

"Doesn't it bother you?" I asked.

"No." He replied so confidently that I almost believed it.

"How is that possible? Because yes, it bothers me."

"We can leave if you want, Carly. It doesn't bother me in the least. Don't get me wrong, I'm a possessive and jealous man, and if you were out hooking up with men from this point on, I'd be red with rage. But I won't fault you for your job, one I was well aware of when I asked you on a date. And I can't fault you for things you've done before we went out. I have a past too, it's not pretty and sometimes it sneaks up and bites me in the ass still, so I won't hold yours against you if you don't hold mine against me."

I just stared at him in awe and disbelief. "You're an angel," I whispered.

He chuckled and shook his head, "No, baby, I'm the devil through and through. You're the golden light in this relationship." He said and then cut me off, "And before you wonder if this is a relationship or not, it is. I'm only interested in monogamy with you, and no one else compares to you now that I've had you."

I kissed him, deeply. Right in the middle of the twenty-four hour diner as men that worked for him stared on with an array of expressions on their faces. And he kissed me back, sliding his hand into my hair and pulling me until I was nearly sitting on his lap.

"Well, should I come back then?" A female voice asked, and I pulled back, covering my mouth with my fingers as Jed laughed and looked up at the middle-aged waitress who smiled down at us.

"Good morning, Marg," Jed said and leaned back, putting his arm behind me on the booth and taking the menu from her and handing it to me.

"Good morning, Jed. Coffee?" She asked, and he nodded, and then they looked at me.

"Coffee would be great, thank you."

"I'll come back in a minute to take your order." she said and walked away with a smirk.

I buried my head in his chest as she did, embarrassed. He laughed and hugged me to him as I looked over the menu. After we ordered, he started asking me about my family and my past. Things we started discussing last night but got too wrapped up in sex to finish.

As I told him about my childhood, I absently played with a sugar packet to distract myself. "I grew up here in Cali, down the coast, and I don't have a tragic story of my childhood like some girls that I work with do. I just—wanted more. So, when I was eighteen, I left and landed here in Shadeport, surfing and working in bars, couch surfing and going nowhere until a girl I met introduced me to Lux. I went one night to see what it was all about and just kind of never left." I shrugged my shoulders. "I loved the atmosphere and the lifestyle. Partying and drinking and making buckets full of money each night was all I cared about at eighteen. Ryker runs a pretty good place there; I was never pressured into doing anything I didn't want to like in some clubs that the other girls worked for before, so I was content to keep doing it."

"But now? You don't sound so sure." He wondered.

"The last few months, I've been less content. I think it had to do with Ellie getting that happily ever after that I never imagined either of us getting someday, and it planted a seed in my brain that this lifestyle I have been consumed with for the last almost five years isn't the most important thing to me anymore."

"So, what is the most important thing then?"

I chuckled and nudged him with my shoulder, "Here's where you run for the hills, I'm about to talk about the future."

He laughed but turned in the booth to look at me head-on, "Tell me about all of your hopes and dreams."

I smiled shyly, dropping my head, and hiding behind my hair. "I want—someone like you," I said and struggled to elaborate, but he stayed quiet, letting me figure it out. "I want someone who doesn't care about my past but doesn't want me to have that as my future either. I want someone I can leave all of that behind for."

"And you think I can give that to you?" His eyes were serious, and I watched the pulse in his neck as he said it.

"Perhaps." I was now questioning everything, but his serious face melted away, and he leaned in, kissing me again.

He whispered against my lips, "I can give you all of that and more, Carly James." He kissed my nose at my sigh of relief and then followed up with, "Say the word, and I'll take you far, far away from here, toots. I've told you that before."

I laughed and leaned into his embrace. "I don't want to go far away from here, just far away from who I've been these last few years."

"Done." He said but didn't elaborate. And he didn't have time to as our food was delivered, but he looked like he was pondering something heavy in his mind but wouldn't elaborate.

"So, tell me," I shoved a forkful of waffle into my mouth in a very un-ladylike fashion, and grinned at his snort, "What was young Jed like?"

He rolled his eyes and took a drink of his coffee. "Young Jed was a pain in the ass that got his ass kicked far more times than I will ever admit to."

I snorted and laughed behind my coffee cup, "Say it ain't so."

"Oh, it is so." He laughed. "I grew up in the foster system and thought being homeless would be easier than living in a group home, which in a way it was, but in a lot of other ways it wasn't. And I got myself in way over my head one day." He got a faraway look in his eyes as he told the story. "I stole from the Shadeport crew, not aware of what a big blunder that had been at the time, and Ryker and Gavin, Elora's dad, were sent to make an example out of me in the streets to keep everyone else in check."

I took a deep breath, sensing the darkness of that memory in his head. "I didn't know you knew Gavin."

He nodded his head and looked over at me. "The greatest man I've ever met."

I smiled at him affectionately, feeling the connection to the love Ellie and Ryker both had for Gavin, and now to know that Jed did too made me wish I'd met him even more. "Tell me more."

He shook his head. "They were only six or seven years older than me; I was sixteen then. Gavin said he saw something in my eyes, a determination to survive that he knew they could mold into a good soldier and loyal crew member, and I jumped at the opportunity to be a part of something, and I never looked back. When Gavin died, Ryker pulled me up, needing people he could trust not to try to steal the new throne out from under him, and they made me into the man I am today."

"They gave you a family. That's why you're so determined to protect Ellie, not because of some obligation or job. It goes so much deeper than that."

He shrugged his shoulders and took another drink of his coffee. "I guess so."

"Does she know that you knew her dad?"

"She knows that I ran with the crew when he was alive, but she doesn't know he's the only reason I'm alive now and not dead in some gutter as a teenage orphan."

"You should tell her." I whispered, "She needs more connections to her dad, I mean, thank God she has Dawson now, a living relative after losing Gavin. But I'm sure she'd love to know about your relationship with him as well. Especially now that she's pregnant, knowing her kids will never have grandparents because Ryker's own are gone too, it weighs heavy on her."

"That baby will never want for anything, Carly." He said, turning an intense stare my way. "Between you and me, Ellie and Ryker, and the crew, that baby is going to have the entire world. I promise you that."

I smiled at him, feeling emotions bubble up in my throat at his intensity. "Do you want to be a dad someday?" I asked, groaning inwardly at asking such a mysterious man about kids, he'd probably rather talk about anything but that with a girl on their first date.

"If it's written in my future to have kids, I'll love every single second of fatherhood." He looked down at my lips and then back to my eyes. "What about you? Ever dream of being a mom?"

"Someday yeah, not while I'm a dancer. But someday when I can be proud of the woman I've become and not feel embarrassed for myself or my kids, then yeah, I'd love to have kids."

"Good to know." He mused.

"Okay, we have to stop," I said, feeling my face heat up.

"Stop what?" he asked, licking his lips, and watching me closely.

"Stop talking about such heavy and important things that hold no bearing on the here and now."

"Hmm." That was all he said, but his phone rang, cutting off whatever else he had to say. He looked at the screen, and I watched his carefree, relaxed face get covered with his dark and mysterious one as he read the message. "I've got to get back." He said, and I knew that duty called.

"Okay, I should get going anyway. I've got to get some sleep before tonight's shift." His eyes darkened even more, but he nodded his head.

We walked outside, but I stopped on the sidewalk instead of crossing the road to his car. "I'll just order an Uber."

"No. Not a chance." He said forcefully. "I'll take you home. I want to check to make sure everything is squared away there, anyway."

"Are you sure? You said you had to go."

"Stop." He said, walking into my space and putting his hands on each side of my face, and then kissing me. "I'm taking you home."

"Okay." I gave in way too easily, and I knew that. But there was just something about being protected that felt—good.

CHAPTER 6 – JED

The drive across town to Carly's apartment was quiet, and I knew we were both weighed down by the Frankie drama, but I hated feeling this riff in the middle of the car.

I took her hand and laid mine on her thigh, holding onto her as I drove, and then placed both of our hands on the stick in the middle as I shifted gears.

"Will you teach me to drive a stick sometime?" She asked, watching my hand shift from fourth to fifth.

"I thought I did that all night last night," I said with a smirk, and she rolled her eyes at me.

"You didn't teach me anything I didn't already know, big guy."

"Ooh, ouch," I said, clutching my heart, and she laughed.

When we got to her place, I parked and walked up with her, watching as she used her new key, and then walked in with her, checking the locks over to make sure they were secure.

The mess was still on the floor in her kitchen, but as I walked in deeper into the apartment, it didn't appear like too much else had been disturbed.

When I got into her bedroom, I stopped in the doorway and leaned on the doorframe.

"What?" she asked, walking around me and looking at the bed I was staring at.

"Just getting visual images of you laid out in that bed committed to my memory spank bank for when you're not around."

She snorted and slapped my chest, sliding her jacket off and hanging it in the closet. She kicked off her shoes and untied the cute little bow at the front of her shirt and then pulled that off. Leaving her in her black lace bra and jeans. She eyed me and raised her eyebrow at me with the ghost of a smile on her lips.

"Like what you see, big guy?" She asked, shaking her hair over her shoulders.

"You know I fucking do."

She laughed and walked into the bathroom, turning on the shower and heating it. "I have dirt in places I never thought I'd have dirt before."

I stood up from the doorway and walked into her bathroom with her and watched as she shimmied her jeans and panties down and took her bra off, tossing them all in the hamper. I know I should have looked away, giving her privacy and respect, but I was a warm-blooded man, and she was goddamn beautiful.

"Do you have time for a shower before you go?" She asked, cocking her head to the side, and walked towards me. Her flared hips swayed with each step, and my hands ached to grab them and pull her to me.

"I have all the time in the world for you, Carly James," I said and when she got within reach, I did just that.

She gasped and then moaned when I wrapped one hand around the back of her head and the other over her hip, crushing her to the front of my body as I drank from her lips.

"Yes." She moaned, sliding my shirt up over my stomach until she couldn't reach any higher and then I pulled from the kiss and ripped it off over my head. Her slender little fingers went to my belt, and I pulled my gun from my holster and set it on her bathroom vanity as she pushed my jeans and boxers down and kicked off my boots and socks, standing naked in front of her.

"Tell me you have condoms here," I said, barely restraining my need for her.

"I might have one that will fit you." She said, raising one eyebrow as she dropped her eyes to my hard cock standing a foot out from my body. "Fuck, you're even bigger in the daylight."

I growled as she walked away from me and opened a few bathroom drawers and found a magnum and brought it over to us. "Get in the shower," I said, taking the condom from her and bringing it with us, setting it on the ledge of her large stone shower. The spray felt amazing on my skin, washing away the grime of sleeping outside and sweating on and off all night but I only took a few seconds to enjoy it before I was on her. I backed her up until she was pinned between me and the wall and lifted her, kissing her deeply as she wrapped her legs around my waist.

"How wet are you?" I growled.

"Drenched and ready." She gasped as I ran my fingers through her pussy lips and pushed three into her body.

"Good girl." I praised, loving how wet she was already. I grabbed the condom and ripped it open, "Put it on me." She took it and slowly rolled it down my length, and when it was on completely I pushed the head of my cock into her, clenching my teeth to keep from pounding her into the wall in one thrust. "You feel like Heaven, Carly. Fucking golden light Heaven."

"More baby, I need more." She begged, and I pushed in deeper, slowly easing myself inside of her until my body was flush with hers. "Yes." She hissed with a long breath, "I've never realized how empty I've felt my whole life until you filled me up."

"Fuck." I groaned and started moving. "Your words are my undoing."

"So, it's not my pussy?" she asked with a chuckle.

To that I bottomed out with one thrust, taking the air out of her lungs, and she quieted quickly but rolled her eyes. "That's my girl."

I fucked her hard, holding her perfect ass in my hands as her pussy sucked me deep into her body over and over again. My skin was on fire, regardless of the mist of the water, from the exquisite feel of being with her. She kissed me, biting my lip, and sucking on my tongue as I railed her. "Yes, baby, just like that." She panted. "Harder, yes, don't stop!"

She arched her back and pressed her head into the wall as she climaxed. Her skin flushed, and her pupils dilated, and I was lost in her beauty. Her orgasm relaxed and she sagged into me, and I spoke against her temple as I held her and kept thrusting. "You're the most beautiful woman I've ever seen before, Carly. You're breathtaking."

She cried out, clawing into me as a second orgasm ripped through her body and clamped down hard on my cock. I shouted with the first spurt of come that tore from my cock from the sheer intensity of my orgasm. I lost my ability to see or hear or think properly as pleasure and bliss overtook my senses as I fucked her hard into the wall.

When the haze lifted, I leaned against her, putting my hot forehead against the cool wall, and gasped in time with her.

"Oh, my God." She moaned, dragging her fingers up the back of my head from my neck and holding me to her. "I'm never coming back from that." She mused.

"Good, then I won't be alone, because that wrecked me." She smiled against my neck and slid her legs down, letting my cock fall out of her body, and then rested her head against my chest as her legs worked to keep her upright. "Let's get cleaned up, and then I really have to go."

"Yeah, me too." She said reluctantly, turning her back, and she started washing her hair. I watched her while she went through her shower routine and couldn't help but wonder what was on her mind as her quietness played on. When we were both done showering, we got out, and I got dressed in my clothes as she sat on the end of her bed in her towel.

I kneeled in front of her and took her hands. "What's bothering you?"

She shrugged and tried to brush it off, but I held my stance and didn't move until she looked at me and sighed. "I don't want to go to the club tonight."

"So don't."

"I have bills to pay."

"Then go to work," I said easily, trying to keep my emotions out of her head.

"It feels—wrong." She whispered.

I leaned forward and kissed her, "Make your money Kit, I'm going to be right here when you're done, regardless."

She smiled softly and took a deep breath, "Good, because I think I'm addicted to your cock."

I laughed, "Oh, just my cock?" I asked.

"Well, it's what I've gotten the most of in the last twenty-four hours so yeah."

"Funny girl." I kissed her forehead and then her lips. "Text me when you get to work and when you leave and when you get home."

She raised her eyebrow at me. "It's going to be like three am when I get out."

"I know."

"I don't want to wake you up."

"I need to know that you're home safe. Text me."

"Okay."

"Good girl," I said, and she rolled her eyes but leaned forward and kissed me again, and I growled as she deepened it. "Careful, or neither of us will make it out of this apartment anytime soon."

"I wouldn't mind."

"Me neither, that's the problem. I have work to do."

"Okay," She pushed me towards the door and stood up. "Get out of here so I can take a nap and get ready."

"Okay," I said. I leaned down and kissed her cheek and whispered in her ear. "Play with yourself before you go to work and think of me when you do it. I want details when I ask later." And then I pulled back and walked away, but when I looked back at her as I got to the front door, she stood with her mouth open and arousal in her eyes. "Be a good girl and do what I said, Carly. I want you to fantasize about me."

"Okay." She whispered. And I winked at her and walked out. When I got back in my car and headed back towards the mansion, I felt myself sliding out of the calm and sated mood I'd been in around Carly, and into the menacing and predatory animal role that I was in when I was at work. Halfway through the city, I spotted a familiar head of blonde hair walking down the street. I looked around and didn't see anyone else with him, so I pulled over alongside the sidewalk and reached over, opening the passenger side door.

"Get in." I snapped.

Mason looked around him and then walked over to my car, leaning down to see into it. His surfer looks made him always look so at ease and carefree, but I knew something darker lurked under his golden appearance because I'd seen it a few times now on jobs. I also knew Elora trusted him most out of the trio of friends she used to run with.

"What's up, boss?" He asked.

"Get in, I've got a job for you," I said, looking forward, tightening my grip on the wheel. He slid into the seat and shut the door behind him. I pulled away from the curb and started back on my drive to the mansion. "Do you know where Frankie is?" I asked, not beating around the bush.

"No man, and I don't necessarily want to if the rumors I've heard are true."

"What rumors have you heard?" I'd been off the streets since last night and needed to know what was swirling.

"That he fucked Carly up and you're hunting him."

"Hunting huh?" I asked, eyeing him where he sat in my passenger seat. He wore a Hawaiian shirt and a pair of tan cargo shorts and flip-flops, and I shook my head, he was never dressed for a fight, and one day that would bite him in the ass. "You know where he is?"

"No way, Jed. Other than his place, Carly's, or jobs, I don't know where he would be. Have you seen Carly? Is she okay?"

I eyed him and didn't detect any insincerity in his voice and nodded. "I just dropped her off at her place. She's fine, she spent the night with me."

His eyebrows raised to his hairline, and he laughed a bit, "Well, it all makes a bit more sense now." I looked at him deadpan, and he elaborated. "Why Frankie went after her when they've been *friends* for years. She's dating you, and he's jealous."

"From what I hear, they've been casual for years. Why would her dating me make him flip a switch so stupidly?"

He shrugged, "No one fucking knows what goes through his mind, Jed. He's possessive and jealous on a good day, and I'm guessing when Carly upgraded to dating you, he snapped."

"You know he's a dead man, right?" I asked, watching his expression.

"I know he deserves whatever he gets for putting his hands on Carly. Regardless of what she does for a living, that girl is innocent in every other way that matters. She doesn't deserve his crazy."

"Good to know." I pulled over along the sidewalk again, right where I picked him up from and he looked around and laughed.

"I wasn't even paying attention to where you were driving."

"You need to be more situationally aware, Mason. I could have been driving you to the shop and delivering you to the butcher there." His eyes rounded a bit, and he swallowed. "And start wearing some actual fucking shoes, you don't need to be fighting in flip-flops. Because you won't win."

"Got it." He nodded and opened the car door and got out. "If I find him, I'll let you know."

"Good. Because if I find him first, it's not going to look good for his two best friends. Zeke, Ryker, and I might start wondering where your loyalty lies."

"Whoa–" He started with wide, worried eyes, but I popped the clutch and tore off down the road, slamming the door shut with the force of my acceleration.

By the time I pulled into the mansion, I was vibrating with anger. Zeke walked out of the garage when I parked, and I looked longingly at the shop, hoping that Frankie was in there, waiting for me. But I could tell by Zeke's face that he wasn't.

"Haven't found him yet?" I asked.

"He's on the run." The words hung heavy in the air, a bitter taste lingering in Zeke's mouth, and I could see the weight of them on him. "He's dead not only for fucking with Carly but for disobeying orders to report."

I nodded and stared off at the concrete building. "Does Ryker know?" I asked.

"I talked to him after you called me."

I nodded again, hating the fact that their vacation had been tainted by all of this. "I have to find him or she's not safe."

"I get it." He said, and he was probably one of the few men in the world that did understand this need inside of me to protect her and shield her from the fallout of our lifestyle. It was exactly what happened to Elora when she fell in love with Ryker, and it was happening again because of me this time. "We'll get him. I've already made changes to the lineup at Lux to watch over her when she's there, and I've updated security at her building with men we can trust. Until we find him, she'll be safer at work and at home than she was before. But she'd be safest here."

I scowled at him, "Yeah, because I'm going to lock her up in my shit-ass studio and make her stay there all the time." I scoffed.

"Something tells me she'll be here full-time sooner or later, and it won't be in your studio, man." He said but didn't elaborate. Zeke was a fucking puzzle on a good day, and this was not a good fucking day. "I've got an order out for Jay and Mason to come in, I'm sure we'll find Frankie through one of them."

"I already talked to Mason," I said, rubbing my hand over my face in frustration. "He said he didn't know where he was and that he wasn't down with him putting his hands on Carly." I shrugged my shoulders. "I didn't get the vibe that he was blowing smoke, and I know out of the three, he's been the most loyal with Ellie so there's hope that he was telling the truth."

"So, we need to find Jay then," Zeke mused. "He's the one who's been problematic, I'm guessing if Frankie is getting help, it's from him."

"I agree."

"Good, we'll find him, and we'll talk to him together." I nodded and then started walking towards my studio when he stopped me with a question. "Did your date go well at least?" He had a smug smirk on his face that I ached to wipe off with my fist given my current frustration level. "You didn't come home, and according to the security at her place, neither did she."

I took a few steps backward, towards my building as I shrugged my shoulders, "Good things shouldn't come to an end too soon." That was all I said and turned around again, walking towards my place as his rich laughter rang out.

"Things are about to get interesting around here." He called and I flipped him off.

When I got inside I stripped out of my clothes from last night and crashed for a much-needed nap, and when all was still and silent in my place, my mind drifted back to the beautiful blonde I was finally able to hold and touch like I'd wanted to do for months. And my dreams were riddled with nightmares about all the ways that harm could come to her because of me too.

CHAPTER 7 – CARLY

I walked into the back entrance of Lux and took a deep breath. The smell of the club calmed me down because it was familiar and pleasant, and I needed all the help I could get tonight.

I was on edge and angsty, and one false move would send me flipping off the deep end of cattiness, which was not a good look. I dropped my stuff off in the locker room and went looking for Theo, skirting around the edge of the club that was already packed and vibing, even for a Friday.

He was at the bar, and when I walked up to him, his eyes rounded as he looked at me. "Don't tell me you're here to quit." He rushed on.

"Why would you think I'm quitting?"

"Because Jed Manning has laid claim to you across the city, and I don't think he's the type of man that shares well with others."

I rolled my eyes, "Claimed me?"

He nodded and rushed on in typical flamboyant Theo style, "Word's all over that you're his, and not to be fucked with." He leaned forward and whispered, "And that Frankie Rivera is a dead man walking. Is it true?"

"Yes."

He squealed and clapped his hands together ardently. "What's it like being Jed Manning's girl? Ooh, I bet he's a fucking brute in the bedroom, isn't he? All caveman and alpha god," He fanned himself. "Oh Lord, I'm hot just thinking about it."

I rolled my eyes again but smiled, feeling lighter that this conversation was at least already started for me. "I don't think I can dance now. But I don't think I can just quit either."

He sighed and put his arm around my shoulders, "I know what you mean, I've seen it happen a million times over the years here. This is an odd position to be in for you and it's new territory, you just have to figure out what you're comfortable with yourself before you weigh his wants and needs into your decision." I grimaced as he made it sound so easy. "How about you work with me as hostess tonight, I could use the help honestly." He said, highlighting the full club with a sweep of his hand.

"Hostess?" I said, trying to imagine that. "I've never done that before."

"You're smart, you'll catch on quick. You can start shadowing me for a few hours and then towards the end of the night you can do some on your own."

"Okay. Thanks." I said, feeling lighter and more hopeful. Hostess was something that would keep my clothes on, while still getting a tip from happy customers when I matched them with girls they liked and catered to their non-sexual needs. I could do that with my head held high with my new change of situation.

"Go get dressed, wear something sexy but classy, and then meet me back out here when you're ready."

"I don't have anything that's not lingerie."

He chuckled and looked at his watch. "Mav's is still open for another twenty minutes; I'll call her and tell her you need help asap and she can help you get set up." Mav's was a designer boutique down the street that a lot of us girls shopped at for going-out clothes, and I had always had good luck shopping there.

"Thanks, I'll be right back!" I all but ran from the club and down the street, and sure enough Mav and one of her shoppers were waiting for me at the door when I got there.

"Hello darling, let's get you dressed, shall we?" The older elegant woman purred as she led me to a dressing room.

"We shall," I said with a full smile on my face.

Twenty minutes later I was walking out of the shop in a black lace and leather outfit that made me feel so incredibly sexy, and almost all of my skin was covered. I wore black leather high-waisted hot pants with a lace off-the-shoulder top that left my tits looking amazing with only the top of my cleavage on display. I had on a pair of black lace heels and a gold Gucci belt around my waist. I already had my hair blown out and my makeup dark and with all of that together, I was a knockout. It was giving Sandy from Grease vibes and I was all for it.

I'd taken a picture of myself in the mirror at the store to send to Jed, proud to show him the change in my work uniform as well as to keep him thinking of me while I was apart from him.

I was typing out a sexy message to send with the picture when I ran straight into someone on the dark sidewalk.

"Oof." I groaned, holding my nose that felt like it was completely crooked on my face. I looked up and stumbled backward as Jay looked down at me.

"Hey Carly, what's up?" He asked as if nothing was amiss and his best friend wasn't circling the drain of life for being a psycho.

"Jay," I said and looked past him to the entrance of Lux. The club was packed, cars lined the streets in every direction, and people lined the sidewalk waiting to get in. "What are you doing here?"

He scowled down at me and stiffened his spine. "Am I not allowed to come to Lux anymore? Now that you're fucking Jed?" The hair on the back of my neck stood up, and I quickly walked around him, heading for the door and the multiple bouncers standing on the sidewalk. "Hey wait!" he said, grabbing my arm and pulling me to a stop before stepping in front of me and holding his hands up. "Sorry, that was a fucked-up thing to say." He sighed and dropped his hands, "It's been a long two days, but that's not your fault."

"It kind of is," I said back, defeated. He gave me a one-sided smile and relaxed. Jay and I had been friends for years, and I hated the idea of losing him and Mason with all of this bullshit.

"You okay?" he asked, leaning his shoulder on the brick wall next to us and lighting up a joint. "I heard he got physical."

I shrugged my shoulders and took the offered weed and took a drag. "He just shoved me around and wrecked my apartment." I handed back the joint.

"What happened?"

"He saw me get out of Jed's car the other morning and followed me into my apartment and just—went wild. I don't get it because he and I both fuck other people all the time. We're not exclusive, or even close. Have you heard from him or seen him?"

"No way, and I don't fucking plan to." He took a long drag off his joint. "I fucked up with Ellie when she first got with Ryker, and I almost fucking died for it. I'm not testing fate twice because I know Ryker is just looking for an excuse to filet me for ever having her before they got together."

I sighed and leaned against the wall. "I don't want him to get hurt, he's my friend, and I care for him. But I don't want him hurting me either."

"I know. I feel the same way. It fucking sucks being stuck with my hands tied. If I talk to him and don't tell Jed and Ryker where he is, I'm dead. If I don't talk to him, I feel like a fucking shit-ass friend to someone who's to thank for getting me into the crew, to begin with. It's a shitshow either way."

"Yeah, I hear you."

We stood there, smoking his weed for a long time in silence before I pushed off the wall. "I got to get to work."

"You're still dancing, even now that you're dating Jed? That surprises me."

"Why would that surprise you? Girls dance all the time when they have boyfriends. Some of them are married, and a lot of them have kids. It's just a job."

He eyed me closely and then just shrugged his shoulders, "You say all of those things," He tapped his finger to his temple, "But I know you, and I know how your brain works. And if you're dating Jed, third in command of the Shadeport crew, then you're not going to be doing half the shit you did before inside of that building."

He didn't have to say what I did, but we both knew. I danced, I had sex for money, I did drugs, I partied and ignored responsibilities in exchange for *having fun*. I never *just* danced.

"I'm not dancing anymore; I'm going to host with Theo tonight and go from there."

He nodded his head as he kicked a stone, "That sounds like a really good fit for you. I bet you take his job before the weekend is over." He winked and smiled in jest.

I took a deep breath and nudged him with my shoulder, "Thanks. I'll see you around. Don't be a stranger, okay." I nodded to Lux, "You know where to find me."

"Yeah, yeah, yeah. Go to work, pretty girl, I'll see you around."

I walked into Lux with a lighter pep in my step and stopped off in the locker room to check my appearance and brush my teeth to get rid of my weed breath.

My phone pinged and I looked down and saw a message from Jed.

Jed: I miss you, have a good night at work.

Jed: DON'T OVER THINK IT, IT'S JUST A JOB!

Jed: But mostly, I just miss you. And now you probably think I'm lame and I'm going to go kick myself in the balls to man up.

I laughed at his banter and sent him the picture of myself in the mirror of the dressing room. I'd held my phone up and cocked out my hip and run my hand through my hair and smiled sexily at the camera for the picture and was excited to send it to him.

Me: Theo is training me to be a club Hostess. Turns out he's more afraid of you than I am, and he doesn't want me to quit the club completely. So, this is my outfit for tonight. Is it crazy that I feel sexier in this than in any outfit I ever wore on stage before?

Me: And I miss you too. I can't stop thinking about you either and please don't kick yourself in the balls. I need them in working order for all of the plans I have for you.

His reply came almost instantly.

> **Jed: Kitten, you look downright sinful and angelic at the same time, you're a complete paradox. You're going to kill it as Hostess, babe. You know that club inside and out and the girls too. It's a perfect fit and I'm happy for you.**

> **Jed: But tell me more about these plans you have for me.**

> *Me: They involve a lot of ball draining. They involve you draining your balls into and onto multiple places.*

> **Jed: Jesus fuck. I'll pick you up from work. Call me when you know what time and I'll be there.**

> *Me: Very funny! Get your sleep, you deserve it after last night.*

> **Jed: I'm not kidding. Turns out I can't stomach the thought of going to sleep without kissing you good night.**

My heart melted and I smiled down at my phone like a love-struck puppy.

> *Me: Are you sure?*

> **Jed: 100%. Tell me.**

> *Me: Okay, I'll be off by three for sure, but I'll call you if that changes to earlier.*

Jed: I'll see you then, go kill it tonight babe.

Me: See you then.

I left the locker room on a fucking cloud, my life was taking a path I hadn't expected, but also one I didn't know I needed until I was already walking down it. I wanted it so bad, so I smoothed my hair down and walked out into Lux with my head held high and determination to succeed oozing from my pores.

Five hours later, and that high never washed off. I'd smiled and schmoozed more men than I thought was possible, and I never once touched them or took my clothes off, and the tips were fucking good.

It was half of what I would have done tonight in the VIP room, but knowing that I didn't do anything that would embarrass me later if it came up, was worth it. I could survive on this wage, and Theo said that it would get better the more I did it. Turns out he'd been begging for a female Hostess but everyone that got hired decided they wanted to dance instead and always left him high and dry. He called this '*divine timing*'.

I didn't know about all of that, but when I called Jed and told him I was good to go, I could hear relief in his voice when he told me he'd be by to pick me up in fifteen minutes. I was so anxious to get to him, which was fucking pathetic, but I didn't care.

I sat at the bar, clinking a drink with Theo on a successful crazy-busy Friday night when my skin started prickling on the back of my neck. I looked over my shoulder towards the front door, and there stood Mr. Giant Dark and Dangerous himself with a sexy as fuck grin on his face as he fist-bumped a couple of guys from the crew on his way to me.

"Hot damn Mylanta." Theo chirped from next to me, but I didn't pay him any attention. I turned my stool around to lean back on the bar and watched my sexy man of mine stalk towards me like he was a predator, and I was his prey.

He wore dark blue jeans and a white T-shirt that hugged his tight muscles and made the black in his tattoos pop as they ran up both of his arms. I knew they covered his back and chest and thighs too, and the dirty little secret of what they looked like when his body was taut with pleasure or rolling in seductive motion.

He walked up to me and slid both hands under the backs of my thighs and lifted me effortlessly and dropped me on the bar top and pressed himself against my aching pussy between my legs as I hooked my ankles around his back. He grabbed my hair and tilted my head and pressed his lips to mine, pushing his tongue in instantly and fucking my mouth with it as his other hand grabbed my hip and pulled me against him hard.

I fisted my hands in his shirt over his tight abs and held on as he drank from my lips like he was on his last breath, and he wanted mine.

"Hi." He said in a voice so deep I could hardly hear it when he finally pulled away.

I chuckled and wiped his bottom lip with my thumb as I eyed him, "Hi back."

"Should I have worn my letterman jacket or my T-bird jacket, Sandy?" He asked, and I smiled brightly at him, glad that he caught the vibe I'd been headed for. "You look sexy as fuck."

"Thank you. And you are perfect exactly how you are." I leaned in until only he could hear me. "You're making me wet just from looking at you."

"You ready to get out of here?"

"So ready." I purred.

He picked me up again and set me on my feet between him and the bar before finally looking over at Theo who was sitting there, with his drink halfway to his lips and his mouth hung open in suspense, watching the show we'd put on unintentionally. "Theo," Jed said, tipping his head to the man who finally remembered himself and closed his mouth, and put his drink down.

He fanned himself and tsked his tongue. "God, Carly, I'm so glad you're done dancing because there's no way I could let you near anyone knowing you have this hunk of a man waiting to do those things to you at home."

I tilted my head back and laughed, even as the blush crawled up my neck at Jed's public display of affection. I'd never had that before, and turned out, I was a fan.

"Let's get out of here," Jed said and pulled me against his side and walked out of the club with his heavy arm over my shoulders, leaving no question about our status.

When we got in his car, I nearly moaned when he started it up and tore off down the street.

"Where are we going?"

"Your place is closer." He said with a wink.

"Perfect." I leaned over the center console and kissed his neck, licking and sucking on the sensitive skin beneath his ear and then nibbling on his earlobe as he drove through the dark city. "I can't wait to have you inside of me."

"Were you a good girl before work?" He asked, sliding his hand between my thighs, and pressing his fingers against my throbbing clit before grabbing another gear.

"How do you mean?" I asked with a smirk.

"Did you play with that sexy little pussy before you left your apartment like I told you to?"

"Yes, I did, just like you told me to." I purred into his ear, and he groaned.

"Tell me how."

I bit his earlobe and slid my hand down his chest and stomach until it lay directly on top of his erection, straining behind the fabric of his jeans. "I lay on my bed, naked, with my legs spread." I squeezed his cock, "And then I took my rose vibrator and held it on my clit as I thought about you, and your massive cock, and your talented tongue and fingers, and how hard you've made me come so many times in the last twenty-four hours, and I orgasmed within two minutes, maybe less. It was a big one too." He groaned and turned to kiss my lips, not looking at the road for a solid fifteen seconds as he drove. "I was so wet I had to change my bed sheets."

"Fuck this," he barked, pulling over suddenly and parking in a dark alley. I squealed when he slammed on the brakes and sat back in my seat in shock and excitement. He reached between his legs and pushed his seat back all the way and tilted it back until it was practically lying down in the back seat. "Take your pants off and ride me."

"Here?" I gasped, looking around. We were parked between two giant brick buildings; I didn't see anyone around but that didn't mean that no one could see us.

"The windows are tinted too dark for anyone to see, and I'll make sure no one is looking in the front. Now get on my cock or I swear to God I'm going to jack off and come all over your pretty tits in that shirt." He ripped his belt open and then his jeans, pushing them down just far enough to free his raging hard-on.

"Yes, Sir," I said softly and pulled down the back zipper of my pants and shimmied them down over my hips and off my feet, taking my heels off as well.

"No panties?" He asked, with a smirk.

"Hard to hide panty lines in leather, baby."

"Hmm." He mused and then picked me up over the center console and into his seat, straddling his legs and his baseball bat. He grabbed a condom from the glove box and rolled it on and then lifted me until his cock was nestled against my entrance. "This is going to be fast and hard baby."

"Yes, please," I begged, holding onto his shoulders as he slammed up into me and pulled me down onto him. I screamed through my clenched teeth as he stretched me open violently and his teeth bit down on my neck, muffling his cry. "Yes, Jed. Just like that." I moaned as he lifted me up and down on his cock.

"You're so tight." His hands held the underside of my ass, and his biceps bulged as he lifted me up and down like he was doing curls in the gym. "Fuck, I'm close already." He cursed.

"Me too. Don't stop." I begged, licking my fingers, and then reaching down between us and rubbing my clit in small, fast circles. I laid my head down on his shoulder as he fucked me harder and deeper while I played with my clit. I bit his shoulder when his hand came down on my ass cheek, branding it with his palm print as he lost control. "Yes!" I screamed, "Spank me again! Harder."

He brought the same hand down over the same spot, and fire erupted in my ass, burning its way into my clit and pussy. I felt myself clamp down on his cock even more as I got closer to my orgasm. He spanked me again and again and I begged and cried for more as I started coming. He grabbed my waist in both of his hands as I screamed out through my orgasm and slammed me down onto his cock, before rubbing me back and forth, grinding my clit on his pelvic bone as he filled the condom up inside of me.

We were both gasping and panting, slick with sweat as we came down from our climax. The windows were fogged up and the car smelled like hot and dirty sex.

"That was the best sex I've ever had." He said quietly, and I stilled at his admission. "Every time I'm inside of you, I tell myself, 'That's the best, right there, it can't get any better.' But the next time I'm fucking you, your body blows the last one out of the water and makes a new best yet."

I chuckled and kissed his neck, up to his ear, and over to his mouth where I leaned in and teased his tongue with mine, sucking it into my mouth and making him moan and his cock twitch.

"I've never been fucked so thoroughly before. You consume every inch of my body when we're together. It's not just sex, it's so much fucking more."

"So much fucking more." He repeated, agreeing. "Let's get to your place so I can eat your pussy for breakfast before we pass out for the next few hours and do it all over again. Sound like a plan?"

"Sounds like Christmas morning to me." I slid over to my seat and pulled my pants back up as he got dressed and ditched the condom. We were only a few minutes from my apartment but by the time he parked in the parking lot and held my hand to cross the street to the building, we were both practically running with wild, carefree smiles on our faces.

When my apartment door shut behind us, he slammed me up against it and devoured me. There was no other word to describe it. I couldn't tell where I ended and he began.

He took me to my bedroom and stripped me bare before shedding his clothes. "Where's this rose?" he asked as I stared up at him in confusion. "The toy you used to play with yourself earlier. I want to use it on you."

My cheeks reddened again, but I nodded to my bedside table, and he wasted no time opening it up and pulling out the small rose toy.

"This little thing made you soak your bed in less than two minutes?" he asked, holding it in his palm and making it look tiny.

"Yes, but it was mostly the mental imagery I was using at that time that got the job done."

"Imagery of me?"

"Yes."

"What were you imagining?"

I smirked at him. "The way you look over the top of me, rolling your hips with your cock buried deep inside of me." He got on the bed and pushed me back until I was lying on my back on the pillows. He pushed my knees open wide and laid down on the bed between them. "I was thinking about how sexy your tattoos and muscles are when you're holding yourself up, and how feminine you make me feel with your big hands and caring touches." He smirked at me and leaned over to kiss my inner thigh.

"What else?"

"I was thinking about how good it felt to have your mouth on me the first time we fucked." His teeth glinted as he smiled before dropping his lips to my exposed pussy.

"Like this?" He asked and swiped his tongue up from my ass to my clit before sucking it into his mouth and flicking it with his tongue.

"Fuck yes, just like that, Jed." I moaned, gripping onto the bed sheets, and pressing my heels into the mattress for leverage.

He growled, and the vibrations on my clit were divine. "I can taste your orgasm from earlier in the car. It tastes so good." He mused and pushed two fingers into my pussy and then brought them out to his mouth and sucked on them. "So good." I watched in wonderment as he played with me like it was his favorite thing in the world to do, and it was sexy as hell.

Past guys that I'd hooked up with, either couldn't bother to go down on me or gave lackluster performances for a few minutes before they got impatient and just put it in.

I never knew what I was missing until Jed showed me.

"You're so good at that. If I were a jealous girl, I'd worry about how many women you've done that to, to get so skilled." I joked, running my fingers through his hair as he chuckled against my clit.

"Tell me something deep, Carly." He said while he watched his fingers disappear in and out of my body. My eyes widened as I watched him.

"Deep? Now?" I asked, laughing a small chuckle at the absurdity of it all.

"Yes, now. Deep like something that you don't tell other people. Something just for me." His dark eyes were glowing as they stared up at me when he lowered his mouth to my clit again. He was a God, laying before me and pleasuring me like this, and a part of me felt so unworthy.

"I've never loved anyone before. I don't even know if I'm capable of it." I said quickly before shame or embarrassment could stop me. His eyes never left mine as he continued to play with me and processed my words. I was worried I'd gone *too* deep, but then he pulled back and gave me his coined one-sided grin that made my thighs quiver.

"You've just never met anyone worthy of your love before, Carly. But now you have, and I'm going to change that for you."

"You're so sure?" I asked.

"Just wait and see, Kit." He said and then turned on the rose, halting the conversation as he eyed it up and figured it out. He put it against my clit, and my back bowed, and my head fell back. "Holy fuck." He mused, watching my reaction to it.

"Yeah." I gasped, fisting the sheets again and rocking my hips. He kept two fingers inside of me and curled them forward toward my G-spot. "Oh, oh damn." I gasped as he rubbed me from the inside as the rose sucked on my clit.

"Have you ever squirted before?" He asked.

"No." I panted.

"Anal?"

"Yes."

"Good."

"Good?" I wondered, trying to focus, but the one-word answers and questions were all I could manage.

"Very good." He replied and he took his fingers from my pussy and dropped them down to my ass. "Is your ass ready to take my cock? Or do we need to work up to it?"

I laughed and reached down to pull the rose off my clit. "I cannot think straight with that thing trying to suck my soul out through my clit." He laughed and sat up, straddling one of my thighs and rubbing his cock against it.

"How prepped is your ass, Carly?"

"I don't know." I stammered, "I don't think I'll ever be *ready* to take your cock there. But that doesn't mean I can't."

"Good girl." He pushed his wet fingers into my ass, and I squealed and arched my back. He turned me over on my side, with my one leg still under him and he brought my top leg up to rest against his chest as he kissed my calf and ankle. This position left my legs spread, and my ass exposed and off the bed. I curled my arm under my head and watched his long fingers wrap around my ankle and hold it against his tattooed chest as his other arm flexed as he pushed and pulled his fingers in and out of my ass.

"Yes." I moaned, arching my back, and pushing my ass into his hand more. Jed pressed my top leg back towards my body, and I hooked my arm around it and held it at my chest, opening me up even more to his eyes and hands. He grabbed the rose again and put it back on me as he pumped his fingers in my ass, and I was lost in a puddle of sensation and pleasure. "Oh. My. God. Jed." I panted, and his predatory smile made me ache.

I pinched my nipples with my fingers, rolling them and pulling on them as he watched in fascination. "You're so sexy like this, spread open for me while I play with your pussy and your ass." He groaned, "God, I can't wait to fuck this ass, baby. I can't wait to feel your body fighting my cock as I push it in real deep."

"Oh God!" I moaned and started coming hard. I shattered underneath him from his dirty talk and the dual sensation of both my pussy and my ass being pleasured. "Yes! Don't stop." My whole body shook as I orgasmed.

"Good girl." He said, taking the rose off as the sensation became too much on my over-sensitive clit. "Are you on the pill?" He asked, and I fought to come back to earth.

"I have the implant in my arm."

"I want to fuck you bare, Carly. I need to fuck you raw." He growled, "And I want to come deep inside of you. I'm clean, I get tested regularly and I always wrap up. But I don't want to with you."

"I'm clean too." I moaned.

"Fuck yes." He groaned and slid forward and turned just enough to press his cock against my entrance. He stayed on my one leg, and I kept my other one folded up against my chest as he slapped the head of his cock against my clit a few times and then pushed inside of me. "Your pussy is so creamy for me." He pressed his fingers that were still in my ass against his cock as he thrust in, and we both moaned. "So, fucking tight."

He picked up his rhythm and fucked my pussy and ass in sync, and I was crazed with pleasure and need. I dug my nails into his muscular thighs as I took his cock, giving him control of me, and he did not disappoint.

"Give it to me, Jed. Don't hold back. Fuck me like you did in the car, I need it like that." I begged, and he leaned over my body and kissed me, shoving his tongue into my mouth, and biting my lips as he quickened his thrusts and fucked me from base to tip over and over. "Yes!" I hissed. He pulled his fingers out of my ass and spanked my ass, the crack through the air was loud and wonderful.

"Now be a good girl and come on my cock so I can come deep inside of your pretty little pussy for the first time."

This man.

CHAPTER 8 - JED

I was going to blow my fucking load so hard. Carly James was the sexiest woman I'd ever met before and she let me fuck her wild in the front seat of my car in an alley, then rode my face and let me play with her ass and her toy and was now milking my bare cock for everything that it was worth as I fucked her through her incredible orgasm.

"Jed!" She screamed, and that was my last straw. I started coming, filling up her pussy and loving the way I could feel the hot silkiness of my orgasm coating my cock inside of her, knowing that she was going to be dripping my come for the rest of the day made me mad with lust for her.

I rolled her over onto her back and laid between her legs as I continued to thrust my cock in long, deep, slow movements that were making her whimper and moan under me. She dug her nails into my hair and held my face against her neck where I latched my teeth onto her skin and sucked, marking her. "How is it so fucking good with you?" I asked hypothetically and then pulled out of her body, sitting up and pushing her legs wide to see the evidence of our mutual orgasms all over her lower lips and thighs.

She groaned and covered her face with her arm, but she let me look. I ran the tip of my finger down one side of her pussy and up the other, gathering my come and her cream on it, and then pushed it back inside of her. "Wouldn't want a drop to be wasted." She moaned from beneath her arm, and I chuckled.

"Your primal side is so fucking hot." she said, pulling me down to lay next to her as she snuggled into my side.

"My primal side is growing stronger and stronger the more times I'm around you. You should be careful, by next week I may be dragging you into my cave by your hair to breed you."

She chuckled and groaned, "Why does even the word breed sound so fucking sexy on your lips?"

"Because you have a primal side too, and it's calling to me to knock you up. Sex was designed to procreate, we just decided at some point along the way to enjoy the act even without wanting the end result to be a baby all the time."

"I can't even imagine having a baby right now, though." She said softly as I ran my hand up and down her spine.

"Me either. But our bodies don't care."

"Well, thank God for birth control."

"Thank God indeed. Because I plan on doing that a whole fucking lot more now that I've blown my load in you."

She buried her face in my neck and wrapped her arms around my stomach, "And branded my neck with your teeth."

I pushed her hair off her neck and leaned up to see the mark I'd left in the heat of the moment. "Did it hurt you when I did it?" I shouldn't have bitten her so hard, but I was lost in the pleasure.

"Yes." She said and then smiled. "But in the best way possible."

"Elaborate."

"It hurt in a good way. Like when you spanked me. Or when you pushed your fingers in my ass without warning me. All of those things hurt, but they also felt good. Like. Really. Fucking. Good."

I rolled until we were facing each other, and I pulled her leg up over my hip. "Yeah, they did, didn't they?"

"Mmh." She hummed and kissed the end of my nose. Her eyes were heavy and the clock on her end table said four am.

"Let's get some sleep. I've got the day off and all sorts of ideas about how I'm going to ravage you. So we need our rest."

"Oh boy." She mused with her eyes closed, and I pulled the covers up over us and turned out the lights and laughed to myself at the way her breathing told me she was already asleep on my arm. Within minutes I passed out with her, content, and sated.

A couple of hours later, I woke up with her ass nestled against my hard-on and my hand holding her breast. She was still passed out, holding my hand to her chest, and looked so fucking angelic. The clock read eight am, and my stomach growled. I didn't want to wake her, but I also didn't want to leave her side. I pulled back, planning on trying to slide from the bed to go make breakfast, but when my hard cock slid from between her ass cheeks, I felt the silky wetness of my come coating her pussy and thighs.

I pushed it forward again, biting my lip to hold back the moan of how good it felt. I hitched my hips low to angle my cock, and I felt her entrance against the head of my cock and pushed forward, impaling her smoothly and effortlessly with the help of the natural silky lube.

"Fuck." I whispered, and she moaned, pushing her ass higher to give me better access as I pushed in.

"Hmm." She hummed, still not moving or anything to tell me she was awake all the way, but I kept going. She felt way too fucking good not to.

I put my hand back on her tit and pinched her nipple and played with it as I slowly stroked myself with her pussy.

"Jed." She moaned in a whisper, stretching, and pulling her legs up to open herself to me more. "What a way to be woken up." She voiced.

"I couldn't help it, my come was making your pussy so silky and wet I just had to feel inside."

She chuckled and held my hand to her breast and squeezed it as she sighed. "Tell me something deep, Jed."

She repeated the words I'd said to her earlier before we fell asleep, and I smiled against her neck. "Now?" I joked.

"Not so easy, is it?" She reached behind her and grabbed my balls, massaging them in her dainty little fingers as I kept lazily fucking her.

"No, I suppose it's not. How deep do you want it, baby?" I asked as I buried myself balls deep inside of her. "The deeper the darker with me."

"I want your deepest and darkest, Jed. I want something that's never seen sunshine before."

I thought about it for a moment and then whispered words I'd never said out loud in the light of day. "I killed my dad when I was twelve after he killed my mom." She gasped and looked over her shoulder at me. "That's when the darkness took hold of my soul and sentenced me to hell."

She rolled over and pushed my shoulders flat onto the bed and lowered herself onto my cock. For a second I was worried we were done having sex after admitting that, but a small part of myself knew she wouldn't shy away from it. She rode me for a moment and then leaned down to whisper against my lips. "I'll be your heaven, baby, stay within my light and I'll bring you out of the darkness. I'll save your soul."

I gripped her hips tight in my hands and fucked up into her body. "Promise?" I was hanging off the edge of her vow of light and was desperate for it to be true. I needed saving.

"I promise." She said confidently, and I believed her. I rolled us both over and twined my fingers through hers and pinned them on the bed above her head as I slowly fucked her. It wasn't rough and brutal like some of the other times we'd had sex.

This was raw.

It was personal.

It was... making love.

Even though neither one of us was in love at the moment, we made love to each other with our bodies. There were no words to describe the emotion passing between us, but we felt it. She kept her eyes open the whole time, watching me intently as I gave her everything she needed and more. She begged and pleaded in incoherent words and broken sentences as I pushed her body past the point of surrender, and when we came, tears slid from her eyes into her hair.

"I'm not sad." She said softly, watching me follow the tears with my eyes. "I'm just—moved." She chuckled softly like it was ridiculous to feel that way. I kissed her.

So slowly.

I moved my lips against her soft and swollen ones, gently nipping at them with my teeth and licking them before softly teasing her tongue with mine. "I'm right there with you, sweetheart."

She sighed and shook it off. "Tell me about your parents."

I rolled until we were nose to nose on our sides again and ran my hand up and down her back. "I grew up in a happy home." Memories assaulted me as I thought back to that time after forcing them dormant for so long. "We lived in the suburbs, had a nice house, they drove nice cars, we went on vacations and had cookouts with our neighbors. I had a good childhood. Until one day I came home, and my mom was on the floor of her bedroom, crying." I licked my lips, looking away from her eyes. "She was beautiful, she had dark brown hair and light blue eyes and she was always smiling and laughing. But that day she was crying, and I walked into her room, and I remember sitting at her feet, confused, because she never cried. At least not in front of me."

I ran my hands up and down her spine, grounding me as anger fought to claw its way from my heart and into my body. "She looked up at me, and her right eye was black and blue, and her lip was split." Carly's eyes widened as she realized what had happened. "She wouldn't tell me what happened, just that she had had an accident. But looking back on it now, when Dad got home that night, he brought a dozen roses and the most expensive bottle of wine he could buy. And plane tickets for the two of them to go away together that weekend, on a whim." I took a deep breath.

"He was groveling and apologizing." she said softly.

"Yeah. The first of many times in the next year or so." I agreed flatly. "The bruises stopped appearing on her face after a bit of time, but then I'd notice that she was wearing long sleeves outside in the sun, or how she'd favor her side after an argument between them. He was beating her, and not only was he getting smart about it, but she was also covering for him. I had a little sister too, who was terrified of them when they got even the least bit loud around each other because she was afraid a fight was going to break out. I tried my best to take her away when it got bad, to shield her from it because she was only eight."

Carly leaned forward and kissed my lips. "You don't have to tell me anymore if you don't want to. I get the picture."

I tightened my arms around her. "I want to tell you. Which is odd, because I've never told anyone else before. Not even Ryker or Gavin." I shook my head and looked back into her eyes. "I guess I trust you more."

She smiled and softened in my arms and nodded for me to continue.

"There was one night, the night before my twelfth birthday, that the argument went—bad. I'd been in bed when her screaming woke me up, and Laila, my sister, crawled into my bed to hide from it. And I snapped." I remembered how much rage filled my body as I tore out of my bedroom on the hunt to hurt my dad for scaring my tiny little sister. "When I got downstairs I found my dad on the couch, naked, fucking some redhead as my mom screamed in agony from the doorway, throwing things and destroying the house. My dad never flinched, he just looked at her while he fucked the other woman on our sofa and smiled like he was a fucking god."

Carly laid her forehead against my chest and tightened her arms around me like she was trying to support me. "I can't imagine seeing that at eleven years old."

"It wrecked me. I couldn't understand how he could be screwing some ugly woman who looked like she was high on meth when the most beautiful woman in the world stood in the kitchen shattering to pieces. That was the first time he ever put his hands on me too."

"No." Carly cried softly. "I'm so sorry."

"I screamed and yelled at him so hard that he got off the other woman and punched me square in the face and then spit on me and then walked away and went back to fucking her like he hadn't just hit his kid. And it was at that moment that I knew none of us were safe around him anymore." My body shuddered as I remembered the pain of my first-ever black eye. "The next day I came home from the park, it was my birthday, but my parents hadn't let me go to school because of my black eye, so I'd snuck out and went to the park on my bike to get away from everything for a little while. When I walked back into the house, I knew instantly that something wasn't right. I could just feel it on my skin. The house was silent as I walked in through the kitchen and living room, and when I got to the bottom of the stairs, I heard Laila's quiet cries from upstairs."

Flashbacks flooded my vision, and my skin prickled as I remembered how afraid I'd been as I flew up the stairs. "When I got to my bedroom, I found my baby sister lying on the floor, beaten to a bloody pulp. She was in and out of consciousness and crying for me, but even as I picked her up and held her to my chest, she was so out of it that she screamed and cried, trying to get away while she screamed my name. I carried her downstairs and to the next-door neighbor's house, who had been friends with our family for years. I opened their front door and walked right in, shocking the shit out of the mom who was cooking in the kitchen, but as soon as she saw Laila in my arms, she ran forward and took her from me and called 911."

Carly kissed my chest again, and I could feel her tears on her cheeks as she took a deep breath in against my skin. "You were so young, but so was Laila."

I nodded my head. "I left her at the neighbor's and ran back next door as the mom screamed for me to come back while she was on the phone with the police, but I just ran harder. I needed to find my mom. If he had done that to Laila, the baby of our family, I could only imagine how bad off my mom was. When I walked into their bedroom, my dad was on top of her in the center of their bed. She was clawing at him and swinging her fists into his shoulders and arms, but he had her pinned and his hands were around her throat. I lunged at him, but he just pushed me off of him and threw me into the wall. And that was when he picked up the butcher knife that was lying next to him on the bed." A cold sweat broke out across my skin as I remembered the sound the knife made as he plunged it into my mom's chest over and over again as I crumbled to the floor in shock and fear. "He stabbed her over and over again while I cowered on the floor in fear."

"It's not your fault." Carly snapped, looking up at me and pulling my head down to look at her. "You were a baby too, Jed. Twelve is not old enough to process all of that."

"Maybe not, but I was a big kid. I was already almost six feet tall and was beefy from football, but I was frozen in place as he stabbed her. Seventeen times." I whispered, scowling at the memory. "The son of a bitch laughed as he did it too, like he had completely snapped and fallen off the sanity wagon. I don't remember exactly what happened after that, but I ran to my room and grabbed my metal baseball bat and when the cops ran in, I was standing over his body on the floor, and his face and head were—pulp. I was covered in blood, and I couldn't even lift my arms from swinging the bat so many times."

"You did the right thing, baby." She whispered and I knew she believed that, and a part of me believed it too. "He could have killed you next, he probably would have."

"I know. But it broke something inside of me, taking his life like that, watching him take my mom's life. The state didn't charge me with murder, though they did try at first until our neighbors testified that there was a long history of violence between our parents. Apparently, they'd heard them fighting but never called the cops because we lived in the type of ritzy neighborhood that didn't want that kind of trouble. The state gave my mom's parents' custody of Laila, but my grandparents thought it would be best if I didn't come with them too because they thought I was a danger to her. Because of the brutality of my dad's murder."

"Oh, my God. No." Carly gasped. I nodded my head, "I got put in a foster home, and ordered into intensive therapy. I haven't seen or heard from my little sister since. My grandparents changed her name and completely hid her from me. And that loss hurt a hundred times worse than losing both parents, how I did."

"You've tried looking for her? Recently?"

"Not for a couple of years now, I'm probably no better for her as an enforcer for the Shadeport crew, then I was as a child murderer."

"Shh." She said, crawling up and holding my head to her chest, "You are not a murderer." She paused and tilted her head. "Well, not for killing your father. I don't know what you've done with your time since then, though I've heard rumors."

I laughed lightly at her honest comment, and she was right. I'd not only killed more people than I could count, but I'd also tortured many of them before killing them. "I'm not a good man Carly, she's better off without me."

"I don't believe that, Jed. You're a far better man than most I've come in contact with over the years, and believe me, that's been a lot of men. And she's no better off without you, don't you wonder if she thinks about you, if she was told why she was kept from you, or if they even treat her right?"

"I wonder all the time, baby."

She pondered that for a moment but remained quiet. There's nothing to be done about it now, so I don't allow myself to hope or want for some miracle to happen. It keeps me from being disappointed and upset over something I can't change.

CHAPTER 9 – CARLY

"I want every detail, every teeny little morsel of information. I want it all!" Ellie gasped and leaned in closer, begging for details of my two weeks alone with Jed while she was away frolicking in some paradise with her sexy-as-sin husband.

"Not a chance." I joked, leaning back on my lounge chair, and adjusting my top. I'd taken to wearing a top since getting with Jed and hated the way it felt but respected him more.

"Oh, come on!" She groaned, "I'm desperate."

"Didn't you get enough spice on your little getaway to keep you sated?"

"Of course I did! I went days without even getting dressed, like no panties or overshirt or anything. Naked as the day I was born, naked. And it was incredible, and it was exactly what I needed from Ry after how hard he's been working lately. But I want to know what my mysteriously sweet giant of a bodyguard did to woo you and leave you looking like you're floating on cloud nine in sexual bliss."

I chuckled and looked at her, "Fine! But it stays between us." I say, staring her down.

"Us and Ryker." She said, nodding her head like she didn't just add a person into the equation, but I wasn't surprised. I wouldn't keep something from Jed if the roles were reversed.

"We've been inseparable since he picked me up for our first date and it's so easy," I said, smiling to myself. "Obviously, he probably wouldn't be so interested in spending all of his time with me if you guys hadn't been away on vacation, and if Frankie hadn't lost his damn mind."

"Can you believe they still haven't found him yet?" she asked, showing me her rarely seen temper. "And why the fuck didn't you tell me about it before Ryker did?" She eyed me angrily.

"Because you were supposed to be getting fucked properly and not worrying about me."

She reached across the space and took my hand, holding it in the space between our loungers, "I always worry about you, the same way you worry about me." I rolled my eyes at her as she tried to look serious. But it was impossible in a bright pink polka dot bikini and her adorable baby bump.

"Either way, it's fine. He hasn't been a problem since that first day, I think the guys all blew everything out of proportion."

"No way, if I had been here, you wouldn't have gone back to work at all after that, or your apartment. You would have been staying here with me and Jed."

"How would I have stayed here with you and him?" I asked, laughing at her pregnant brain.

"Because he lives here, you would have spent your nights in bed with him and your days out here with me, like this." She said so matter of factly.

"Wait!" I leaned forward, taking my sunglasses off, "Jed lives here? How did I not know that?"

She eyed me and took her glasses off, shielding her eyes with her hand. "Haven't you guys stayed at his place at all or even talked about it?"

"No."

"He lives here on the grounds, in the barracks." She hooked her thumb over her shoulder to the large building behind the garage overlooking the deep lawn. "Zeke and he both live there. They each have really cute little apartments there."

"Huh," I said, sitting back and mulling that information over in my head. He'd never invited me to stay with him, and after the first night he picked me up at the club and took me to my place, we'd just gone there every night. But Ellie and Ryker got home this morning, so would that mean he'd be back to staying here twenty-four seven and I'd be on my own?

"So at least tell me this, is the sex as hot as I imagine it to be?" She asked, with a mischievous smile on her face.

"Hotter." I played with her, fanning myself. "He doesn't have a normal dick; he has a fucking baseball bat between his legs, and the man knows how to use it."

She squealed, clapping her hands together dramatically, "I was hoping he was hung; it would have been a shame for him to be so big everywhere else and not where it matters most."

"Perfectly put." I nodded and took a sip of my mocktail margarita we drank now that she was pregnant. I wasn't going to rub it in by drinking in front of her even though she'd told me numerous times that it was okay.

"So..." She said and turned in her seat to face me. I put my glasses back on and turned to face her, tuning into her shift in conversation.

"Remember when we talked before I left, and I said I wanted to run some things by Ryker first before I shared with you?"

"Of course, I was wondering when you were going to tell me."

"Well." She said, rubbing her hands over her belly. "I want you to move in."

I raised my eyebrows at her and shook my head in confusion. "Sister wives with you and Ryker isn't exactly my cup of tea, girl." She rolled her eyes, "But if you ever ditch him I'm game for lesbian motherhood with you."

She laughed and poked my nose. "I don't mean into the house with us, enough people are lurking around catching us having sex in random places as it is. I mean onto the property here."

"Like in the barracks?" I asked, eyeing the bland building behind us.

"No, there's a cottage on the other side of the shop that I think would be perfect for you two."

"Whoa, us two? What exactly are you thinking here, Ellie?"

"Yes, you two, you said it yourself, you haven't slept alone in weeks. If you're here on the property, you'd be even closer to him to do it more."

"Huh," I said, trying to imagine living here in their world.

"The cottage is adorable; it's two bedrooms and it's all been updated recently. Ryker had originally built it to house Zeke, but then Jed and Razz were living here too at the time, and the barracks were better suited for them all. And think about it, Frankie wouldn't be able to get to you here. You'd be safer here, which would help me relax."

"I don't know what to say, I'm not sure I could afford it now that I'm not dancing."

She huffed at me and brushed it off, "You're not paying a dime to live here. It's all paid for anyway, if you want, you can pay the utilities or whatever, but you don't have to. And Theo told Ryker that you guys are splitting days anyway, so you won't even be at work as much anymore. And think about it," She grabbed my hand again and pulled me to sit next to her on her lounger, "Wouldn't it be fun living here, being so close when this little one is born?"

She put her hand on her belly and looked at me hopefully. "Yeah, it would be a dream," I answered truthfully. I shook my head, shaking the daydreams of having a family from my mind. "What if Jed doesn't want me in his space though? He didn't even tell me he lived here, El, what if he doesn't want that?"

"It's not his space Carly, you're my family, and the cottage is not even visible from the barracks or the main house, so he wouldn't even know you're there if he didn't want to. It's fucking perfect. And besides," She shrugged and played with her dark hair where it fell from her bun. "Ryker's probably already told Jed he's getting a promotion from my guard and enforcer to the right-hand man with Zeke."

"What?" I gasped, "What do you mean?"

"He doesn't have time to date if he's my guard, that's just the bare basics of it, and I won't stand in the way of him finding happiness. Zeke and Ryker had already been discussing how they'd noticed a switch in him the last few months. He's not content anymore only having the crew in his life, so they want to help him find balance like they do."

"Zeke has a balance between crew and life?" I asked, scoffing. "That man is here more than Jed is."

"True, but it's different for him." She said with a flip of her hair, not elaborating. "Regardless if you move in or not, Jed will have a lot more free time on his hands starting today."

"What if he doesn't take that as a good thing? What if he resents me for losing his job guarding you, you know how seriously he takes that job, El. I can't believe Ryker agreed to let someone else guard you when he knows that Jed is life or death serious about your safety."

"He will see the benefits of the switch eventually, even if he doesn't right away. It's not a demotion, believe me, he'll have a ton more responsibilities, he'll just be able to delegate them himself instead of always taking the orders down the chain."

"Yeah, maybe," I said, thinking it over in my head.

"Come on," she said. Standing up, she pulled on her gauzy cover-up and slid her feet into her sandals. "Let's go see the cottage and then you can decide once you have all the info."

I slid my sandals on and tied my sarong over my hips and followed her as we walked the cute paver pathway past the buildings, she'd just informed me were the barracks and the shop.

Jed had told Zeke to take Frankie to the shop when he called him after Frankie had blown my phone up while we were on our first date, but he never told me what it was or why he would go there.

When we walked past the path to it, Ellie walked the long way around instead of past the front doors. I looked in the doors and saw men, heavily armed, standing right inside them and shivered. "What exactly does Ryker use the shop for?" I asked, unable to draw my eyes away from the doorway.

Ellie shrugged, "You wouldn't like that answer." I turned and eyed her as we walked, and she laced her arm through mine and pulled me along as she worked out how to answer it. "That's—where my mom died."

Elora had told me about how Ryker had captured her mom and killed her in front of them right after it had happened. She'd been distraught about how she didn't react the way she thought she should have and was worried about what that said about her. I'd assured her over and over that she was not the bad guy in that situation, but we hadn't talked about it further.

I looked at the large building again and took a deep breath. "That's where they're going to kill Frankie, isn't it?"

"Maybe." She pursed her lips. "They'll make him wish he was dead at least. I don't know if they'll kill him, though. But I suppose only time will tell once they finally find him."

"Hmm." I pondered it all over in my head and followed her. "How did Ryker find your mom? Wasn't she down in South LA?"

"Yeah, he has connections and allies everywhere, though."

I stopped walking and pulled her to a stop. We stood alone on the long path with no one near. "If I asked Ryker for help to find someone, would he do it without telling anyone else or giving me a rash of shit for it?"

She raised her eyebrows and mulled it over. "Depends on who it is, honestly. But if it wasn't for anything bad, I'm sure he'd help. He loves you as much as I do Carly, there's not much he wouldn't do for you if you asked him nicely." She wiggled her eyebrows.

"You mean if you asked him nicely, for me." I laughed.

"Well, if you insist on me trading sexual favors for real favors with my husband, I guess I have no choice in the matter." She said sarcastically, but I knew she was more than willing to negotiate with Ryker with sex.

"Good to know."

"So, who are we looking for?" she asked as we started walking again.

I contemplated my answer, not wanting to betray Jed, but I needed to give her some details if I was going to get help. "Jed has a little sister he hasn't seen since he was twelve. I can't go into details because it's not a good story to tell, but he's looked for her before with no luck."

"I had no idea Jed had any family; I knew he'd been in the crew since he was a teenager, but he doesn't talk about his past."

"Your dad got him in when he was supposed to punish him for stealing from a convenience store in Shadeport territory. Gavin told him he could tell there was something about Jed that would make a good soldier for the crew and took him under his wing. That's why he's so obsessed with protecting you, he was close with your dad."

Tears came to her eyes as she listened to my story. "I had no idea." She said quietly.

"I know. I told him that he needed to tell you, but I also knew he never would. He cares for you deeply because he was given a second chance at life by Gavin, and without him and Ryker, he probably wouldn't be alive today."

She slashed at the tears and shook her head. "That man is such an onion."

I laughed, confused. "An onion?"

"Like Shrek. He has so many layers to him, I'm always surprised by him left and right."

I chuckled and rolled my eyes, "Girl, you don't even know half of it. Maybe between you and I together, we might get to know half of him someday."

She laughed and agreed, and we started walking again.

We followed the path around the side of the shop and the cottage came into view, stopping me in my tracks. The word cottage didn't do it justice.

It was the size of a medium house, and it was beautiful. It was nestled against the woods that lined the property, and it was white with black shutters on the windows and dormers in the roof that made it look like the house had a smiley face on it. Flowers lined the front porch, and two rocking chairs sat by the front door. "Wow," I whispered.

"I know, right." Ellie sighed, looking at it. "If Ryker wasn't so high maintenance, I'd insist on us living here, but you know that would never fly, and instead I think it's perfect for you and Jed."

"It's so beautiful."

"Come on inside, let's look around." We walked around the house, and it was breathtaking. It was fully furnished with farmhouse-chic décor and light-colored furniture. The kitchen was large, and I imagined cooking all sorts of things in the oven. The master bedroom was on the first floor with an attached bathroom that had a large shower and soaker tub, and I swooned, imagining taking baths in it.

"I'm sold," I said, deadpanning as she pulled me upstairs to look at the bedroom and loft space that was open to the floor below.

"And this is where little baby Ryker can sleep when Auntie Carly and Uncle Jed babysit so Mommy and Daddy can have wild crazy sex all over the house and make baby number two."

Laughter bubbled up in my chest and erupted into full belly clutching, side holding, mirth as I imagined just that. "I'd love every second of it too. With or without Jed."

"Without isn't an option babe, he's hooked, and you're sold." she said with a shrug. "It's a done deal. And now that you'll be living here, you and I can be even bigger pains in the asses of our men." She cackled, "Can you imagine how much trouble we can get into together twenty-four-seven?"

"Oh Lord, I'm scared to even think about it."

We walked back to the mansion laughing and planning, and as we stepped in the back patio door, Ryker came flying into the kitchen with Jed hot on his heels.

"Where the fuck were you?" Ryker snapped at Ellie and me.

Ellie's anger bristled at his tone, and I groaned, knowing they were full on going to go at it. I looked at Jed, who stood behind Ryker with his own hands on his hips, and felt his anger like a full-blown caress on my skin. And I couldn't help the twinge of anger that I felt residually in my system from finding out that he lived here and never told me.

"We went for a walk." Ellie bit.

"Where? We've been looking for you two for fifteen minutes."

"I didn't realize I owed either of you a play-by-play of where I go on the property here, I'm not your pet. I'm your wife."

"And I am your husband, and I had no fucking clue where you or my baby were!" He bellowed, and I watched his fear turn into rage. Rationally, I knew this conversation needed to end before he had a coronary or she went into labor.

"We just went out back–" I started, stepping around Ryker towards Jed.

"Don't you dare, Carly!" Ellie snapped. "He isn't my boss." She held her finger up to stop me.

"But he is mine." I deadpanned. "She was showing me the cottage." He deflated a bit, and she rolled her eyes.

"Oh." He said, dropping his hands from his hips as if he had just remembered they had discussed me living there before.

"It's amazing, but I'm not sure I want to live there if this is going to happen every time she comes to see me or something."

"Live there?" Jed asked, finally stepping into the conversation.

"Yeah, unless the idea of me living a couple hundred yards away from you is a no-go because turns out you live here at the mansion too. Who knew?" I asked sarcastically, letting him know I was less than pleased that he hadn't told me himself.

"I think it's a great idea." He said, never breaking eye contact with me. "I can keep you safe here."

"Safe," I repeated, underwhelmed by his response.

"You're a real pain in the ass, you know that?" Ellie sneered and drew our attention to where she and Ryker stood toe to toe.

"Don't fucking tempt me, Ellie."

"To what, treat me like an adult?"

"To spank you like the fucking child you're acting like."

"You wouldn't dare!" She snapped, "We don't use sexual pleasure in anger, remember!"

"Oh, I'd enjoy myself while I did it." He said with a sinister and predatory smile on his face.

"That's my cue," I said, turning and walking out of the kitchen, neither of them even acknowledged my exit though as they were both locked in a stare-off. When I got to the back patio and headed towards my lounger where my bag was, Jed caught up with me.

"Hey. Are you mad at me?" He asked.

"What gave you that impression?" I snapped and then sighed and rolled my shoulders. "No. I'm not mad. I'm just confused."

His shoulders fell, and he walked over to me, pulling me down on his lap on my lounger until I was straddling him. "Confused about what?"

"Why didn't you tell me you lived here?" I asked, holding his gaze, waiting to see some sort of clue there.

"Why does it matter?"

"I don't know why," I answered truthfully. "I guess now that they're back, this is your priority, and it just seems like I won't see you at all now that I know that you live *and* work here."

"But you're moving in here, so what does it matter? We'll all be here." He said as if it were so simple. He leaned forward and kissed me, and I let him because I needed to calm down, and his touch was usually soothing. When I pulled back, I looked him in the eye.

"And work? What about that?"

"What about it? I had this job with these obligations when we got together, it's not like I changed up after I committed to you. I can't change how much I have to work."

My eyes flickered back and forth between his as I waited for more, but it never came. He wasn't going to tell me he got promoted, and he was going to keep his cards close to his chest. I nodded, seeing the red flags popping up all around us. "Okay," I said softly and got off his lap, grabbing my bag from underneath. "I'm going to go get dressed," I said, not looking him in the eye as I walked away, afraid he'd see how upset I was, and I didn't want that because I didn't even know why it upset me so badly.

I guess standing in the center of the large house, surrounded by people I cared for greatly, but not feeling significant to any of them in that moment, left me feeling insecure and doubtful that I even wanted to try to fit in here amongst their tight circle.

In a way, I didn't realize how much of an outsider I was amongst them all.

When I got inside, I walked past the now quiet kitchen and into the guest bath in the hallway and got dressed. When I came out, Zeke was walking down the hallway with his keys in his hands.

"Hey, Slim." he said, pausing when he saw me.

"Are you headed somewhere?" I asked.

"Yeah." He answered, without much other info.

"Can I catch a ride with you to my place, or at least as far as you're going in that direction?" He watched me closely and then looked over his shoulder to where Jed sat on the lounge chair still, waiting for me.

"You running?" he asked with a disapproving look on his scary face.

"You going to rat on me if I am?" I challenged.

After a minute, he chuckled and shook his head. "You and Ellie are just the same when it comes to that shit, and it irritates the piss out of me."

"Fine. I'll just get an Uber. Thanks anyway." I said, shrugging my shoulders and walking towards the front door.

"Wait, dammit." He grumbled, nodding his head towards the garage, and I followed him. He got into a sleek black Audi sports car, and I slid into the passenger seat. "I'm telling him as soon as I drop you off."

"That's fair," I replied, looking out the window.

He backed out of the garage and then drove down the driveway. "What'd he do?"

I smiled into my lap at this bizarre conversation with a man that used to terrify me. "Are you going to ask me about my feelings next?"

He smirked and kept his eyes on the road as he drove. "He's a bit dumb when it comes to feelings Carly. He and Ryker are a lot alike in that sense."

"Are you trying to tell me you're the wise love guru of you three stooges?" I asked, trying to keep the smile off my face and failing.

He laughed and nodded, "In a way, I suppose. I'm just the only one who knows how to use my mouth to communicate and not fuck everything up, I guess. So what did he do to upset you?"

I sighed, "He didn't do anything."

He paused, "And that's the problem, isn't it?"

I grinned again, rolling my eyes at him. "You're astute, you know that, right?"

"Love guru, darling." He drawled. "Now answer the question."

I looked out the window, embarrassed about trying to express my feelings with a man who always seemed devoid of such things. "I don't fit in anywhere. There's no place for me there, no matter how hard I try to pretend there is."

He watched me out of the corner of his eye, but I didn't meet his gaze as shame and insecurity washed over me.

"How do you mean?"

"Ellie has Ryker, and Jed has the crew and his job, so, in turn, he has Ryker and Ellie, and they will always come first to him. And I respect that, I do. But I just—" I faded.

"You just want to come first to someone." He finished for me.

Tears burned my eyes, and I blinked rapidly to keep them at bay. "Ellie wants me to move into the cottage, but I think it's just because she's lonely since Ryker locked her away in there after the kidnapping. She said Ryker promoted Jed, but he didn't tell me that when I asked him how my living at the mansion would change anything at all. And I know why he didn't say anything about it, because it wouldn't change anything, not really. He'd still be consumed with the crew, and I'd just conveniently be there when he was available. But he'd never be there when I was available, and that's not how I picture my happiness."

He hesitated, "How do you picture your happiness?"

"Being the very sun his world revolves around. Being the very breath his lungs ache to fill themselves with. Because that's how I give my love, and I can't settle for any less in return."

"You shouldn't settle for less, Carly. Not ever, not even for Jed."

"I know," I said sadly and looked out the window, watching the city pass by. "I just thought it was finally my turn to matter." He didn't say anything back to that, and there wasn't anything to say, so we just rode in silence until he pulled up in front of my apartment. "Thanks for the ride," I said and smiled at him.

"Give me your phone for a second." He said, and I handed it to him, ignoring the texts and calls from Jed that had come through in the last few minutes. He dialed a number and hit send, and then his phone lit up with my number on the dash. "There, now you have my phone number. If you ever need someone, whether it's to protect you or talk to you, or just someone to give you a ride somewhere, call me. Don't hesitate and don't overthink it, just dial the number, and hit send. Got it?"

I looked over at him as tears finally broke over my eyelashes. "You can't be nice to me, Zeke," I said in a whisper.

His brows dropped over his eyes in a scowl. "Why can't I?"

"Because I don't know how to let you be."

"Well, I guess we're going to learn a few things from each other as we go because I'm actually a nice guy."

A giggle bubbled up, and I dashed at the tears and took a calming deep breath. "I can't wait to see what I can teach you in return," I said sarcastically.

"Me neither, slim." I rolled my eyes at the nickname he'd taken to calling me when I started coming around Ryker's with Ellie when they first got together.

"See you later, cue ball."

He roared with laughter, and he rubbed his hand over his shaved head when I got out and walked into my apartment lobby. On the elevator ride up to my floor, I texted Jed back, not bothering to read the ones he sent me before that.

> Me: I need some space. I'll call you in a few days. Please respect that.

Next, I texted Ellie.

> Me: I'm fine. I'll call you later. Love you.

When I got into the safety of my apartment, I triple-locked my door and stripped down and crawled into my bed that smelled like Jed, and cried for all of the things I didn't realize I'd wanted until I felt them slip between my fingers.

Chapter 10 – Jed

I fucked up, royally. I wasn't sure exactly where I went wrong, but I knew I did when I came inside to find Carly when she didn't come back out to the pool and instead found her gone. I texted and called her, but she just ignored me until she sent me that message.

Space.

That was the last fucking thing I wanted to give her right now.

I sat at the kitchen counter, phone in hand, trying to figure out what to say to make things right, but I wasn't even sure where I'd gone wrong. In the time I'd gotten to know Carly, I'd seen her bite her tongue and keep her feelings to herself multiple times to save face and keep everyone around her happy.

And today she did it to me. I'd hurt her, and she'd put her brave face on and slipped away without a word.

Ryker and Elora walked in, laughing, and touching in a way that screamed, '*We just fucked our problems away*' and I groaned inwardly. A part of me was jealous of their ability to do that, but another part of me was wise enough to know it wouldn't work for everyone as effectively as it did them. But they had twenty years of history to fall back on when they had issues.

"Where's Carly?" Ellie asked, grabbing an apple out of the basket on the counter while Ry sat down on the stool next to me and stole it from her, and took a giant bite.

"I don't know," I answered truthfully.

She paused, and so did Ryker, "What do you mean you don't know?" She snapped, walking around to stand on the other side of the island so I couldn't avoid her glare.

Zeke walked in from the garage at the same time and glared at me too. "Is everyone pissed at me all of a sudden?" I snapped, lashing out.

"You tell me," Ellie said, still not sure what happened.

"I don't know yet," Ry answered.

"Yes." Zeke retorted.

"Fantastic." I bit out.

"What happened?" Ellie asked, but I just shrugged my shoulders, truly clueless.

"Fuck if I know, we were talking about her moving into the cottage, and I must have said something wrong because the next thing I knew, she was gone. I don't even know how she left."

"Me," Zeke said, leaning against the counter across the kitchen and crossing his arms. "I took her home."

"Why?" I yelled. "Why get involved?"

"Because that girl deserved to have someone in her corner for once!"

"What's that supposed to mean?" Ellie countered.

"Let me ask you three a question, and I think you'll get your answer from that." He started. "Ryker, who's your main priority day in and day out?"

"Ellie." He answered instantly.

"Right," Zeke turned to Elora, "You?"

"Ryker."

"As it should be. And you, Jed?" he asked, looking intently at me as he waited for my answer. But I could see where this was going.

"The crew."

"Bingo." He said, pursing his lips. "Yet Carly is the only one who would give her life for all three of you, without fail, and without hesitation."

Ellie deflated a bit, and a sad look crossed her face.

Zeke kept going though, riled up in a way that I hadn't seen from him before. "She doesn't matter that way to any of you." Ellie tried to cut in, but he held his hand up and silenced her, "Before you even try to reason with me here, I just watched her cut herself open and lay her beating heart out for me to see, so I know better. And I know that she has zero sense of self-worth, and I also know that you asking her to move in here for your selfish gains, to fight off your loneliness, was a low blow and a shitty thing to do to your best friend." He snapped, pointing at Ellie.

"Zeke," Ryker warned, not liking his tone. But Zeke kept going.

"And you," He leveled me with his stare, "Why did you refuse to squash her fears of feeling like a second priority to you by telling her about your new job description? Instead, you kept your mouth shut about it and made her feel like an inconsequential piece of ass. Ellie told her about the change to how things are going to be done around here, but when she asked you about it, you just deflected and solidified that she doesn't matter to anyone."

I didn't say anything to him because I knew as soon as he started lying into me, what I'd done. Truth was, I was on edge about this switch-up because I thought at first it was a punishment for something, perhaps for my failure to keep Ellie safe when she was kidnapped. But now I saw Ellie's hands all over it.

They were trying to make it easier for me to date Carly, to have a life. And I'd gone and ostracized her instead.

"You know what she said to me when I asked her what her idea of happiness looked like?" He asked, not waiting for me to answer him, and instead just told me. "She said she wanted to be the sun that your entire world revolved around. She wanted to be the breath that you ached to fill your lungs with. Because that's exactly how she gives her love. And you couldn't even be kind to her in a vulnerable moment."

God, that gutted me, because when I told her that there weren't words to describe how she made me feel, those were the words I had been searching for.

"Go to her," Ellie said to me, looking sad and guilty.

"She asked me to give her space. I have to respect that." I said, staring at my hands on the counter.

"Then I'll go to her," Ellie said and started walking from the room.

"Don't," Zeke commanded. "Respect her request for space. She's tough and she'll be fine, but she's raw right now, that was clear. Send her a text or something, but wait until later to show up. Let her feel her feelings before you try to fix everything because fears like hers are deeply rooted and they aren't something you're going to fix with just words."

"He's right," Ryker said, sighing and leaning forward on his elbows. "She's only going to change how she feels about herself when we change how we treat her."

"I hate this," Ellie said, tearing up.

"I know," Ryker said, standing up, pulling her into his arms and comforting her. I got up and walked out the back door, raw and on edge as I played Zeke's words over and over in my head.

It had only been a few weeks that I'd had her as mine, and I had already fallen for her and fucked it up. Maybe I should just end things while I was down, save her from the pain my stupidity would no doubt cause her again in the future.

But even as those thoughts crossed my mind, I knew I couldn't walk away from her. I didn't think about my destination until I was standing in my apartment closet, pulling clothes out and throwing them onto the bed.

I was going to figure this out, I was going to fix this. I had to.

I took trip after trip across the lawn as I took all of my belongings and personal effects to the cottage in the back of the property and moved in. If she was going to forgive me and give me another chance, I was going to be here, ready and committed to putting her first when she did.

It was Monday morning, and she still hadn't called me. And that killed me.

Four days and nights without her.

Ellie had gone over that same night and spent the night with her, much to Ryker's dislike, but she wouldn't give in to his demands to stay at home and bring Carly there where they were both safe. He'd posted men at every entrance of the building and outside of Carly's door, twenty-four-seven from that moment on, protecting her the only way she'd let him.

I slept at the cottage every night since then too, making small changes I hoped Carly would like when she finally came over. Praying she'd come over.

But I couldn't wait any longer with the radio silence from her end. I needed her.

Needed.

It wasn't a choice or a decision; it was necessary.

And I wanted to prove that to her.

I stood outside her apartment door and dismissed the two guards in her hallway; I didn't need witnesses if she ended things with me for good.

I knocked and waited to hear her inside. Glancing at my phone, it was only eight in the morning, which I knew was early for her. She'd be asleep because she worked last night, and I knew that because I'd parked outside the club and watched everyone walk in and out, aching to go in to her but forcing myself to stay in my car.

I knocked again. And this time I heard her walk to the door.

"Who is it?" She called from the other side, a few feet back from the door.

"Jed," I said firmly.

A long pause passed before she finally turned the lock and then opened the door, standing in her kitchen looking like a fallen angel. She had her hair piled on top of her head in a messy bun and wore a short baby pink cotton robe with white lace trim, her legs and feet were bare, and it made my mouth water.

"Hi." she said softly.

"Hi." I leaned on the doorjamb and just stared at her. "Can I come in?"

"Yeah." She backed up and let me in, and I shut and locked the door behind me as I followed her over to the couch as she sat down, crossing her long legs under her.

"I'm sorry it's so early for you," I said, sitting down in the chair across from her.

"It's early for you too, I saw you parked outside Lux when I left last night." Her stare was steady.

I grimaced, "Sorry."

"Don't be, I actually liked seeing you there."

"You did?"

She nodded and bit her lip. "I wanted to call you so many times, but after so much time had passed, I didn't know what to say and I didn't know if you even wanted me to call."

"Of course I did." I blurted out, leaning forward. "Carly, I've been in agony these last four days." She tilted her head as if she were trying to crack some hard code. "The only reason I stayed away was because you asked me to, but don't think for one second that it was easy or that I didn't think of you every second while I did it."

"I made a big deal out of nothing." she said, embarrassed as a flush crawled up her neck. "I overreacted and let my feelings get the best of me."

Standing up, unable to keep the distance between us, I sat down on the coffee table and put my hands on her bare knees between my legs on each side of her tiny body. "I misunderstood my reassignment with Ryker and Zeke. I thought I was being punished for failing Elora with the Wellingtons." I admitted out loud for the first time, exposing myself in hopes of proving the truth to her. "I thought they took me off her detail because I had failed, and then when you questioned me about work, I got defensive about it, not even understanding what you were asking of me at that moment." Her eyes got sad as she covered my hands with hers on her knees. "They were trying to lessen my duties, so I had time for you, time to dedicate to you and show you how fucking important you are to me."

I could tell she didn't believe me, so I continued, "The first time we had sex here, you had said it wasn't just sex, it was so much more. And I felt that in my soul, Carly. I felt that in a part of me that had been dormant for so long. Until I first touched you and you brought it to life again. I'm falling for you. I'm falling in love with your soul in a way I never knew was possible, especially after only being together for a short period. And I'm so sorry I ever made you feel optional to me because you are no more optional to me than air is." Her pretty blue eyes swam with tears as she climbed into my lap, straddling my legs as she held my face close to hers as I finished my speech, "You are the sun and the stars and the air between there and here, Carly."

She cried harder and kissed me like she had waited her whole life to hear those words. And I didn't realize it until that moment, but I'd waited my entire life to have someone worthy of saying them too. Someone who wouldn't abandon me either.

"I'm sorry I'm a mess, I'm tired and obviously delirious." She apologized, wiping away her tears.

I stood up with her in my arms, "Don't worry about it Kitten. Let's go get some sleep, and then we can talk about where to go from here."

"I like that plan." She mused and held onto me as I walked us into her dark room. I laid her down on the bed, and she undid her robe and took it off, revealing a matching lace nightgown underneath. It was baby pink and had thin straps and a deep V-neck that barely contained her tits. It was sexy as fuck, and I was going to have a hard time sleeping next to her while she looked that good.

I growled at her, and she smirked, biting her lip. "I didn't get dressed with you in mind." But she loved the effect she had on me, planned or not.

"Hmm." I hummed and then decided I'd play dirty right back. I pulled the collar of my black t-shirt off over my head and tossed it on the ground and dropped my head to hide my smile when I saw her eyes drop to my abs instantly. Unbuckling my belt, I pushed my jeans down until I stood before her in my black tight boxer briefs. "I can't sleep in jeans."

"Hmm." She deadpanned and then shook her head, laughing. She crawled up the bed and slid under the covers, and I joined her, turning off the light and pulling her back against my chest. I wrapped both arms around her and held her tight, taking a deep breath for the first time in days. "I missed you." She whispered.

"I missed you too. Let's not do this to each other again."

"Deal." She said with a light laugh, snuggling deeper into my arms.

She fell asleep quickly, and I lay there listening to her rhythmic breathing, letting it lull me to sleep.

When we woke up again, it was early afternoon, and I ached to get her into the new place. It was like a part of me needed her there to feel settled, like it was a fresh start for us.

"I have a confession to make," I said, sitting at her table drinking a cup of coffee as she made herself a smoothie.

"Uh-oh." I smiled at her and waited until she sat down across from me to start. She was wearing that baby pink nightgown without the robe on, and I was having trouble containing my need for her, but I knew this conversation had to happen sooner rather than later.

"I moved into the cottage the same day you asked for space."

She held my stare and set her drink down, "The cottage that I was told I could move into?" She asked for clarification.

"I was hoping we could move into it together, and I wanted to be there when you finally came back to me. I wanted to be ready to show you my commitment to you."

"You want us to live together?" She asked, chewing on her bottom lip.

"Yes. I'd meant it when I said I thought it was a good idea that day in the kitchen."

"You'd also said it was a good idea because you could keep me safe, not because you wanted me near you."

I nodded my head, as more pieces of the puzzle of Carly James fell into place the more we talked. "I didn't get to that part, I suppose." I chuckled and leaned forward, taking her hand in mine. "The most animalistic part of my very being wants to provide for you and protect you, Carly. Maybe that's because of what happened when I was a kid, who knows? So yes, my first thought when you and Ellie sprung that on me was that I'd be able to keep you safe if you lived on the property with me. I also understand now, how that may not have been the romantic answer you'd been hoping for, but don't think, for one second, that I didn't want you to move in because it would mean that you and I could move our relationship forward."

She let me hold her hand, but she tilted her head and pondered that, so I kept going.

"I want to live with you Carly, I want to work on building something with you full-time. I have a ton more free time now, time I'd like to commit to you, and I know that you aren't working seven nights a week now either, so I thought perhaps you'd like to commit some of your free time to me too."

"I have never lived with a partner before, Jed. What if I drive you absolutely bonkers?" She asked, and I could see the actual fear in her eyes.

"I've never lived with anyone else either unless you count Zeke, and we both know he's a fucking bear even to be near, and we haven't killed each other yet. And you're far more agreeable, especially if you wear sexy little nighties like that around all the time."

"That seems easy enough." She mused and then looked curiously at me.

"What?"

"What if I had said I didn't want to live with you?"

I laughed and rubbed my hand over my face as I took another long drink of my coffee. "I suppose I'd have moved back out, but I would have taken back all of the things I've done to the place the last few days too."

"What have you done?" She asked, leaning forward with worry etching her eyes, "I loved everything about it."

I chuckled and leaned forward, kissing her nose gently. "You'll love the upgrades, I hope. And you'll just have to wait to see them until we get there."

"Let's go." She stood up, drinking down a large sip of her smoothie, now in a hurry to get to our new home.

"Calm down, we need to pack some of your stuff to take with us so we can stay there for a while."

"Oh right," She turned around the kitchen, looking at stuff. "I really only need clothes and toiletries, right?"

"Yeah, there is a fully stocked kitchen and it's furnished."

"Perfect, less packing time." She winked at me and went to her bedroom. I finished my coffee, washed my cup out, and followed after her, helping her pack clothes, shoes, bathroom stuff, and some personal things that she wanted to take with her.

When we pulled into the driveway at the mansion, I drove past my normal parking spot and drove out towards the cottage, and parked in the driveway next to it, and she smiled sweetly when she saw some of the changes I'd made.

On the corner of the large wrap-around porch, I hung a daybed swing with a bright white mattress and an array of soft-colored cushions on it and a big cozy blanket laid across the end.

"Is that for watching the stars on?" She asked as I helped her out of the car.

"That had been my original idea." I said and winked at her, "But for some reason, star gazing gets you all horny, and I ended up missing most of the show last time."

She gasped, covering her chest with her hand in pretend shock. "You're blaming me for that? You're the one who brought a strip of condoms on a first date."

I chuckled and grabbed a couple of bags and walked up the walkway with her as she looked over the hanging baskets I hung off the porch roof too.

"These are so pretty." She said, fingering the petals of the bright flowers.

"They look pale compared to how pretty you are," I said with a wink and opened the front door for her.

We walked into the living space, and I set the bags down on the new couch I'd bought. It was slate blue and matched the new chairs on each side of it that had a blue and cream pattern on them.

"You picked these out yourself?" she asked in awe.

"Yeah, the brown leather didn't really feel cozy. And I want this place to be all sorts of cozy and warm."

"It's perfect." She said, twirling in circles and then falling into me, where I held her against my chest.

"You're perfect. I can't explain to you how excited I am to live with you, Carly James. I can't wait to wake up every single morning with you next to me."

"Me neither." She smiled at me. "I never want to leave this house. Ever."

I chuckled at her, "I doubt Ellie will stay away once she knows you're here. She's been chomping at the bit the last few days to tell you about this, but I wouldn't even let her in here to see until you did."

"I love it." She whispered. "But I think I've forgotten what the bedroom looks like, so maybe you can show me that room next." Her voice was low and sultry as she wrapped her arms around my waist and bit her lip.

"I think you'll be pleasantly surprised with what I've done in there."

We walked across the room and into the bedroom, where I'd done the most work and I leaned against the doorjamb as I watched her take it all in.

I wanted the bedroom to be classy and a bit girly for Carly, she deserved to have a space to feel feminine in. The furniture before had been large and masculine because it had been furnished for an enforcer, but it was now our space and I wanted her to be comfortable here too. I bought a brand-new white king-sized bed and picked out white bedding for it. I added a blush-colored area rug over the dark hardwood floors to make it more comfortable on her feet. I even added a thick plush armchair and table in the corner by the windows for her to read in, something I'd learned that she loved to do, during our alone time before Ry and Ellie got home. Thick rose gold curtains hung on the windows to block out the sun when she needed to sleep in after working late, and it all paired well to make the room look bright and feminine.

"This is beautiful, Jed." She whispered, covering her mouth with her hand, and shaking her head. "You did this for me?"

"Of course, I wanted to make sure you were comfortable here with me and felt like it is as much your space as it is mine."

"I love it." She took a deep breath and stepped into my arms. "I have to be honest with you about something, and it might make you change your mind about this whole thing." She said, nodding towards the bedroom behind her.

"What?"

"I'm falling in love with you." She whispered. "And I'm fucking terrified of it."

CHAPTER 11 – Carly

He stared down at me with the ghost of a smile on his lips as his hands tightened around my waist and he pulled me in tighter against his body.

"Why does it scare you?"

I shrugged, trying to keep my emotions in check. "Because I've never felt worthy of anyone else's love, I've therefore never given my own. I don't know how to love anyone, I meant it when I said I wasn't sure if I was capable of it."

"And I meant it when I said that you'd finally met your match and that I'd teach you how to love Carly." He threaded his fingers through my hair and pulled me tight against his chest as he lowered his lips to mine, kissing me in a way that left words unnecessary. "I'm in love with you, Carly." He whispered against my lips. "I realized it when you walked away after I handled everything poorly."

I took a shuddered breath as his words warmed me from the inside out. "How am I ever going to earn this?" I said, highlighting the beautiful space we were standing in. "How am I ever going to feel worthy of all of it?"

"Time. And constant reassurance. And lucky for you, now that we live together, we're going to be around each other a hell of a lot more, so I'll be here to show you how perfect and worthy you are. We're perfect for each other."

"I think so too," I said and sighed, laying my head on his chest.

"Can I show you the shower next?" he asked gently.

"I'd prefer it that way." I smiled up at him, and he leaned forward and pressed his warm lips to mine, gently without deepening the kiss like we usually did, but for now, it was perfect and exactly what I needed. He put his hands on my hips, gathering the large shirt I was wearing, and then pulled it off over my head and laid it on the bed.

His eyes roved over my body, and I felt warmth coat my skin as his gaze caressed me.

I stepped back and pulled his shirt from his belt and then off over his head. I leaned forward and kissed the center of his chest and let my fingers rove the muscles of his abs lightly like feathers.

He growled and kissed me, deepening it just as I was hoping he would. "You know how to touch me like no other woman ever has." He smiled against my lips. "I'm not a gentleman, so women aren't gentle with me, but your touches, your kisses, they're so soft and sensual, it's my undoing."

"I like undoing you, Jed." I purred as I pulled his belt free and then undid his pants and pushed them down with his boxers to his feet.

"Fucking hell." He groaned and stepped out of them after kicking off his shoes. Using his thumbs, he slid my shorts down to my ankles. He kneeled in front of me again and lifted one leg, then the other, pulling my shorts free of my legs, and then leaned forward and kissed my stomach. On his knees, his head still came up to my chest, and he rested his face against my skin and took a deep breath. "I'll never be able to explain to you what I feel when you touch me." He looked up at me and his dark eyes were glowing in the sunlight from the window next to us. "I'll never be able to capture the strength of it into words to describe it to you." He took my hand and placed it flat on his chest, over his racing heart, "But I want to try to show you, anyway. Because I need you to know how committed to you, I am, how committed to this I am."

Tears burned the back of my eyes again as I leaned down and kissed him passionately. Showing him without words how much it meant to me to hear and see him trying. He stood up again and carried me into the bathroom and straight into the shower, turning the hot water on and letting it cascade over us as he set me on my feet.

He soaped up a washcloth with his manly body wash that I loved, and he started washing my body, touching every inch with his talented hands. He was igniting an inferno inside my belly with each touch of his skin on mine. When I was clean, I took the cloth from him and washed his body, paying extra close attention to his cock as I fisted him and rubbed the cloth up and down over his hard length. "I don't need anything baby. I just want to take care of you." he said, gritting his teeth and clenching his fists as I worked my fist up and down.

"I know." I lowered my hand and washed his balls and upper legs. "But I need you." He kissed me and pinned my hands above my head.

"Finish washing your hair and stuff, and then we'll get out. I've taken you dozens of times, but never in our new bed. And I desperately need to feel you under me in our new space, I've fantasized about it so many times."

I shoved him backward, close to breaking, and begging him to take me right here, and quickly washed my hair and rinsed it out as he did his.

We got out of the shower, and he quickly dried my body off before drying his and then he carried me back to bed, tearing down the covers and laying me in the center of it on the pillows. "Fuck, you're so sexy." He moaned, running the head of his cock back and forth against my clit, getting me more aroused than I already was.

"I need you. Don't make me wait, I'm ready." I panted, begging him to fuck me already. Other women would kill for a man to give a fuck about foreplay, but I was desperate to be filled up with him. I didn't want his fingers or mouth, I wanted him.

He smiled at me with a predatory glint to it and leaned down over my body. He pushed my knees open wide, hooking one over his arm, and laid down between them. "I'm going to fuck you so good, Carly."

"Please." I gasped. He spit on his hand and then rubbed it over the top of his cock to help lubricate it up and then pushed inside of me, splitting me in half in one brutal thrust. I screamed and clawed at him as I rocked my hips back and forth underneath him when he hit bottom. "Yes."

"That's my good girl, taking my cock however I give it." He started fucking me hard, driving me into the comfortable mattress as I wrapped my arms and legs around him to hold on through the brutal assault.

"More, Jed, I need more."

He reached down and pinched my nipple, pulling it hard, and then slapped the flesh and pinched it again and it was exactly what I needed to fall over the edge of my orgasm. My skin burned and tingled as pleasure shot through my body. I felt the way his cock slid into me easier as my orgasm coated his skin and he groaned, rocking his hips against my clit.

"Roll over." he demanded, pulling out and sitting on his heels. He grabbed my waist and flipped me over until I was on my hands and knees, and then he impaled me again. I dropped down onto my forearms and spread my legs wide, arching my back and pushing back into him with each thrust. "Holy fuck." He moaned, "Your ass was made to be fucked like this." He grabbed two big handfuls and shook my ass, letting it ripple. He held still and pushed his hips forward while leaning back on his hands. "Twerk your ass for me, baby."

I grinned. "Are you demanding to see my superpower?" I asked him, looking over my shoulder at him. "I'm a dancer, Jed, I can shake my ass in ways that will leave you stunned."

"Do it." He brought his hand down hard on my right cheek, the sound of his slap vibrated through the air and my clit as I moaned.

I rocked forward and back quickly, shaking my ass in rhythm that fucked me on and off of his cock at the same time, and smiled into the bedsheet when a long line of curses fell from his lips as he watched.

"Just like that baby, fuck that feels good." His hips jerked, and I could tell he was losing his hold on his ability to stay still while I played, and a few seconds later his big hands wrapped around my hips and held me still while he railed into me.

I put my hand flat up on the headboard, holding me still as he owned my body, making it his. I slid my knees out from under me, lying flat on the bed with my legs twisted together tight between his massive thighs and he followed me down, never pulling out while we moved.

He raised like was doing pushups and then his hips started moving as he fucked me. I gripped the pillows around me and screamed as he bottomed out deliciously, drawing another orgasm from my toes to crash over me. "You're rubbing my g-spot baby. Fuck that feels so good." I whimpered. "Don't stop."

"Give me another orgasm, come on my cock again, Kitten, I need it." He commanded and laid over my back, snaking his hand under my body and sliding his fingers through my lips, pinching my clit.

"Just like that, yes just like that Jed." He kept fucking me like that until I was on the ledge of yet another orgasm. "I'm going to come; you're going to make me come again. God fucking damnit Jed!" I screamed as another orgasm chased every nerve ending in my body.

I buried my face in the pillow to scream, but he grabbed my hair and pulled my head back, so my screams filled the room. "Let me hear you, sweetheart. I want to know exactly what I do to you."

He groaned and his hips jerked madly before I felt his cock start jerking inside of me and I knew he was filling me to the brim with his come. When his climax was over, he rolled off my back and lay next to me with his hands in his hair, panting like he'd just run a marathon.

I watched his body in fascination, from his ink to the expansive muscles on his arms and chest, and down further to his somehow, still hard cock where it lay against his stomach. I scooted down to kneel between his legs and looked up his body as he dropped his arms and looked at me.

"What are you doing?"

"Tasting us," I said as I fisted his cock and licked up the side of it. I distinctly tasted his salty come and the sharp bite of my arousal on him, and it made an intense combination. He groaned and hissed, jerking his hips as I swirled my tongue over the top of him. "You taste so good."

"You look sexy as hell, freshly fucked, and flushed, sucking on my cock in our new bed, you're so fucking perfect."

I hummed and smiled as I took him deep into the back of my throat. "We're perfect."

"Damn fucking right, we are." He agreed, threading his fingers into my hair, holding my head in a gentle way but with authority behind it so I knew exactly what he wanted from me. He wanted me to take him down the back of my throat, and he wanted me to suck hard as I did it. That's what he liked the most, and I loved watching him come unraveled when I gave it to him.

I worked him down my throat, humming each time my lips touched fresh skin before I gagged and pulled back off of him. It was impossible to deep-throat him without gagging, but I knew how to control most of it to give him incredible pleasure at the same time.

"That's it, baby, just like that." He praised, and I watched his ab muscles flex as his hips jerked up to match my movements. "Fuck you feel so good, you do that better than anyone else. Ever."

I pulled up off of him with a pop and bared my teeth as I let them lightly scrape the head of his cock. "Don't talk about other women's blowjob skills in our bed."

He chuckled and tightened his hands in my hair and pulled my teeth off his cock. "Come on Kitten, show me your claws." He sat up and pulled me up until our faces were even, and he put one hand around my throat with his other hand still tight in my hair. "Do you have any idea how impossible it is it even remember the faces of the women I've been with before, since meeting you? How blind I am to any woman I meet these days because all I can see is you and your beauty?"

"Good." I bit out, stroking his wet cock with my tight fists. "I don't want you ever even thinking about anyone else. Ever again."

"Then be a good girl and ride my cock so I don't have the brain power to even try."

I crawled forward and impaled myself on his rock-hard cock, letting the silkiness of his come lubricate my pussy for the invasion of his massive size. "Yes." I hissed, holding on to his wrist where he still held onto my throat. "Tighter," I begged and his fingers tightened around my throat, leaving me the freedom to breathe, but giving restriction against blood moving into my brain, making me feeling high and euphoric. "Just like that, Jed. You fuck me so good."

He held my neck, keeping me hovered above his lap as he fucked his cock up into my body. My tits swayed on each side of his enormous arm, and I felt my eyes flutter closed as pleasure burned up my spine.

"You're going to come again, aren't you?" He demanded through clenched teeth. "Your pussy can't help it when my cock is fucking you. You're always so hungry for my come. Open your eyes and look at me when I make that pussy orgasm again."

"Yes." I cried, looking straight into his eyes as he rolled his hips and fucked me savagely. "You own me, Jed."

"That's right, whose pussy is it?"

"Yours!" I cried, feeling my orgasm cresting, and pushing my body through a convulsion as every muscle in my body tensed. "It's your pussy, baby."

"Good girl." He grunted, feeling me clamp down on his cock. "You're such a good fucking girl."

I screamed into the sky as he kept fucking me through my orgasm, making it roll on and on through my system. I sagged into his arms, leaning my forehead against his as I came down from my orgasm while he lazily pushed his cock in and out of me. "Aren't you going to come?" I asked, noticing how he was slowing down instead of speeding up, chasing his release like he normally did.

"I have other plans for my orgasm." He said with a smirk, and he slapped my ass.

"Oh?" I asked, leaning back to look at him. "What are they?"

"It's a surprise. I want you to go to the kitchen and kneel in the center of the island."

"What?" I gasped.

"You heard me. On your knees in the middle, and I want your legs spread under you with your eyes closed. Don't open them until I tell you. Now go." He pulled his cock out of my pussy and slapped my ass, pushing me towards the door.

I crawled off the bed and looked back at him as he lay back on the pillows and put one arm up behind his head and watched me walk away.

He looked like a god lying there, all tattoos and muscles and hard steely cock standing straight up, dripping wet with my orgasm coating it.

"Fuck." I moaned and then ran from the room to the kitchen. I looked out the giant windows overlooking the yard between our house and the mansion and bit my lip when I saw gardeners pruning the flower beds a hundred yards away.

"Get up there, Carly," Jed ordered from the bedroom still.

"Yes, sir." I quipped and climbed up onto the cold marble countertop and kneeled in the center of it as he had instructed. I spread my legs wide and closed my eyes, taking a deep breath and feeling the excitement and arousal burn through my system.

I worried that the gardeners were getting closer to our house as I kneeled there open and exposed with my eyes closed, but didn't open them to look and see, following Jed's orders to a T.

I heard the soft padding of his bare feet across the hardwood floors as he walked into the kitchen and the hair on the back of my neck rose. He walked over to the windows, and I heard him opening up one after another. In the quiet of the house, I could hear the voices of the gardeners carrying in on the breeze and bit my lip to stop the moan and smile that tried to form.

His deep voice vibrated through the air as his fingertips traced down my spine, slowly. "You look so beautiful like this, obeying me."

Tingles broke out over my skin as his fingers dipped between my ass cheeks and down over my wet core. "Bend over and put your forehead on the marble, raise your ass into the air." I slowly lowered my face down, pressing my hands flat to the cold countertop, and laid my forehead against it. "Good girl." He said, letting his fingers rub over my lower lips before he slid them back up to my ass and rubbed them against the puckered flesh. "Can you guess what my plans are yet?" He asked, pushing one finger deep into my ass and swirling it around, stretching me out.

"You're going to fuck my ass?" I whispered. "Here?"

"Right here." He said and I could hear the smile in his voice. "I'm going to spread your ass wide open right here in the bright kitchen, in front of the open windows."

I moaned and pressed back against his hand, and he slid another finger into me. "Please," I begged.

"Tell me you want me to fuck you like this. Beg me to fuck your ass here on the kitchen counter."

"Please, Jed, I need you to take my ass. I crave the feeling of you fucking me there and coming inside of me."

"Tell me you want to be heard and seen by the men in the backyard." I paused, anxiety and fear trying to claw their way from my heart. "Say it, Carly." He demanded.

"I want you to make me scream so the gardeners hear me and look over and watch you rail me."

"Mmh." He moaned. "You want them to get hard watching you, don't you? You want them to want what's mine, even though they can't have it."

Being a stripper played into my exhibitionism kink over the years, but I'd never told Jed about it.

"Tell me I'm right, Carly, because your pussy is dripping, and not just with my come anymore."

"You're right." I panted, "How-how did you know?" I asked, wanting desperately to look at him.

"I just had a feeling, between fucking you outside the first time, and then in the front seat of my car. You were on another level of sexual high each time."

"Fuck." I moaned as he scissored his fingers in my ass before adding a third one.

"That's exactly what I'm going to do to your ass. And we're going to draw a crowd while we do it."

"Please, Jed." I begged, "Are you sure you want them to see us?" He was so possessive usually, letting other men see me naked while he took something from me for the first time, seemed intrusive. Even for me.

"Fuck yes, I do. I want everyone to know exactly what's mine. I want them to know I have the sexiest woman in the world, screaming my name when she comes."

"Yes." I lifted my head and arched my back, but kept my eyes closed still. "I need it."

He pulled his fingers from my ass and got something from the cabinet and then pulled me backward to the edge of the counter. My feet dangled off the edge and he pulled my ass down until my pussy hovered right above the cold marble. "I want you to stay just like that, spread nice and wide for me, okay?" He said, grabbing both ass cheeks and pulling them apart.

"Okay." I panted.

I listened as he opened a jar and then set it down on the counter next to me seconds before cold goo pressed against my opening as he pushed his three fingers into me quickly, lubricated with it.

"What is that?" I asked.

"Coconut oil. It doesn't dry out like a lot of lubes do."

"You sound like an expert at anal," I said, trying to fight down the jealousy that bubbled up inside of me. His teeth latched onto my ass cheek, and he bit down roughly, drawing a high-pitched scream from my lips.

"There are the claws again, Kitten." He purred, using his oil-covered fingers in my ass, and then rubbing my clit with her other hand. I mewed, falling back down onto the counter fully as pleasure rocked me. "Your scream got some attention." He said, smiling against my ass cheek.

"Let me see," I begged.

"You want to watch them as they work closer to the noise, knowing exactly what's happening in here?"

"Yes." I panted.

"Those men work for Ryker, which means he'll know your dirty little secret." He growled, but as he said them, his fingers pumped harder into me, and his teeth latched onto my ass cheek again.

"That makes *you* horny, doesn't it?" I asked, feeling the proof of his arousal pressed against the bottom of my foot. His cock jumped when I rubbed my foot back and forth over it. "Do you want Ryker to know you fucked me in front of his men?"

"Yes." He groaned, thrusting his hips against my foot again. "He fucked Ellie in the back seat of the car, with Zeke and I upfront one time. And it unlocked something inside of me." He answered truthfully.

"Did you watch them?" I asked, imagining Ryker and Ellie having sex and feeling like a creep for it, but I couldn't deny the fact that I was so close to an orgasm while I did it.

"No, but I listened to them. He fucked her right into the back of my seat, and I listened to them talking dirty to each other the whole time."

"And you liked it?" I panted.

"Yes." He hissed, pulling his fingers from my ass. "Just like you do."

"Yes, I do." I felt the hot head of his cock press against my ass as he rubbed more oil over it and then pushed it against me. "Open your eyes." He commanded. I opened my eyes as he grabbed my hair and pulled my head up off the counter, lifting my top half towards him as he pushed his cock into my ass for the first time.

"Oh, my god." I moaned, elongating the syllable as his cock burned its way into my body.

"Good girl." He praised, holding me by the hair and the hip as he pressed deeper, slowly inching his cock into my body until I felt his hips press against mine and he rolled them. "Holy fuck, your ass is swallowing my cock, Carly. You're so tight."

"You're so big!" I hissed, feeling a cold sweat break out over my skin. "I'm not going to be able to sit for a week."

He chuckled and pulled out all the way, I groaned as I felt my ass gape for a second before it tensed closed. He pushed his cock into me again, slowly going all the way in and then pulling it out all the way again, letting it gape and starting it all over again.

"Do you have any idea how sexy you look with your pussy dripping my come onto our brand-new countertop and your ass gaping open when I pull my cock out of it? Fuck you're the sexiest woman in the world."

"Fuck me." I hissed. "Please."

"Scream it." He commanded, as his large hand came down hard on my ass cheek as his other one tightened in my hair and pulled me up until I was sitting up with my tits exposed and my pussy open between my spread legs facing the large sliding glass doors overlooking the patio and the gardeners. One of them was looking towards the house and they were considerably closer than they were when I climbed up here.

There were four of them in total, and I recognized two of them from the crew. They weren't gardeners, they were crew members.

"Holy fuck." I gasped as Jed chuckled in my ear.

"You know them, don't you?"

"Yes." I panted.

"Then scream so they know exactly what I'm doing to you. Beg me and scream it for them to hear."

I panted and rolled my hips as he thrust into me with more vigor. "Please fuck my ass," I said loudly, but nowhere near a scream.

"Louder." He said, slapping my ass, the noise echoing off the walls around us.

The one that was looking to start with nudged one of the other guys and they both were looking in the window now.

"Please, Jed. Fuck my ass!" I begged with a scream as he bottomed out in one punishing thrust. "Yes!" I hissed and he pulled my head back to look up at the ceiling as he started fucking me hard.

"Good girl. Let me hear whose ass this is." He growled against my ear.

"It's yours, it's your ass." I panted.

"Good girl." He praised again. I held on tight as he fucked me like a man possessed, screaming his name over and over again as he rode me hard, pushing me toward my orgasm. When it crested over my body, he wrapped his hand around my throat and buried his other one in my pussy, pumping two fingers into me and rubbing them against his cock, making himself moan and groan.

When I opened my eyes again after my orgasm released my body, all four men were facing our home and watching Jed fuck me on the kitchen counter. Before I could think about it or say anything, Jed lifted me off the counter, carrying me still on his cock, over to the sliding glass door. He pushed me forward until my tits were pressed flat against the glass with my toes barely touching the ground as he crouched behind me, slamming his cock deep inside of me over and over again.

I pressed my hands flat to the glass and came again, the exhibitionist in me loving the attention and the feeling of being owned by Jed.

"That's my girl. You take my cock so fucking good like this. I'm so deep in your ass."

He was fucking me so hard; my tippy toes were barely touching the floor anymore as he held me against the glass.

"Come for me, Jed, fill my ass up with your come. I want to hear you scream my name as I screamed yours." I ordered, stepping out of my usual role and filling one based solely on need at the moment. I needed to own him in this second too.

"Fuck!" He bellowed. Slamming into me so hard I was afraid the glass was going to break. He roared my name over and over again as his come branded the inside of me like lava as he came until it dripped out around his massive cock. "Holy fuck," he gasped, panting, and fighting for air. He pulled me off the glass and pulled out of my ass, as we both watched his come drip down my thigh and land on the floor between my spread legs. "That just destroyed me." He said, dragging me away from the glass and against the wall next to it. He turned and yelled out the door, "Get back to work!" And then slammed the door shut. We paused to catch our breath, foreheads touching. Then, he kissed me gently, his hands wandering over my breasts and stomach before finding and sensually massaging my clit. He pulled his fingers from my pussy and licked them clean and then smirked at me as he picked me up and carried me away from the giant windows.

I chuckled into his neck as he smiled into my hairline, carrying me into the bathroom and setting me on my feet next to the giant soaker tub. He turned the water on, poured some Epsom salts in, and then pulled me into his arms, kissing my forehead before capturing my lips in a kiss so sweet and tender it brought tears to my eyes.

We went from dirty anal fucking on the kitchen counter, to tender and gentle next to the bathtub in less than a minute, and my emotions were all over the place. Jed pulled back and wiped his thumbs over my tears as they fell over my cheeks.

"Are you hurt? Did I fuck this all up?" He asked, with worry etching his perfect face.

I shook my head, struggling past the bubble of emotion threatening to choke me, and smiled up at him. "That was so perfect," I said, trying to find the words. "I didn't know I could have it all. To be consumed by an alpha man like you, and feel fulfilled with adding things like that to an already out-of-this-world sex life... I'm just overwhelmed."

"Thank you for giving me this. For trusting me completely like that, it means so much, Carly." He smiled and kissed me again before helping me sink my battered body down into the steaming water. "Relax, let the salts ease your body for a while."

"You're not joining me?" I asked, leaning back into the cushion on the side.

"No. If I got in there with you right now, I'd be buried deep inside that ass again in mere minutes."

I chuckled, shrugging my shoulders. "I wouldn't complain."

He leaned over and kissed me deeply, letting his tongue play with mine for a long time, before pulling back and kissing my forehead. "You would later when you couldn't stand or sit down."

"Hmm, good point."

He lit some candles and dimmed the lights and walked out of the bathroom, leaving me in peace and quiet as I let the happiness I'd felt the last few hours settle into my bones.

This was good.

I deserved this.

I was worthy of this.

CHAPTER 12 – JED

I walked into the club, keeping Carly pressed against my side as the crowd parted ahead of us to let us through. Behind us, Ryker had his arm around Elora's shoulders the same way, shielding her and pressing her through the crowded dance floor on the way to our table in the back.

Today was Ryker's birthday, and Elora *insisted* that we go out and celebrate. She was over six months pregnant at this point, and Ryker hated the idea of bringing her out to a club for his birthday, but she hadn't been able to be swayed at all on it.

So, the compromise was that we had to come to Erotiq and that way he could ensure Ellie and Carly's safety better while we were here. But even surrounded by crew members, I was on edge and couldn't relax. Frankie was still at large, which irritated me like no other. Mason and Jay had reported every single day like they were supposed to, and Ryker and I both had men on each of them, following them and monitoring their comings and goings to watch for any sign of Frankie anywhere, but still, we hadn't come up with anything.

He'd disappeared without a trace, but we both knew, sooner or later he would run out of money. And that's when he'd get desperate and sloppy. And that's when Carly was most at risk of being hurt by him because desperation made people do really stupid shit.

It had been heaven living with her the last two months; it was our slice of heaven in the back corner of Ryker's land. Every single night, she fell asleep in my arms, and every single morning I kissed her goodbye before I went to work. She worked at Lux still, but only three nights a week as a Hostess, and she picked up the role of social media promoter for both Lux and Erotiq as well, which she was able to do from home unless she needed pictures or videos for campaigns and posts.

She was thriving, and it was incredible to watch happen. It was like she was a butterfly, breaking out of a cocoon and fluttering her new wings, right before my eyes. I was so fucking proud of her and how she was working so hard to build a new image of herself.

I looked across the club, noting the way the added security for tonight blended in with the crowd, but stood out to me because I had stationed them all there.

"Are you okay?" Carly asked, leaning up to my ear so I could hear her over the music. I looked down at her and nodded once, before moving my eyes back over the crowd. "We don't have to be here if you don't want to be." She added, pulling on my sleeve when I didn't look at her.

"It's fine," I said, a bit harsher than I intended to, but I was on edge and hated this. And by the looks of it, so did Ryker.

We got to our booth, and we put the girls on the inside of the U and sat next to them, shielding them from the crowd with our bodies.

The bottle girl came over instantly with drinks for the table, including mocktails for Elora. Carly drank the virgin drinks even though there were plenty of other options available because she didn't like rubbing it in that Elora wasn't able to indulge.

She was that kind of friend.

And I loved her for it.

And she loved me, and it was the single best feeling in the world.

"So, I was thinking…" Elora started, leaning forward on her elbows, and I groaned, and Ryker rolled his eyes.

"I'm not going to like this, am I?" Ryker asked, kissing her temple, and putting his hand on her belly.

She shooed him off and then winked at him to soothe the rejection. "I was thinking we should all go away on a vacation somewhere. Before the baby comes, somewhere that there is no Frankie and no worries and you two can just be doting partners and not crime bosses."

"Doting partners?" I asked with a raised eyebrow. "I thought I already was that." I looked over at Carly and she was trying but failing to hide a smile behind her glass as she shrugged her shoulders. "Did you know about this plan?"

"She mentioned it this morning. I told her you two would never go for it," Carly said. Something about the way she said it, like she was talking about the weather, kind of hurt. Was I really so predictable that she would know I wouldn't be down to walk away from work completely for a while to dote on her?

"Where do you want to go?" Ryker asked, looking between the two girls.

"Somewhere warm and relaxing," Elora said easily as she steepled her fingers together in front of her.

Ryker nodded, "Wherever you want to go, just let me know and I'll make it happen. But I'm not going to be okay with going much later than this in the pregnancy. So, figure it out quickly and we'll go soon."

"Just like that? I'm surprised." Carly asked him, stunned by his amicable ways.

"A chance to take my beautiful wife away from here and the danger lurking around every corner, I'll jump at the chance every time." He said, gaining a swoony grin from Elora, but I didn't miss the way his comment wounded Carly.

She blamed herself for Frankie's psychotic flip already, and Ryker talking about it so flippantly only wounded her more.

She dropped her eyes and her smile on the glass in front of her and remained quiet. My anger bubbled up at his lack of tact and how it hurt her, but I tread carefully because I didn't want to embarrass her in front of them.

"Count us out. We already have plans to get away just the two of us." I said confidently, taking a sip from my bourbon.

Carly turned to look at me with pinched brows at the same time both Elora and Ryker looked at me, confused.

"Why can't we all go somewhere? It might be our last chance to get out of town, just the four of us, before we're new parents." Ellie said, and I finally saw the selfish streak that Zeke mentioned before. I hadn't seen it before now, and I knew it came from a good place, but it was still selfishness.

"Because we want to go away as a couple, our relationship is still new, and don't we deserve to have a couple's getaway like you guys have had a dozen or more times already?" I asked pointedly, not backing down.

Ryker cleared his throat, catching on. "He's right, let them have their alone time, we just got back from a two-week trip all alone, Doll. They deserve that too."

Elora pouted but dropped it. I looked over at Carly, who was still looking up at me with questions in her eyes, and I leaned down and kissed her.

"Dance with me?" I asked.

"You want to dance?" She sounded surprised.

"I want to dance with you."

A smile graced her perfect face, and she nodded eagerly. I slid from the booth, nodding to Ryker, and held my hand out for Carly to help her stand up. She was wearing a ruby-red dress that was absolutely to die for. It had thin straps, crossed over her back and it was short, falling only to mid-thigh and with a slit in it over her thigh that made my mouth water. I pulled her behind me and walked onto the chaos of the dance floor as I felt her press herself against my back and wrap her fingers around my belt to stay close to me.

When I got to the center of the floor, I turned towards her and pulled her flush with me and kissed her, dragging my tongue across her lips as she melted into me. I wanted to distract her from everything swarming around in her head that she didn't even need to tell me was there; I just knew.

"Tell me something, love," I started, "Do your panties match your dress?"

She smiled at me and rolled her hips, pressing her belly against my erection, which was swelling more and more by the minute. "What makes you think I'm wearing any panties?"

I growled at her and put my hands on her hips and lowered my thumb down to the sexy-as-sin slit that ran from the bottom of her dress up to her hip. "Are you?"

"Find out for yourself." She challenged me, and I gladly stepped up to accept.

I slid my thumb into the opening and ran it up her leg until the tip of it touched the soft spot of her hip, and I felt no band of panties resting there. I raised my eyebrow at her as she bit her lip and rocked her hip, so my thumb pressed against her pubic bone.

"My little kitten wants to play, huh?" I asked, swaying with the fast tempo of the music as I put my palm flat on her stomach and slid my fingers under the hem of her dress, and ran my fingertips through her wet pussy lips. "Fucking hell." I groaned.

I used my body to shield her body from any prying eyes as I slid two fingers deep into her pussy and swayed my hips back and forth to pump my fingers deep into her with each movement.

"Yes, baby." She moaned, wrapping her arms over my shoulders, and holding on to me as she rode my hand in the middle of a packed dance floor. "Don't stop." She panted against my lips as I bent down to her height.

"Never. I want that pussy to come on my fingers, I need it to cream up and loosen so I can fuck you hard in a few minutes." Her eyes rolled and her lips parted as I pushed her closer to her bliss. "That's it, baby, be a good girl and come for me right here, right now."

She leaned forward and bit my peck, suffocating her moan as her inner muscles clenched down hard on my fingers, spasming and rolling her orgasm over her entire body.

"Jed, oh my god." She panted. "It feels so good."

"I know, kitten, I know just how you like it." When her muscles started to relax and her body started going limp in my tight arms, I pulled my fingers from her body and smoothed her dress down. "I need to fuck you. It's not going to be nice or sweet either. I need it to be carnal and rough, are you up for it?"

"I'm up for anything you need from me, Jed. I want you to take your pleasures from me exactly how you need them."

"Good," I said and turned her body, drawing her back behind me and walking away from the dance floor. Ryker caught my eye as I walked away from the table, and he nodded to the office upstairs with a knowing grin, permitting us to use it as Elora leaned against his side, playing with the buttons on his shirt.

If my predictions were right, it wouldn't be long before they were headed up themselves, so I needed to get there fast and empty myself inside of Carly. I got to the bottom of the stairs, and Skills moved out of our way as I pushed Carly up the steps ahead of me.

"No one but the Lawson's come up, understood?"

He nodded and turned to look back out over the crowd as I walked up behind Carly, shielding her exposed ass in her short dress with my own body. She ran up the last few steps and I gave chase, excitement racing through my veins as she squealed and pushed through the office door with me hot on her heels.

As soon as we were in the dimly lit room, I slammed the door shut and pushed her against it, ripping her dress up over her hips and exposing her cunt.

"Is it okay that we're in here?" She asked, panting, and pulling my shirt open before biting my chest.

"Would you stop if it weren't?"

"No." She giggled and then moaned as I pulled her straps off her shoulders and exposed her tits to my greedy mouth. I sucked one nipple, pulling it deep into my mouth and flicking it with my tongue. She bucked her hips off the door, and I ran two fingers through her creamy lips.

"Nice and wet for me." I mused, letting my teeth scrape over her tight nipple before moving to the other one.

"I need you to fuck me, Jed. I need it harder than you've ever given it to me before."

"Careful what you wish for, baby."

"Give it to me." She demanded, and I wrapped my hand around the back of her neck and spun her around and pushed her across the room until her ass hit the top of the desk. She climbed up on and spread her legs as I pushed my pants down, freeing my cock.

Her dainty fingers with their bright red painted nails slid down between her drenched lips and rubbed her clit as she pinched her nipple, watching me. I grabbed the back of her thighs and pulled her ass off the desk completely and forced my cock into her tight pussy, knocking the air straight out of her lungs as she held on to the edge of the desk, digging her nails into the wooden surface.

"Fuck!" She screamed as I slammed into her, shaking the desk over and over. "Just like that!"

"Take my cock, Kitten." She groaned with the pet name I'd taken to calling her and her pussy gushed as her orgasm got closer to the surface. "You feel so fucking good." Her arms gave out, and she wrapped them around my neck, and I lifted her and fucked her on and off my cock in the air, loving the way her tits shook with each punishing thrust. "You knew I'd fuck you like this when I found out you were bare beneath that dress, didn't you?"

"I was sure hoping so." She panted. "If not, I was going to fuck myself when we got home and make you watch."

"Tease." I groaned and walked us over to the couch, but instead of throwing her down on it so she could ride me, I dropped her to her feet and bent her over the back of it. I put my hand flat in the center of her shoulder blades and pushed her face down over the back cushion until her feet left the floor and her pussy opened to my waiting cock. I buried myself deep, pushing her further over the back until her face was buried in the cushions. I slapped my hand down hard on her ass and pulled her back up and onto my cock as she screamed.

"Oh my god!" She cried. "You're pushing on my g-spot so fucking hard."

I grabbed both of her arms and pulled them behind her back, using them for leverage to keep her held where I wanted her because with each thrust she fell forward over the edge from the viciousness of it.

"You look so fucking sexy like this, with your arms pinned, forced to take my cock however I choose to give it to you."

"Mmh." She moaned with her head lolling back and forth.

"I think I'm going to buy some bondage to tie you down in the center of our bed or spread eagle over the dining room table. Fuck, the plans I have for you, baby."

"You like me defenseless?" She gasped, moaning, and rolling her hips with each thrust. She was so close; I could feel it in the way her pussy twitched and spasmed after each time my cock pulled out of her.

"I like you at my mercy."

"You have no mercy." She said and sighed pleasantly. "I love being your fuck toy."

"That's exactly what you are right now, Kitten. Mine to move and bend how I want and all you can do is take my cock wherever I put it."

"Fuck!" She hissed and started coming on my cock. "Fuck! Fuck! Fuck!" She screamed.

I kept fucking her savagely until I couldn't take it a second longer and felt my cock start filling her up as my orgasm took over my entire body. I roared into the open space of the office and slapped her ass as I emptied myself.

I let go of her arms and she folded over the back of the couch as we caught our breath. I grabbed both of her ass cheeks and pulled them apart, looking down at where her body was impaled with my cock, and licked my lips. "You are single-handedly the sexiest woman on this earth." I praised her.

She chuckled and looked over her shoulder at me. "You're saying that while looking at my asshole—that's weird."

I smacked her ass again for her sass and then slowly pulled out of her, growling when the opaque proof of my orgasm slid out onto her outer lips when my cock finally fell free of her body. "Don't move," I said, pulling her cheeks further apart and kneeling behind her.

"What are you doing?" she asked, looking at me over her shoulder still.

"You have tasted the combination of our orgasms, but I never have," I said and as she gasped in shock, I leaned forward and ran my tongue up her slit, gathering both of our come on my tongue before pushing it all back into her pussy. I growled as the mix of our tastes exploded on my tastebuds and made my cock stiffen to full-staff again. "Fuck Kitten. You've been holding out on me." I licked her again, using my thumbs to pull her pussy open wide and tongue fucked her before sucking on her clit.

"Jed." She moaned. "It's too much." She writhed between my face and the couch, but I didn't relent.

"It's not too much, I want this. And you're going to give it to me." I said, running my fingers up her slit, gathering more of our orgasms, and pushing them into her ass. First one, then two, and finished with three. I pumped them into her as I went back to sucking on her clit. "Not a drop of my come will go to waste where you're concerned."

She moaned and spread her legs wider and bucked her hips. "How is it possible that it feels good, after how many times you've made me come in the last twenty minutes?"

I chuckled against her clit, and she hissed, pushing back onto my face hard. "That's it, Kitten, ride my face." I used my whiskers against her and rubbed my face back and forth as I continued to finger fuck her ass. "Such a perfect little sex toy. So, fucking perfect for me."

"Yes!" She cried. "Only for you."

I pulled my fingers from her ass and switched hands, pushing two fingers into her pussy and driving my tongue into her ass as she shrieked and bucked against the couch. "You're going to come again, baby. I want you to come on my face to hold you over, and then when we get home, I'm going to fuck this perfect ass so many times in a row. You'll have no voice left from screaming my name."

"Jed, please baby. Please make me come on your face, you've got me so twisted up."

"Shh," I said and pushed my tongue back into her as I fingered her pussy and rolled her clit with my thumb and seconds later both of her holes tightened up and she climaxed. Her back bowed and she screamed as her legs shook and she begged me to fuck her again. She was desperate for me the same way I was desperate for her. "I got you," I said to her as she came down from her catastrophic orgasm. I lapped up her pussy and her ass and then stood up behind her, pulling my pants up and tucking away my erection before helping her stand up. "Let's get the fuck out of here. I want to spend the rest of my night inside all three of your holes."

"I love you." She mused with a sated and sleepy smile on her face as I put her breasts away and kissed her deeply. She climbed up my body and deepened the kiss until I was tempted to just lay her out on the couch again and fuck her again, even if Ryker and Elora came in but something caught my attention out of the corner of my eye.

I walked over to the glass windows overlooking the club below and cursed when I saw Diesel Ames and his VP Ripper and two others walking through the club toward Ryker's table. Razz and Zeke were sitting with him and Elora, and Ryker's eyes were on the Reaper crew walking towards him, and his face was stone cold.

"We need to get downstairs. Now," I snapped. Carly looked out the window down to the table as I set her down on her feet and helped her arrange her dress and hair, so she didn't look so freshly fucked.

"Who is that?" She asked, watching as they walked straight to the table.

"Diesel Ames and his Reaper MC crew," I said, but just then they all started walking towards the stairs. They were coming up to the office, which meant this was a business meeting. "Fuck." I pulled Carly over to the wingback chair and made her sit down in it. "Whatever happens, you have to keep your mouth closed, okay? Don't make yourself a target for these men. Do you understand me?"

She nervously nodded her head, and I kissed her. "Aren't these the men who took Monica Wellington? As a slave?"

I sighed and ran my hands down her arms. "No one will touch you, stay by Elora's side no matter what. And if Ryker tells you guys to leave, do it. Don't argue."

She nodded and was about to say something, but the door to the office opened right as I leaned back against the wall, crossing my arms and my ankles to look like Carly and I were having a casual conversation. I watched as Ryker, Elora, Zeke, Razz, Diesel, and Ripper walked in. Ryker was first, and his eyes held mine as he led Elora over to the other wingback chair directly next to Carly's. He kissed her forehead as she sat down but didn't say anything else to her as he walked to his desk and sat down. Where I stood, I was close enough to touch Carly and Elora both, which is no doubt why Ryker put her there and stepped away.

Diesel was unpredictable on a good day, and showing up unannounced on Ryker's birthday evening to discuss business wasn't good.

Diesel and Ripper both nodded to me as they stood in front of Ryker's desk, Zeke stood to his right, and Razz leaned against the wall on the other side of Elora's chair. We protected what was ours. Diesel's eyes fell on Carly, sitting with her legs crossed in the chair, and to her credit, she looked completely unaffected by this encounter, and I knew her poker face had been perfected from her years of dancing. But I barely contained the growl that fought to curl my lips back at him as his eyes roved over her long legs and lush tits. But I couldn't show my hand yet, not without knowing what his intent was. I couldn't dare put Carly in any more danger than she'd already been put into from my association with her.

"Sorry to interrupt your evening, Ryker, but there was something that needed to be discussed sooner, rather than later." Diesel started. Ryker watched him contemplatively, not speaking, before he nodded to the chairs in front of his desk, telling them to sit.

If they did, that was good. It meant that it was a friendly meeting. If they chose to stand, in an offensive position, then it was about to get ugly.

Diesel walked around the front of one of the chairs and sat down in it and ran his scarred and tattooed fingers over his lips as he looked at Ryker.

"What is it, Ames?" Ryker said, keying his frustration up and letting Diesel hear it.

"There's an MC, The Youngblood Club, out of Nevada that is encroaching on my territory. I've been friendly with them over the years because they stayed on their side of the border and didn't bother me much."

"And now that's changed," Ryker said.

"Yeah, and there's been a change in leadership. Their new Prez is no longer playing by the rules. He's making a big problem for both me and you."

"Me?" Ryker asked, raising his brows. "I haven't heard a single thing about any MC in the area but the Reapers. How are they a problem for me?"

"You may not have heard about the MC themselves, but I'm guessing you've heard chatter about girls going missing."

Elora leaned forward in her seat as Ryker stared at Diesel, trying to figure him out.

"They're taking girls from Shadeport?" Ryker leaned his elbows on his desk and his entire demeanor changed.

"They're taking girls from the entire West Coast," Diesel confirmed. "Just in the last week I've had four go missing off my streets, and those are just the ones that people went looking for, I don't know if there are more."

"Streets? You mean hookers?" Elora asked.

Diesel turned to her and addressed her the same way he would any King, which was saying a lot about his respect for her. "Hookers, strippers, homeless, down and outers. Anyone who might be hard to track down."

"Trafficking?" Elora asked.

"Most likely, though I haven't heard of any new rings in the area, and I–personally know of the one that operates around here."

"You know of a sex trafficking ring going on in our streets and it's still fucking running?" Elora seethed.

Diesel ignored her, knowing that was a lost battle and I looked her in the eye and shook my head. To be honest, Ryker, Zeke, and I found out about the ring a few weeks ago and were working on getting it shut down. But it wasn't an easy thing to do, there were a lot of big-money players in on the action and we had to do it in a way that would shut it down for good, or someone else would just fall into the empty space and make another one, and it may be even worse than the small one that operated currently.

I laid my hand on Carly's shoulder, "Any girls inexplicably absent from Lux lately?" I asked, as she looked up at me with her big blue eyes, and I knew the answer before she even answered.

"Three girls have not shown in the last week." She started, turning her attention to Ryker. "It's not unheard of for strippers to leave town without a backward glance, they're usually chasing a dream. But they left without even cleaning out their lockers, it could be connected."

Diesel and Ripper watched her closely, "You work at Lux?" Diesel asked with a glint in his eyes that annoyed me.

"She's family," Ryker said authoritatively and drew their attention back to him, sparing me from dismembering them in the middle of his office.

"Well, then obviously the Youngbloods are a problem for you as well if they're getting girls off your streets too, straight from your club. My guess is they have someone who used to be inside your crew, giving them info to get the girls easily without detection."

"Clearly." Ryker snapped. "I'll look into them, and we'll meet again in a few days. Until then, watch your streets closer and I'll watch mine."

Diesel nodded, aware that the meeting was over, and stood up. As he walked away, he turned back to Ryker with a cautious look on his face. "I only know of the local ring because it's where I sold Monica Wellington when I was done with her."

Carly stiffened in her chair, and I stood up off the wall and pulled her to her feet, putting my arm around her and comforting her. This was the first time that she had seen this side of our life firsthand.

"My bet is if you or I went to the Youngbloods, looking to make a purchase, that would be our best way into their ring. Which you know is the only way to shut it down."

"I'll call you in a few days." Ryker reiterated, putting an end to the conversation given Elora and Carly's reactions.

"Diesel," Elora called as he neared the door once again. He and Ripper turned to her as she stood up from the chair, holding onto her belly as both of their eyes dropped to her hands. Ryker eyed them, and Razz stepped closer. "Did you make her life as bad as you promised you would?" She asked about Monica and his vow to hurt her. Elora's own blood thirst for Monica came from the woman's role in the death of Gavin Dax, Elora's father.

Diesel smiled a charming smile that I'd never seen in the ten years that we'd been doing business with him. "I made her regret the day she was ever born, and I added in a few extra special treatments along the way and made sure she knew they were from you and Gavin."

"Good," Ellie said, with her spine straight and head high. "I'm glad she suffered."

He comically bowed to her and then left, with Ripper right behind him. Razz followed, making sure they left without any incidents and as soon as the door was shut behind them, Carly sagged into me.

"I'm sorry," I whispered against her hair and held her tight. "I would have gotten you out of here before if I'd had time."

"I'm fine." She said, taking a deep breath, "I have to get better at dealing with men like that if I'm going to be around you guys like this."

"Jed's right." Ryker said, "You shouldn't have had to hear that, though I suppose it does involve you, anyway. I need the info on the girls that went missing, anything the club or the other girls might know about them so I can look into them."

She nodded, "I'll get what I can for you."

"Good, thanks." The air was tense, and the appeal of celebrating no longer felt right as Ryker adjusted his jacket and sighed, "Let's go home, El." He said and held his hand out to her. She walked over and hugged Carly and then followed him to the door, where he turned as he opened it, "Feel free to keep using the office if we interrupted anything earlier." He winked at Carly, and she blushed to her ears.

"Thanks, but we've got a bed for the rest of our activities," I said, and Carly snorted and leaned into my side, burying her face in my shirt.

I drove Carly home, and I spent the rest of the evening using her body to make us both forget the woes of the rest of the world for a little slice of time.

CHAPTER 13 - CARLY

Two weeks had passed since the meeting with Diesel Ames, and three more girls had stopped showing up for work at Lux, and no one had heard from them. Ryker and Jed were working hard to protect girls at all costs, upping security and even recruiting new members to the crew. My anxiety was high every time I came from or went to the club, desperate to get home safely, while also dreading seeing another unplanned space on the lineup.

The entire crew was working tirelessly to find any of the women or leads where they went. Jed and I had argued endlessly when he told me he knew about the local sex trafficking ring in Shadeport, the one Monica had been sold into. I couldn't believe that Ryker and he had known it was happening and hadn't blown it up or something. But logically after talking to him, I realized it wasn't always a physical place that could be taken down like that. It was a network of people and places that all worked in the shadows to move women around the city and sell them to the highest bidders, whether that be an hour at a time, or once overall and into ownership.

My stomach ached every time I thought about the women who were living through such an excruciating life with no one to protect them.

Elora and I were protected nonstop, and it felt wrong to have armed guards with us wherever we went when women all over the city trusted the Shadeport Crew to keep them safe and were left wanting.

I'd put all of my energy into working with the three dark and dangerous men in charge to find the women and it had also caused issues with Jed when I was pulling late nights with them so often when he wanted me to be as far away from all of it as possible. But I had gotten closer to Ryker and Zeke in the process and respected their business dealings after seeing them in action.

I understood a bit more about Ryker and Ellie's relationship too, because I saw just how desperately Ryker worked to protect her and make her safe in a world full of things that went bump in the night. And I saw how she stood at his side through it all, not behind him. It was humbling to see such an enigma of a man and woman work so well together, and a part of me wanted to lead with Jed like that someday. I wanted to help and be useful to the Shadeport Crew, not just be someone who tagged along with them.

Frankie still hadn't been found, and it was assumed he was long gone, out of the city, and moved on somewhere else, but I couldn't shake the feeling that I wasn't so lucky. I still felt his presence near and couldn't explain how or why when Jed or Ryker would ask how I knew, but I just did. He didn't leave town, and he wasn't done ruining my life.

"Ready to go, Kit?" Jed asked, stepping into the kitchen of our house as I rinsed out my coffee cup.

"Ready," I called back, grabbing my jacket, and walking towards him. It was Thursday morning, and we were off to our weekly breakfast date at the diner across the city that he had taken me to the morning after our first date. He leaned against the wall and looked downright sinful in light-wash jeans and a white t-shirt. His dark hair was growing out on top but still faded short on the sides, and it gave him a perfectly, just fucked look that made me itch to ride him like a bull in a rodeo.

He grinned at me knowingly as I got caught eye-fucking him, and he took my hand and led me from the house towards his car. I wore a pair of dark jeans and a flowy black top, feeling the coolness in the air as winter got closer. We rode across the city with the windows down and the music up louder than should be acceptable at eight am on a weekday, but there was just something that felt good about today.

Ryker and Ellie were on that last-ditch getaway in the Napa Valley Region she had wanted, close enough they could get home to her doctor and hospital if needed but far enough away to enjoy their time away from the craziness here. Jed and I were planning on leaving and going away soon, hopefully to somewhere warm and exotic but neither of us felt right leaving with the possibility of the Youngblood crew making more problems for Shadeport.

Jed opened my car door for me and held my hand on the way into the diner, and I relaxed into his touch and our routine. He was feeling touchy, and even after we slid into our booth at the back of the restaurant, he kept his hands on me in one way or another.

"I love you; you know that, right?" He asked at one point, catching me off guard.

"Yeah. I know that." I laughed nervously. "Why do I feel like there is a but coming next?"

He smiled at me and shook his head. "No, but; just wanted you to know how loved you are at this exact moment."

My heart swooned a bit, and I leaned over the table and kissed him, intending it to be soft and gentle, but instead, he threaded his fingers through my hair and held me over the table as he deepened the kiss, tasting my lips and tongue like it was the last kiss he'd ever get from me.

"Hey, Jed!" A man said loudly, interrupting our intimate moment, and I fell backward on the bench. Jed turned quickly, taken by surprise, and caught off guard and I knew that didn't happen to him often.

"What's up, Flynn?" Jed asked, and I watched the mask of Shadeport's notorious enforcer slide back over his features.

"Nothing much, I got an envelope for you. Some dude paid me to find you and give it to you."

The hair on the back of my neck stood up as the guy handed over a thick yellow envelope to Jed as he paced back and forth in a way that indicated he was a tweaker. His eyes were glassy, and he scratched his arm until it nearly bled.

"What dude?" Jed demanded.

"Ah man, I don't know, one of your crew but I can't remember his name. The Latino, he runs with those other two dudes all the time. The surfer and the pretty boy with girly hair."

Flynn twirled his finger over his head as he described a man bun, and my blood ran cold.

"Mason and Jay?" I whispered, and Jed looked at me out of the corner of his eye. He looked around the diner, and so did I, noticing more than a few stares our way as business went down in broad daylight.

"Yeah, those two!" Flynn said, hopping from foot to foot. "You know, man, you were a lot farther away than he said you'd be, and

I rode my bike all this way—" He left the sentence hanging but his expectation was clear.

"Did you open this?" Jed snapped, holding the envelope up to the man, but his eyes bugged out and he shook his head and entire body.

"No way, man! I wouldn't do nothing so stupid!" He said, and I believed him, and it looked sealed.

Jed leaned forward and grabbed his wallet, fishing a twenty out, and handed it to him. "Get lost, Flynn, and if anyone ever tries to pay you to deliver something to me again, I'll fucking grind your bones. You don't work for the crew! Stay out of crew business."

Flynn snapped the twenty out of Jed's hand and held his up, "No problem, Jed, I hear you loud and clear, I'm gonna keep my bones right here in my body." He slapped his hands over his arms and legs.

"Get the fuck out." Jed snapped.

Flynn ran and shoved his way through the front door without a backward glance, and Jed glared after him.

"It was Frankie, wasn't it?" I asked in a whisper.

"Let's go." He stood and held his hand out for me and pulled me to my feet before nodding to a few men on the way out to his car. His head was on a swivel when he helped me in and then got in behind the wheel and turned the car on, burning rubber as he pulled away from the curb.

"Where are we going?" I asked, nervousness filling my bones and anxiety about what was in that yellow envelope above his visor.

"Home." That was all he said, and he didn't leave much room for discussion on it, so I sat quietly in my seat as he tore through the city.

When the gates opened, we pulled in next to the garage instead of by our house, and Zeke was waiting for us.

"What happened?" He asked when we got out of the car, and Jed shook his head, vibrating with anger. I stood to the side, unsure of what my role here was.

"Got a delivery from Frankie at Marg's. Frankie paid Flynn to deliver it to me." He held up the envelope.

"Flynn the tweaker?" Zeke asked, eyeing the envelope. "This is the first time anyone has seen or heard from Frankie in months."

"Guess we were stupid to hope he had cut town," Jed said under his breath and then growled, ripping the envelope open and looking inside. His face hardened even more as he stared at what was inside, and by the time he looked up at Zeke, his eyes were downright murderous.

"What is it?" I asked. But he didn't answer me.

He *wouldn't* answer me.

Zeke went to take the envelope, but Jed snatched it away. "No!" He roared. "I want his fucking head on a fucking platter. I'm going to rip it off his fucking shoulders with my bare hands." His violence surprised me, but Zeke didn't even blink.

"What is in the envelope, Jed?" I asked again, knowing it had to do with me somehow. When he once again didn't answer me, I ripped it from his hand as he paced.

"Carly, no." He ordered, but I ignored him, opening it, and acid burned in my throat as my stomach rolled.

"No," I whispered as I pulled out pictures and screenshots from videos that were printed out. I was the focus of all of them, naked, being fucked in various positions at different points over the last few years. "Oh, my God." There was a note inside the envelope I pulled out next, and my eyes burned with tears as I read it.

> *The whole city has seen her naked and has felt her grinding in their laps, some of them have even paid her to spread her legs.*
>
> *But do you want the rest of them to see her taking cock like the little whore that she is?*
>
> *How would you feel knowing every man is jacking his dick off to our girl's first porno?*
>
> *Give her back, and I'll keep them to myself. Fuck around and I'll send them to everyone I know, and I have more than just this.*
>
> *Did you know the Queen used to walk around naked when she stayed at Carly's?*

Frankie had recorded us having sex and was now using the recordings to blackmail Jed. And he had pictures or videos of Elora too?

"No," I whispered in pain. My decisions could not affect her, not like this. God, not with the baby on the way.

Jed paced the driveway like a caged animal, waiting to strike the first chance he got, but Zeke was still lost. I handed him the note, keeping the pictures to myself.

His face darkened horrifically as he read it, and then he looked up at me. And for a split second, I saw his anger, aimed at me before he covered it.

This was all my fault.

I was a stripper who thought she could be worthy of something more, and it was going to destroy my best friend. My chest ached, and I watched every bit of happiness slip through my fingers as I realized I was going to lose Jed over this.

My head throbbed as I thought over and over, desperate for some way to get her and me out of this mess. But I knew I only had one option; leave Jed.

It was the only way Frankie said he wouldn't share the pictures. I couldn't hurt Ellie by having nude pictures of her shared with the world. And I couldn't shame Jed by people seeing his girlfriend in a sex tape. I was the common denominator in this whole thing.

"I have to call Ryker," Zeke said angrily.

"No, just wait. We need to find Frankie. We can't put that fear on Ellie, she won't handle it well."

"He needs to know that there are nude photos of his wife potentially being shared right now."

"It will destroy her!" Jed yelled back, and for the first time since being romantically involved with him, I was jealous of my best friend. He hadn't once said anything about me and how this was affecting me. His priority was once again Ellie.

And I loved that she had that, but a part of my heart ached to be cared for too. I was so stupid to think that I could ever measure up to her like this. That I could ever have this life.

Zeke pulled his phone out and sent a text out, and a second later Razz and a couple of other crew members came out of the house, faces poised for war. And when they looked at me, I felt their wrath aimed directly at me. And I stepped back from them as my heart broke.

I'd never matter.

I was so out of my element here.

A peasant in a kingdom pretending to be royalty.

Silently I stepped back again and then turned and walked away as they continued to argue and strategize, and none of them even noticed. I walked around the garage, instead of going towards our house, I walked down the long, sunbaked driveway, each step echoing in the stillness, and ordered a car as a wave of despair washed over me. Forcing my feet to keep moving, I put one in front of the other, over and over again down the street when my car pulled up outside the main gate of the village.

I didn't look back as I climbed in, I just ordered the driver to take off. I couldn't look back.

When we were away from the mansion, I opened my phone and unblocked Frankie's number and dialed it. He answered on the second ring.

"Well, hey baby, did you get my package?" His voice rang through the phone, and I cringed, as tears fell from my lashes.

"Why are you doing this, Frankie?" I asked, hating the way my voice shook.

"Because he doesn't get what's mine."

"You fucked around all the time! Why is this any different?"

"Because he already has everything, Carly, he doesn't get you too."

"You're the most wanted man in Shadeport right now, you know that, right." I sneered.

He chuckled and I heard him taking a drag on his joint. "Yeah, but let me ask you a question babe, am I wanted because I threatened you and Jed, or because I threatened the Queen?" I didn't answer him, and he chuckled into the phone. He was poking every insecurity of mine, and he fucking knew it. "That's what I thought, no one cares about you. Not like her."

"Whatever." I snapped. "I left. I'm done, and you win. Okay?"

"Well, I'm glad to hear you say those words, but talk is cheap. Actions are a hell of a lot more persuasive."

"What the fuck does that mean, Frankie? What do you want?"

"You, Carly." He snapped, and I heard his anger for the first time since he answered the phone, and I shivered remembering the way he held his hand around my throat and cut off my windpipe. "I'm going to text you an address, and you're going to go directly there. Do you understand?"

"What address? For what?"

"Just do as you're told, baby, and everything will be fine. Go straight to the address and call me when you get there. If you tell anyone from the crew where you're going, I'll press send on the videos of me fucking you while you beg me for more, like a dirty whore, to the entire city, and everyone will know who you belonged to first. Got it."

More tears fell from my eyelashes as I accepted defeat. "Got it."

"Good girl. I'll see you soon, baby."

He hung up, and a second later a text came through with an address outside of Shadeport and I scowled at my phone. It was near Nevada. What the fuck was he doing?

I switched my destination with the driver, giving her an extra-large tip for the inconvenience, and then watched out the window as my heart ached in my chest. Something inside me told me that I had just kissed my old life goodbye. I'd never be free to return if I gave in to Frankie's demands.

I wouldn't be worthy of Jed by the time Frankie was done with me. I knew it.

My phone rang in my lap, and Ellie's face lit up the screen. I held my phone, contemplating what to do next, but I knew I had to answer it. If nothing else, to say goodbye.

"Hello?"

"Carly! Thank God, where are you?" She snapped; I could hear the anxiety in her voice.

"Calm down, Ellie, I'm fine." I tried to lighten my voice, but it was useless.

"Bull shit. Where are you? Zeke just called Ryker and told him what Frankie is doing. I'm so sorry, babe. Why did you leave? Jed's freaking out."

"I'm just going to a hotel for the night, Ellie. It's all my fault, I'm just going to let things cool off for a bit."

She sighed, "You don't understand Carly," Her voice dropped, "Frankie signed his death warrant when he sent those pictures of you to Jed."

I shook my head back and forth as more tears fell, and a sob escaped my lips. "No El, he signed it when he wrote your name on the letter. Before he did that, he simply pissed some people off, nothing more."

"Oh, babe." She said sadly, "You're wrong. Jed is irate because he threatened you! How could you think it would be safe to leave right now? What if he's waiting for you somewhere?"

"I have to fix this."

There was a commotion on the other end of the phone, and then Ryker's deep commanding voice filled my head. "Carly, do not go to a hotel, do you hear me? Have the driver turn around and take you back home. We're on our way there now. You're not safe!"

They were coming back home because of me. Ellie needed this vacation so badly, and it was ruined. Because of me.

"I'm sorry this ruined your plans, please just stay there, Frankie won't be a problem any longer. I promise." I rushed on, trying to convince him to just let it be. "Ellie deserves this vacation."

"Fuck that, Carly, you're family. We're not staying here with all of this going on. Now do what I told you to do, damnit."

"I can't," I whispered. "I can't risk him destroying her like that. I'm doing this for her."

"Doing what?" His voice sounded haunted, "You let me worry about that piece of shit!" He exploded through the phone, and I could hear Ellie yell at him on the other end. "I'm going to get every last picture and video of you girls back from him, I promise. I won't let that dirtbag hurt you two."

"I won't let him hurt her either, Ryker. She's the only one in my life who's ever deserved my loyalty because she gave me hers. It's time I repaid her for some of that. I have to go. I have to end this." I said quickly. "Tell her I love her, and that I'm sorry."

"Carly! Don't you dare fucking hang up–" But it was too late, I ended the call and turned my phone off to save the charge.

When we got to the address on the Nevada border, there was another car waiting for me in the abandoned parking lot. The driver of my car eyed me cautiously, but I just put my brave face on and thanked her again. She looked like she wanted to say something but held her tongue. Which I was glad for, I already knew this was a mistake. But I had no choice. I'd die to protect Ellie.

When I stepped out, the man waiting looked like the worst kind of thug. He had greasy hair and beady eyes and skin that looked like it hadn't been bathed in two months straight.

"Carly James?" The man asked as his eyes dropped over my body.

"Who are you?" I asked, frozen in place. But he just smiled at me with a sick gleam in his eye.

My brain was screaming at me to get back in the car that brought me here as she stayed put behind me. But my heart knew Frankie would release those photos if I did.

I took my phone out and turned it on and dialed Frankie, and he picked up on the first ring.

"Get in the car." He ordered.

"Who is he?"

"Get in the fucking car, Carly!" He ordered. "It doesn't matter who he is, just fucking do it."

"Frankie, please," I whispered.

"Get in the car!" He screamed, and my feet stepped forward of their own accord towards the man that leered at me.

"Okay," I whispered again, looking over my shoulder to the woman in the car behind me. She was looking between me and the man but then gave me a sad smile and pulled away, reading the vibes that this was nothing she wanted to be involved with.

"Good girl." The guy leaning against the car said, and Frankie chuckled into my ear. He opened the back door, and I stepped to get in, but he held out his hand before I could.

"Give me the phone." He said, and now that I was stuck up close to him, my skin crawled as his scent invaded my nose.

"What? No." I snapped, holding my phone to my ear, but he reached forward and ripped it from my hand with a chunk of hair and then shoved me into the back seat and slammed the door. "Give me back my phone!" I screamed, but he ignored me and chucked it into the weeds as he got in the driver's seat.

It was only then that I realized another man sat in the passenger seat, but I couldn't really even describe him as a man, more like an ogre. He turned and looked at me as I shrank against the back door. His yellow eyes scanned my body as his tongue licked his lips. The driver looked at me in the rear-view mirror and smiled his predatory grin at me again and nudged his cohort. "He wasn't lying, was he?"

The ogre just leered at me longer and then smirked, showing his yellow teeth under his patchy dirty facial hair. "She'll fetch a pretty price for sure. Especially once we let the buyers sample her pussy first."

"What?" The words fell from my lips as panic truly set in. I grabbed the handle of the door but it was broken and barely hanging on, rendering it useless as I clutched at it. I turned towards the driver again, ready to fight my way out of the car if I needed to, and saw a leather vest hanging over the seat behind him. On the back of it was a large patch with a picture of two giant knives, dripping with blood.

Under the knives were the words 'Youngbloods' and 'Nevada Charter'.

No!

CHAPTER 14 – JED

S he left.

She ran away from me to protect Ellie.

"Fuck!" I roared as I destroyed the garage, throwing anything I could get my hands on. Both of my hands were bloody and torn to shreds from the rage I'd been throwing for the better part of three hours now as more and more time passed with no word from Carly.

She had told Ryker that she had to 'end it' and protect Ellie. That meant that she talked to Frankie, and he told her to do something in exchange for the pictures, and she was going to do it. He'd said in the letter to give her back to him and he'd keep the pictures to himself, but I knew better. He'd release them regardless because he was kicked out of the crew.

Ryker's Audi roared down the driveway and skidded to a stop outside of the garage that I'd torn apart as he and Ellie climbed out. Ryker took one look at me and put himself between me and his wife.

He wasn't wrong to do that either, I was unhinged and crazed.

"We'll get her back."

"We don't even know where she is. What if he has her?" I snapped. "They could be anywhere!"

"We'll find her." He said again with authority, but I shook him off.

A black car came down the driveway, escorted by the shack guard, and pulled to a stop behind Ryker's Audi. I walked out of the garage as a middle-aged woman stepped out of the car and walked behind the guard. She was wringing her hands together as her eyes flicked from me to Ryker and back.

"Mr. Lawson, this woman said she had information about Ms. James." The guard said and then motioned for the woman to step forward.

"Do you know where she is?" I snapped, and Ellie put her hand on my arm to calm me down.

The woman continued wringing her hands as she looked at me. "I was her driver when she left here a couple of hours ago, I think she's in trouble."

"What happened?" Ellie asked.

"She hired me to take her to the Hilton downtown, but a couple of minutes into the ride, she made a phone call, and it got intense. She was talking to someone, asking him to stop doing what he was doing and not to hurt anyone. And then when she was done she changed her destination with me and paid me extra to make the switch."

"Where was it," I asked, feeling relieved that we might have a direction to go in at least.

"Almost to the Nevada border." The woman said with a grimace.

"Nevada?" I asked in a quiet voice of disbelief.

"There was a car waiting for her there, with a man who looked—scary. She hesitated to get in with him, but the guy on the phone screamed at her so loud I could hear it. But before she got in the car, the guy ripped her phone out of her hand and threw it into the bushes. That's how I knew she was in trouble, and I knew that I needed to come here and at least tell you, Mr. Lawson." She said with a small nod, looking down to the ground. "She seemed scared but kept trying to calm herself down."

My blood boiled again, and my heart ached for the love of my life. Frankie had her.

"What did the guy look like in the car? What did the car look like?" Ryker asked.

"He was older, maybe forty or fifty. He had a giant bald spot on top of his head and looked dirty. They got into a tan SUV, it was older and rusted.

"Did he have any tattoos or anything?"

She looked down again and thought about it before looking back up, "Yes! He had something on his neck." She pointed to the side of her neck under her ear, "It was like two knives or something crossed over each other."

A cold sweat broke out over my body as I realized what logo that was.

"Youngbloods," Ryker swore and yelled out in frustration.

"Oh my God!" Ellie cried, and Ryker grabbed her before she collapsed to the ground, falling into a fit of hysterics. "If they have her, we'll never find her! They'll... they'll..." She said, unable to finish the sentence.

"They'll sell her." I finished, and a flashback of my father's beaten and pulverized face flooded into my vision. Something snapped inside of me, and I felt the change happen in a way that took over every inch of my body. Gone were my restraint and ability to think logically. I had only one goal, and I'd die to complete it. "I'm going to burn this world to the ground to get her back," I said to Ellie. "I promise you that."

Ryker pulled his phone out, and he dialed Zeke and barked orders to him. "Youngbloods have her. Arrange a conversation with their new President. Tell them they have something that belongs to me and that I'll decimate their entire family lines to get it back!"

CHAPTER 15 – CARLY

The mask over my face made me nearly hyperventilate in fear. The duct tape covering my mouth and tying my wrists behind my back cut into me as I fought against them both. Fear assaulted me the longer we rode in the car, but on top of that, was the anger.

The blinding rage consumed me in a way I'd never known before. Frankie had sold me to the sex traffickers that Diesel Ames warned us about. And Jed and Ryker had no idea where I was or who I was with. I tried to remain calm, but I was failing.

When the car finally stopped, I tried listening to what was happening as the two guys got out, and then all of a sudden my door opened, and I was dragged from the back seat by my hair.

"Get off of me!" I screamed and fought back, kicking, and throwing my body away from the hands that held onto me.

The men grunted and cursed as I lashed out until one landed a punch to my stomach, knocking the air out of my lungs and doubling me over.

"Careful!" The driver snarled. "Marks on her skin will make her pull less cash, you know that!"

"Fucking cunt got my nuts!" The ogre yelled back, but I couldn't breathe to fight back as he lifted me over his shoulder and carried me into a building. It was cool and damp, like a basement and I could hear muffled music and voices from upstairs. I heard multiple locks and doors being opened and closed as we walked through the basement until we walked through one final door and the ogre threw me to the floor in a heap.

Female voices hushed as soon as we walked into the room, and I tried desperately to get my hands free.

"Stop fighting, you cunt." The ogre snapped and wrapped his hand around my throat and shook me violently. My head whipped back and forth, and my teeth rattled, disorienting me and catching me off guard.

He ripped the mask off my face, and the dim lights of the room were bright against my sensitive eyes as I looked around.

It was a dingy basement, cold concrete walls and floors were what I saw first, and then I saw the women, cowering in every corner of the room.

Most were young like me, some were older, but more than anything, they were scared. Fear burned in their eyes as they watched the men standing over me. Another door in the room opened, and a woman walked in, wearing a long silk gown with feathers around the cuffs, like something Marilyn Monroe would wear. She was tall and rail-thin with long black hair and eyes that matched. She had a face full of makeup, and I could tell at one point in her life she was beautiful, but now, she just looked worn out.

She watched me with a severe gaze as she walked towards me. "Who's this?" she asked, never letting her eyes fall from me where I sat on the floor.

"A gift from our new friend. He said she was a beauty, and he wasn't lying." The driver said, leering at me, and I scowled at him as best I could with my mouth taped shut.

"She looks too high-class to be a gift." The woman said, raising her eyebrow and looking at the man.

"He needs a new crew to fall in with, turns out he pissed off his old boss and is on the run. This was a token of good faith."

"A nobody on the run from a powerful man is not the type of person we do business with!" She snapped, finally showing emotion. "That brings trouble to our doorstep, idiots!"

The men faltered and looked at each other. "But look how pretty she is. He said she was a stripper, so she's got skills. With the big timers coming to you for new pussy, we thought you'd be happy to have some quality cat in-house for them."

My stomach rolled, listening to them talk about me as if they were discussing the weather. The woman watched me closely. "What boss is the new guy running from?" She asked.

"Uh—I don't know." The driver said, shrugging his shoulders. "He didn't say. We picked her up at the border."

Fire erupted in her eyes as her lips pressed into two thin lines. She looked down and nodded to me. "Do you know who sold you?" She asked straight.

I nodded once.

"Do you know who his boss is?" She asked again.

I nodded once again.

"Take her tape off!" She ordered, and the ogre stepped forward and ripped the tape off, taking a layer of skin with it, and I spit in his face the second my mouth was free. He reared back and backhanded me quickly, pain exploded in my cheekbone, and I fell over onto the concrete.

"Don't fucking touch her, you idiot!" The woman screamed. "If we have any hopes of staying out of the shit drama that kid brought to our doorstep, we need to offload her quickly, and we won't be able to do that if she's bloodied up! Fucking imbecile."

I sat up, keeping my knees bent and feet flat on the floor as I spat a mouthful of blood onto the ground next to me and glared at the man.

The woman huffed and turned, "Star! Get something to clean her up with!" The girl she ordered stood up from where she was sitting on the ground with a couple of younger girls and walked to the sink in the corner, wetting a rag and then walking back to me. She kneeled next to me, keeping her eyes downcast, and I looked at her closely as she brought the rag up to my lip and gently dabbed at it. It stung, and I reared back, and her eyes snapped up to mine.

"Don't move." She whispered. "I'm sorry." Her eyes were dark, bottomless pits with zero emotion in them as she dropped them back to my lips and went back to dabbing at them. The lights in the room were dim, but I could just make out the faint flecks of gold in her brown eyes and something inside of me warmed. Her nose was small but sharp and her eyebrows were dainty and dark over long black eyelashes. Her lips were a perfect cupid's bow of rosy, pink flesh. I couldn't tell how old she was exactly, my guess was mid-twenties, though something about her eyes called to me. I couldn't place what it was or where it was from, but I felt like I knew her from somewhere.

She pulled back, looking up into my eyes again, and the corner of her lips turned up in a sad smile. "All better." She stood up and quickly walked back over to the corner where she had been sitting on the floor on a bare mattress with the others and wouldn't meet my gaze again.

The woman in charge walked forward and sighed. "Now we will have to wait for that to heal before we put her in the auction."

The man who hit me had the decency to look sheepish and backed away, remaining quiet.

The woman looked at me again and asked again. "Who is the boss?"

I stared at her and wondered what to do. I knew Ryker's power spread far and even farther than that, spread his dark reputation. If this woman was afraid of Ryker, perhaps she'd let me go if I told her, it was him. But if she was an enemy , she might make my life worse because of it.

I didn't know what to do.

"Answer me, girl!" She snapped her fingers in front of my face.

I licked my lips and took a deep breath. "Ryker Lawson."

Her eyes widened, and her lips parted. The men behind me cursed, and murmurs from the other women in the room filled my ears.

"Ryker Lawson is hunting the man that sold you to me?" she asked quietly, fear flashing in her eyes.

"Your biggest problem isn't that he wants Frankie," I said evenly, trying my best to seem confident and strong.

"Then what is my biggest problem?" She asked, stiffening her spine like she didn't like being challenged like this.

"Your biggest problem is that I'm the girlfriend of Ryker Lawson's right-hand man, Jed Manning, and the best friend of his wife, Elora. And you three have just made yourselves the biggest targets of the entire Shadeport Crew and their allies."

The woman's face fell and then her rage exploded, "You fucking idiots!" She screamed; red-faced, at the two men. "He'll hang our bloody corpses from the streetlights in his city for this!" She picked objects off the tables and threw them, destroying the place in her attempts to injure the two lackeys. The women cowered, crawling further into the dark corners, hiding from her anger, but I just sat there, not backing down at all. "Lock her up!" She screamed, throwing her hand towards me. "I need to figure out what to do!"

"We've already called a couple of big wallets about her," the driver said, "Titus is banking on her making him a big amount in the next two days. He'll be pissed if you don't sell her."

"Titus isn't the biggest monster in the closet anymore, you fucking asshole! This is my business; I'll decide what we do. Now lock her up!" She cried again, and the ogre lifted me off my feet and dragged me over to the edge of the room and threw me down on a ratty old mattress. I kicked at him as he grabbed my ankle and shackled me to a chain in the floor. Panic overwhelmed me as I saw it was only about ten feet long; I was defenseless like this. I couldn't get away or fight. He cut the tape off my wrists and ran to get out of my reach before I could strike, but I still tried.

They followed the Madam out of the room, locking a bolt over the metal door when they left, and finally the girls started moving from the shadows, and I watched in horror as twenty or more of them came out into the room.

They were sickly thin and desperate looking, and I recognized the beady look in some of their eyes—they were high. I just didn't know if it was by choice to block out what happened to them here or if they were controlled that way.

"Carly!" Willow ran to me and hugged me tightly . She worked at Lux with me and went missing last week.

"Oh my god!" I pulled her to me and then ran my hands over her arms and face, checking her for injuries. "Are you okay?"

"Physically I'm fine, but—" She widened her eyes and shuddered, "Carly this place is hell."

"Where are we?" I asked her, the other girls looked on like they were looking to me for guidance.

"Nevada, I don't know where exactly, but it's a brothel. They sell girls here every single night, some get pimped out every twenty minutes to different men, some get sold to someone as a slave, and they leave with them and never come back. Tell me Mr. Lawson is coming for us!" Her eyes were frantic as she clung to me.

"I don't know, Willow," I said honestly. "I don't know if they know where I am. Frankie set me up."

"He set all of us up, girl. Sabine and Darcy were here when I got here, and they both got pulled the same way I did. We got grabbed on our way home after work by the Youngblood MC."

"Jesus fuck." I groaned, holding my head, and trying to think.

The metal door opened, and a tattooed man stepped through, wearing a leather vest. He had curly black hair and a full black beard, and tattoos covered every inch of skin on his arms and neck and face. "You." he said, pointing to a girl that was half-conscious in the corner. "You're up." He commanded.

She slowly stood up and walked over to him, in a trance, and he grabbed her by the throat and shook her like a rag doll. "Wake up! You're going to be a good girl and do everything you're told to do to make your client happy, and if you do that, I'll give you a nice big hit when you get back." He held up a bag between his fingers of what looked like cocaine, and she grabbed for it slowly. He pulled it out of her reach and then shoved her towards the door. "Be a good girl now." He said and smacked her ass as she stumbled through the door. Before he followed after her, he looked over at me on the ground, shackled, and paused.

He licked his lips and walked over toward me. The girls who had congregated scattered away, except for Willow, and I steeled my spine and kept my eyes locked on his.

"Well, if it isn't the new girl that comes with the highest reserve bid in the history of our humble little club here." He fingered his beard as he looked down at me. "Yeah, you're a sexy little thing, aren't you." He squatted down right at the end of the mattress and grabbed ahold of the chain and pulled. I scrambled, trying to grab onto something to keep myself from being pulled towards him, but he was too strong to fight.

He dragged me down and grabbed my ankle as I kicked and fought against him. I landed a kick straight to his face, but he quickly grabbed both of my ankles and stood up, pulling them straight up into the air until I was hanging upside down.

"Put me down!" I screamed and swung my arms, trying to hit him in the crotch as he laughed sinisterly at me.

"Or what?" He challenged. "You're going to end up on your back one way or another. You're new pussy, and from what I hear, you're a dancer, so it's not like you're not used to spreading those sexy little thighs for men like me, anyway. My guys are going to tear you up before we sell you off to some shlep that likes to keep little girls like you naked in kneeling cages hung from the ceiling. He'll fuck your body with his cock and anything else he wants to for his joy, baby. You're going to be just a body with three holes in no time at all, and you'll be begging to be owned by someone sane like me."

"Sane! You're a fucking psycho if you think you'll live long enough to get your dick wet ever again, you piece of shit!" I snapped, but he dropped me on my head, and I landed in a heap on the concrete floor as the other women watched on.

"You think so, pussycat?" He asked, grabbing my legs, and pulling me towards him once again and forcing them apart as he leaned over me. He grabbed a fistful of hair and twisted my head to the side and ripped my shirt open, revealing my bra to his ugly eyes. "Then I guess I should probably just go ahead and fuck you right here and now in case I don't get the chance again." He laughed and wrapped his hand around my neck as he fought with my jeans.

"Get off me!" I hissed, fighting him nonstop. "I'll kill you!"

He laughed again as he ground his hard-on against me. "Fuck yeah, baby, fight back, that's how I like my pussy. I like bitches that have fire in them!" He tightened his hand around my neck, and I couldn't get any air in past the restriction.

I struggled against him as he got my pants undone and was working on pulling them down my body when the girl that had cleaned my face up, Star, stepped forward holding her hands out.

"Titus! Madam said she couldn't be touched; she's got a big buyer for her and apparently, if she's touched before he gets here tonight the sale is off." She said quickly, swallowing when the man tore his stare away from me and looked at her.

"Big buyer, huh?" He sneered and looked back down at me.

"Biggest she's seen in all her years," Star said confidently, but I knew she was lying.

"Hmm." He said and rolled his lips as he looked down at my exposed body and then stood up. I gasped for air and scurried away from him, back to the mattress, and Willow pulled me against her, wrapping her arms around me as he kept his eyes on me. "This isn't over." He told me. "I will taste that fucking pussy before you're gone." he said, pointing his finger at me as his nostrils flared.

I kept my mouth shut because I didn't dare challenge him when he'd finally let me go.

He turned to Star, who had backed up away from him, but I saw his intent seconds before his hand shot out and grabbed her hair, dragging her towards his body. "I guess your pussy will have to do for now then."

"No!" I exploded, but Willow clamped her hand over my mouth and turned my head away as he dragged Star over to the table in the center of the room. I fought Willow off and threw myself to the end of my chain and tried to get to her, but I couldn't reach her as he pushed her over the edge of it and I screamed in horror as he shoved her pants down and took his dick out.

My screams vibrated off the concrete as I scratched and fought to get to her as he started raping her.

She closed her eyes and screwed her face up in pain as he did it, but she never made a sound. Willow and a couple of other girls dragged me back away from them and held me down trying to calm me down but even over my screams and sobs, I could hear his grunts and moans as he raped that poor innocent girl for standing up for me.

I cried as my heart felt like it was bleeding out. I would have given anything to take away her pain at that moment, even volunteered to be raped by him if that was what it took, because she didn't deserve it, she'd helped me and was being tortured for it.

It didn't last long, but every single second was agonizing. He chuckled as he kissed her cheek, petting her hair back away from her face after he finished. I watched on in hysteria as he zipped up his jeans and walked away, staring at me the whole time. "Don't worry baby, you'll get your turn." He said, blowing me a sadistic kiss and then slamming the large metal door shut behind him.

I gaped in shock at Star as she stood up and righted her clothes and wiped at her tears quickly. She wouldn't meet my eyes as she took a couple of deep breaths and calmed herself.

"Why?" I whispered, "Why would you do that for me?" My face was wide with shock and revulsion as I tried to understand her self-lessness.

She licked her lips and wiped at a few more tears that had fallen over her lashes and stiffened her spine, standing tall and nodding her head as she finally looked me in my eyes. "Because I owe Jed Manning my life, however pitiful it's turned out to be, and I couldn't just stand by while Titus raped his girlfriend." She sniffled. "Because I have real hope that you're going to get out of this alive, and you don't need any more scars to your soul when you get back to him."

I shook my head in confusion and looked her over, trying to wrap my head around it all. And then it dawned on me.

Her dark features.

The gold flecks in her brown eyes.

The sharp nose.

"Oh, my God." I gasped, covering my mouth as a silent sob of agony ripped from my lungs. "You're Laila. You're Jed's sister."

CHAPTER 16 – JED

I pulled up outside the Reaper MC Clubhouse and got out of my car. It was a Thursday, but they were apparently throwing a party. Riders eyed me up as I walked past them with a menacing look on my face. Ryker had been trying to get in contact with the Youngbloods MC all day, but they were lax on their secretarial duties, and he kept hitting dead ends.

And I was done waiting, knowing exactly what type of environment Carly was in right now. I couldn't let another second go idle without doing something to actively get her back.

"Jed," Ripper said when I walked into the clubhouse. Riders and girls littered the entire space partying, but when the patched members saw me speaking with their VP, they all shook off their old ladies and stood on guard.

"Where's Diesel?" I asked.

"He's busy," Rip said, crossing his arms over his chest. "I can tell him you stopped by."

"This ain't a social call, Rip." I snapped and pushed past him towards the office in the back of the room. He held a hand up to keep his men from tearing me to pieces on my way, not that I would have stopped if they tried.

I had nothing to lose at this point.

I got to the office door and pushed it open, catching Diesel getting his dick sucked by a roadie in his office chair.

"You mind, boy?" he asked, hardly sparing me a glance.

"Youngbloods took my girl," I said, ignoring formalities.

His eyes snapped to mine, and he pushed the girl between his legs off, smacking her ass as she stumbled away. He put himself away, and when Rip shut the door behind her, leaving the three of us alone, he leaned forward on his desk.

"The blonde from the other night? You know that for sure?"

"The guys spotted taking her had the Youngbloods crests on their necks."

"Fuck." He murmured. He looked past me to Ripper. "You hear anything today?"

I looked over my shoulder at his second, and he nodded, though he looked like it pained him to do so. "Word is traveling fast that they've got a new load of fresh pussy hitting the market tonight. There's a lot of talk about one in particular. A blonde dancer."

I growled as my pain surfaced again.

Diesel watched me closely.

"You have a way to get in on the buy?" I asked.

Diesel nodded, running his hand over the top of his head down to his man bun. "Once we use it though, we won't have another unexposed ticket into the place."

"There won't be a place left standing once I get Carly out of there."

"Is that a Shadeport Crew-wide statement?" He was asking if the entire crew was going in.

"Every last available member will be involved."

"Good." He said, standing up and adjusting his vest. "Then we'll ride with you. Rip will get the invite, and you and I will go in. Once they know they're surrounded, they'll come out guns blazing, but the crews will just pick them off as they run."

"None of the girls get hurt unnecessarily, and you don't get to keep any of them either," I said, raising my eyebrow at him in a way that dared him to challenge me.

He grinned evilly, "I've got something keeping my hands full at the moment, son, don't worry about that."

"Good. I'll organize the meet up at Erotiq, and we'll ride from there. One hour."

"We'll be there." He said, holding his hand out. I shook it, feeling the power behind it and also feeling the psycho beneath it as well. He was exactly the type of ally we needed for this.

By the time I got to Erotiq, Ryker, Zeke and the crew were there, waiting for me in the parking lot. It would be almost ten before we got to the address in Nevada that Diesel had given me, and the auction was set to start at ten thirty. We had no room for error here if we were going to pull this off.

"We all set?" Ryker asked me as he put on his jacket over his shoulder holster.

"All set. They'll be here in ten minutes."

"Good."

"Where's Ellie?" I asked, surprised to see him here at all, knowing so many of his enforcers were riding with me.

"In the safe house. Dawson and his crew are watching over her."

Dawson was Ellie's grandfather; his crew had saved her from the Wellington's when she was kidnapped so I knew without a doubt that she was safe. "Good, I'm sure he's enjoying having her to himself for a while."

Ryker chuckled and nodded his head. "Yeah, though I don't expect her to stay for long once we get Carly back home."

"No, I don't expect her to either." I looked over at Zeke as he geared up with a vest and other tactical gear like the rest of our men not going into the brothel. "We clear on the plan?"

"You flush them out, we pick them off. We'll come in if need be." Zeke said.

I nodded and looked at the ground. "Thank you, both."

Ryker just scoffed, "She's family, Jed, the same way you are." His stoic face was sincere, and I looked away, fighting back the emotions that had been brewing all day. It wasn't the first time he'd called Carly family, but it was the first time he'd said it about me. And that fucking meant something because I'd lost all of my family years ago when my parents died.

Laila was still out there somewhere, but I didn't have any hope of finding her anymore. She was better off without me, I just had to accept that.

Rumbling caught my attention, and I turned as the Reapers pulled up into the parking lot alongside all the Shadeport crew. They were fifty riders deep, next to our seventy-five. Rumors said that the Youngbloods were a smaller MC, with numbers somewhere in the forties or fifties, so if that was the case, we should be able to strong-arm them with no problem.

I just hoped we didn't have too many casualties in the process. And I prayed to God that we were able to get there before Carly suffered something that broke her. She was the love of my life, and I'd use my love to help her heal whatever had happened to her there. I just needed to get her home first if I was going to be able to do that.

"Let's ride," Ryker said, finishing up briefing Diesel and his men and gearing up. Diesel got into my car with me, and we took off, breaking every speed limit on the way, daring one of the local police departments to try to fuck with me right now.

When we got to the building where Ripper said the auction would be held, my palms started sweating as I looked at the bricks imprisoning Carly.

"This is where they house and sell the girls?" I asked, and Diesel nodded his head. "We're on the buyer's list?"

He nodded again, "JT and Derek are the names we are using. They don't ask for proof; most people don't give their real info, anyway. Word is, they do a catwalk of sorts, showing off the girls that are for sale, and then the bidding starts."

"As soon as I see her, it's game over. I'm not waiting a second longer."

"Works for me. The sooner we get in and push them out, the sooner we take them all out."

"Let's go." We got out of the car and walked to the front door of the nondescript building in the middle of nowhere. The parking lot was full, a mix of beater and luxury cars that cost more than the entire building parked next to each other. I guess money didn't differentiate the psycho in men willing to buy women like they were property, forcing them into slavery for a flock of different uses.

I wore my usual black suit, and Diesel wore a black and white flannel over his black jeans and bike boots, leaving his cut with Ripper. There was no denying we were powerful and dangerous men, even without labels on our bodies identifying exactly who we were. The bouncers at the front door were Youngbloods, and they all stood taller when we walked up.

The leader of the group stood with a clipboard in the center of the group and nodded when we got to the door. "Are you on the list?"

"Yeah, TJ and Derek," Diesel answered, stepping forward.

The guy looked down at his list and then back up at us, raising an eyebrow. "I've never seen you two here before." he said, eyeing us as he tucked the clipboard under his arm. "How'd you get a spot here for tonight's event, it's very elite?"

"You going to stand here and bullshit business on the sidewalk or are you going to let two guys who got a personal invite from Titus into the actual event?" Diesel bit back, not used to anyone bullshitting him. But I couldn't let him mess this up before we even got in.

I stepped forward, "We've just never been interested in the quality of pussy you've had before. But we got word that it's been upgraded lately."

The blood looked me over, eyeing me up, "You must be talking about the blonde." He said with a sinister smirk on his face. "She's drawn quite a crowd tonight, looks like we've got a new supplier that's earned a lot of future business if he keeps sending such quality bitches our way." He stood to the side, and one of the other bloods opened the door to let us in. As we were about to pass him, he called out, "The new supplier, a young Hispanic kid, he was at the bar last I knew. I'm sure if you don't see something that tickles your fancy, he'd be more than willing to come through next time if you let him know what you're looking for. For an added price, of course." He winked, and his friends laughed, and Diesel pushed me forward and into the club.

When we walked into the dimly lit room, we walked forward to a hostess desk, and a woman in a long black silk gown walked forward.

She was older but had an air about her that screamed authority. She was in charge here.

"Gentlemen." She said as she glided up to the desk. "What a pleasure to have some new faces here this evening. I guarantee you, we have anything you're looking for. Follow me and I'll take you to a booth, the lineup is about to start." She clapped her hands together in front of her like she was giddy and excited, and my hands ached to bounce her face off the floor for being a disgusting human being, knowing for a fact that she was probably sold just like this at some point in her life, pointing her down this path of disgust.

We followed her to the booth along the wall, on the way there, I let my eyes rove over the other men in the room, sitting and waiting for the show to start. "Here we are." She stood to the side as Diesel and I sat down, keeping our heads on swivels. "Here is your bidding button," She slid a wireless controller across the table, "When you want to bid, press this button and your light on the table will light up and your bid will be registered. We have an incredible lineup of girls tonight, ranging from sales for the night to full ownership so I hope you handsome men brought your checkbooks. Any of my girls would be blessed to get bought by either of you." A wicked smile crossed her face, "Or by both of you." She winked and then walked away.

"What a despicable woman." Diesel sneered.

"From the man that sold a woman to a place just like this." I deadpanned back.

"Wrong. I sold Monica directly to a man, using a place like this to facilitate the trade only. And the man I sold her to will treat her far better than I did. Which was still far better than she deserved for what she did to me and Elora both."

"Hmm." I hummed, not willing to get into it right now when I was so on edge. I looked towards the bar and didn't see Frankie sitting there like the bouncers had said he would be. If he was here, and he made us, we would be dead before we even knew it. But the booth was dark, and I knew we sank into the shadows far enough to ignore detection now that we were seated.

The lights on the stage lit up, casting a warm glow on the worn wood as the Madam walked out with a microphone and a man who looked like he'd been dragged under a semi-truck across the country a couple of times.

"Titus," Diesel said quietly, nodding to the stage.

The Youngbloods President stood with his vest on next to the madam as he looked around the room. His cheek looked like he'd recently taken a punch there, and I couldn't help but wonder who would have been brave enough to take a swing at the man controlling this shit show.

But I knew the answer to that before I even finished the thought.

Carly.

She was scrappy and a fighter if she needed to be, her street smarts would have given way to instinct if she was threatened, and she would lash out and hit a man like Titus without thinking twice.

Fucking hell, please let her still be in one piece.

"Gentlemen! Thank you all for coming to our little club this evening, I love seeing all of the new faces tonight and look forward to the beginning of new relationships from here on out!" The crowd cheered and clapped for her, and my stomach rolled. "We have an incredible lineup for you tonight, we'll start first with the girls that are going to be available for the evening only, and then we will move on to the girls that are looking for new homes completely. So, sit back and enjoy the parade, and we will start the bidding after that."

The DJ in the corner turned on music, and the curtain parted, and girls started walking out onto the stage and then down the steps to walk through the crowd. The looks on their faces were all the same; like they were dead inside.

I couldn't help but wonder how many times these girls had made this walk, or how many times they'd been forced into prostitution, without getting any of the money from it. I was all for normalizing sex work when it was consensual and safe, but this wasn't either of those things. This was slavery.

Ownership.

They all wore dresses of some sort, with their hair and makeup done to make them look high class, but more than a few of them had track marks on their arms and glazed eyes as they passed by us. They were either drugged to be kept in line, or they used it to get through this life as a coping mechanism.

I clenched my fists on top of the table and forced my feet to stay planted on the floor when all I wanted was to run straight through that stage and find Carly and get her the fuck out of there.

Women walked past our table, some of them looked down at us and smiled and flirted, while some others acted like they were walking death row. But none of them were Carly. I didn't look at their faces after a while, my stomach rolled thinking about what they were going to endure, and I cowered out, staring at my hands on the table as they walked by.

The madam took the microphone back, "Thank you, ladies! Alright, gentlemen those women are all available for the remainder of this evening only. We have a limited number of rooms upstairs available for rent, or we can facilitate other lodgings if you'd like. But save your bids until you've seen the girls that are available to be taken home for good. We have quite a few diamonds in our lineup tonight." She said with a breathy laugh, and then the music started again.

"Our inside guy said your girl was in this group," Diesel said as women started walking across the stage again. These women were less dazed.

They were looking around the room with crazed eyes as they were pushed forward by blood members and forced to walk the plank. Third from the front was Carly.

The breath was sucked right out of my lungs as I watched my soulmate walk across the stage in a turquoise blue lace cocktail dress that hugged every single curve. She had a gash in her lower lip and bruises around her neck that looked a lot like a pair of hands made them. Her hair and makeup were done in a way that she never would have chosen, and I started to stand up from my seat to get to her.

Diesel put his hand on my shoulder and pushed me back down. "Wait."

"I can't." I snapped.

"Just wait, she'll walk by our table, and we'll make our move then."

I took a deep breath, knowing he was right, and forced my tight muscles to relax as she walked down the steps and started walking around the room. Men cat-called and grabbed at her as she walked with the other girls, and a growl started in my chest, aching to get to her. Her eyes traveled the room, and the second they found me in the darkness, they widened and watered as tears threatened to fall. I started to stand up as she got closer, but she shook her head no and put her hand up slightly, stopping me.

"What's going on?" Diesel asked.

"I don't know," I said back, watching as she got closer to our table. The panicked look never left her face as she got within three feet of me, but she didn't stop, just slowed down.

"Carly—" I started, but she cut me off.

"Laila is here." She hissed with a scared look on her face. "Rescue her!"

She walked past my table, and my blood roared in my ears as my brain tried to process what she had just said.

"Who the fuck is Laila?" Diesel snapped, leaning forward with his phone out, ready to give the command.

"Hold off!" I bit back, pushing his phone out of his hand.

"Who is she? Is she worth losing your girl?"

"She's my sister." That was all I could say. Disbelief roared through my brain as I tried to figure out what to do.

Our plan only left enough time to save one girl, but now I was forced to decide.

What the fuck was I supposed to do?

CHAPTER 17 – CARLY

As soon as I got back to the holding room, I ran to where Laila stood against the wall. She had walked in the first round, and I knew for a fact that Jed never would have recognized her, she was only eight when she was taken away from him. And I knew that he was micro-focused on looking for my blonde hair in the lineup, he would have easily missed her walking right past him.

"You have to listen to me." I snapped, grabbing her hand, and forcing her to look at me. Ever since she was attacked and told me that she allowed it to happen because of her relationship to Jed, she had been quiet and lifeless. Like somehow, she'd given up now that she'd repaid a lifelong debt. She looked up into my eyes, and I could tell she was trying to focus, but I could also tell she had so little life left in her that it was hard. "Jed is here," I whispered, not trusting even the other girls to hear the news in case one of them ratted him out to the guards in a case of misplaced loyalty.

Her pupils dilated, and she blinked a couple of times as she fought to pay attention. "What?" She whispered back.

"He's here, he's going to rescue us. I told him you were here. You have to fight though, Laila!" I begged, "You have to focus and stay with me if we have any chance of getting out of this alive, okay?"

"Okay." She said, with more conviction, but I could see the doubt in her eyes too, and I knew instantly what she was thinking.

"You deserve to get out of here Laila, you are worthy of being rescued, so don't you dare start thinking up some bullshit scheme to get me out of here safe by sacrificing yourself! Do you hear me? We are all going to get out of here."

"Okay." She said again and tightened her hand in mine.

"Line back up!" A man yelled and started shoving the girls back in line to stand on the stage as the bidding started. The Madame walked into the room with a proud smile on her face as she walked over to me. I let go of Laila's hand and tried to separate myself from her, I didn't want to give away that she was important to me in case they tried to use it against us.

"Darling, you are the belle of the ball tonight!" She said in a honeyed voice I hadn't heard from her yet. She fingered a blonde ringlet of my hair and smiled down at me affectionately. "Every man has come tonight just for you. So, we'll start the auction off with a bang that way the men don't hold back on their bidding to save their money for you."

"Ryker and Jed will kill you if you do this," I said firmly. "But they won't just kill you quickly. Their specialty is torture; they get off on the pain they inflict." I was trying to scare her, and for a moment I thought it was working. Her eyes widened, and I saw the fear in them before a sinister smile curled her bright red lips.

"You'll be long gone out of my hair before either of them even realizes we had you to start with, dear." Her smile fell from her lips as she pulled my hair and pushed me towards the door. "Now get the fuck in line!"

I stumbled forward into line and tried to think of what to do when the man named Titus that had attacked me and raped Laila walked into the room and leered at me. "Well, hello again poppet." He said and licked his lips. "Change of plans." He said and pulled me from the line with an iron grip on my arm and dragged me along behind him as I fought to get free.

"What change?" the Madam asked, marching over to us.

"A special request. Money up front for her."

"I don't care what was offered up front, we do the auction as we planned. We could get so much more money that way!" She snapped, going red in the face. "This is my house, my rules Titus!"

"The man who bought her paid ten million, wiring it now." He said, and she shut up instantly.

"Ten million?" She asked in disbelief, and I fought the churning of my stomach as I prayed, somehow, that it was Ryker or Jed that paid that amount. But I knew that was impossible.

"And he wanted her little pet too," Titus said, nodding to where Laila stood with wide eyes watching the whole scene unfold.

"Star? She wasn't on the slave walk though." She snapped.

"Does it fucking matter what order they walked in? A man is paying ten million dollars to buy them, I'm not about to be picky about it." Titus said, cutting her off. "Star, let's go, grab your shit."

It was Jed. There was no one else who would buy us both. It was him.

Laila grabbed the small bag of things that she had and walked forward toward me, and I grabbed her hand in mine. Titus watched us, and my skin crawled with the intent in his eyes. "I bet you two look real pretty in a little bit, eating each other out and taking his cock." He tsked his tongue. "I'm just mad I didn't get a taste first." he said, looking down at my crotch before tilting his head. "But with ten million dollars, I can buy all the pussy I want." He finished with a grave laugh and started dragging me out of the room again.

He pulled us through a dark hallway and up a different staircase than the one we'd used to go on stage. I looked back at Laila and mimed for her to stay quiet as we scurried along behind him. When we got to the top, we exited the building straight into the parking lot. It was pitch black out, and the only light was directly over the door, casting the rest of the parking lot in shadow.

There was no one there though, and I looked around in a panic.

Where was Jed?

Just then, two headlights turned on directly across from us, blinding us as the car roared to life, and I nearly fell to the ground in relief when I recognized the purr of Jed's muscle car rumbling across my skin.

The car pulled forward and stopped ten feet away, and my eyes burned with tears as Jed stepped out of the driver's side with Diesel Ames getting out of the passenger side.

"Looks like you both will be stuffed full of cock after all." Titus joked menacingly and jerked me forward. Jed's eyes flashed as he watched me get shoved around like a rag doll, I gritted my teeth to bear it without letting on that he was about to regret it. Jed looked away from me to where Laila stood with her hand in mine, still with fear radiating off her body as she stared into the eyes of her brother for the first time in eighteen years. I couldn't begin to imagine what either of them was thinking at that exact moment, but I felt their grief from here.

More Youngblood members came around the building and out from the door behind us as the transaction was about to be done. I looked around, counting men as I tried to figure out what to do.

"Did the wire go through?" Titus asked one of his men, who had a tablet in his hands, and checked.

"Yep, ten large sitting pretty in our account." The biker said with a rotten-toothed smile.

Titus laughed and shook his head, "I don't get what it is about this girl that makes you think she's worth so much goddamned money, my man. I never got to personally get a taste of her, but her friend here has been one of my favorites over the last year or so. She's damned tight too, for a whore anyway." He said and laughed, and I had only a second to react before Jed grabbed the gun from his waistband and started firing shots.

I ducked and ripped my arm out of Titus's grip in his surprise and tightened my hand around Laila's as we ran behind a car parked to the side. I saw the flash of guns from beyond the parking lot, hundreds of guns, and held Laila tight as we hid. Youngbloods ran from the building, shooting back and getting slaughtered as they encountered a firing squad of Shadeport Crew and Reapers in the darkness.

"Oh my God!" Laila screamed as she clung to me.

"Shh," I said, holding her tighter, "It's okay, it's Jed's guys. It's okay."

I poked my head up over the hood of the car but couldn't find Jed in the chaos and prayed that he was okay. None of this would be worth it if he was killed because of me and my stupidity in trusting Frankie.

Just then, I caught movement out of the corner of my eye and saw the piece of shit ex-friend that had sold me into slavery cowering behind a car much like we were, and something inside of me—broke.

Men fell all around us with their weapons lying in their dead hands as Jed and Diesel's men walked forward from the darkness and decimated them all. A man fell to the ground next to the car we hid behind, and his gun skidded across the dirt to my feet. I didn't make the conscious decision to pick it up, but before I knew what I was doing I had the large, cold metal gun in my hand and felt the heaviness of it in my palm as I looked back up to where Frankie hid with his back to me.

"Stay here." I said quietly, "Stay down."

Laila looked up at me with crazed eyes, "What are you going to do with that?" She asked, looking down at the gun in my hand.

"Kill the man that started all of this for me," I said confidently, and I felt every word as I said it.

I crouched behind the car and jumped behind the one next to us and didn't look back as I dodged bullets ricocheting off the metal and brick around me until I was one car away from where Frankie kneeled on the ground.

I stood up, suddenly unable to hear any of the chaos around us anymore as I only had eyes on one thing.

The back of Frankie's skull.

"Frankie." I sneered, and he whipped around and looked at me, his eyes rounded with shock as he stared at me.

I squeezed the trigger, feeling the gun jump in my hand, and then squeezed it again over and over until it stopped firing and started clicking in my hand. My arm shook from the recoil and my palm tingled where it squeezed the grip painfully tight.

"Carly!" I heard in the quietness around me like a loud echo as Jed's voice roared from behind me.

I felt wetness on my face and wiped it away with my hand and looked down. It was red.

Frankie's blood covered my face and arms as he lay in a heap at my feet, multiple bullet holes in his face and chest. And then I started shaking.

A hard body crashed into mine, and Jed's strong hands ripped the gun from my fingers and tossed it on the ground as he tore me away from Frankie's dead body. He shielded me with his body as the first sob escaped my lips.

I grabbed handfuls of his jacket and shook as I screamed into the night, all of the fear and rage ripping from my body as shock set in. I screamed over and over again, the noise piercing even my own ears as Jed tried desperately to calm me down.

My voice gave out, and I crumbled in his arms, feeling all the emotions at once.

"Shh, baby." Jed soothed. "I've got you. It's all over, Carly. I promise you're safe, I'm right here."

I sobbed as he wrapped his hands around my face and tilted it up to look at him and he kissed me, molding his lips to mine in a way that forced me to feel the pain he'd felt the whole time too and I took it. I took every ounce of pain from him and let my love for him wash it all away.

"Is he dead?" I asked, taking a shaky breath when he finally pulled away.

"Yes."

"Good," I whispered, staring up into his dark eyes. Eyes with gold flakes like Laila's. "Your sister." I gasped and looked around his arm to where I'd left her, but Jed pulled me back, shielding me from looking out over the carnage.

"Diesel's got her. She's safe." He said, pushing my hair back.

"Carly." Ryker's voice called from behind Jed, and he turned with me in his arms until I saw my best friend's husband. He sighed and sagged a bit when he saw me standing there, safe. "Thank fuck." He walked forward and pulled me out of Jed's arms, and I was pretty sure Ryker was the only person in the world that Jed would have let me go to right now. Ry crushed me against his chest and took a deep calming breath and then pulled me back to look at him. "Are you okay?" he asked, looking over the blood on my body.

I nodded, "It's Frankie's." He looked past me to where Frankie lay on the ground. "I killed him," I whispered.

Ryker looked over at Jed and then back to me. "Good." He said confidently and held my stare. "Kill or be killed, Carly. That's the code we live by, and you're as much a part of this as we are now. You're part of this family, don't ever fucking forget that again."

I nodded and felt his intensity, and so did Jed because he pulled me back and into his arms. Diesel and Laila walked up, he was holding her up as she shook worse than I did, and I wanted to comfort her but knew doing so, covered in blood, wouldn't help.

They came to a stop in front of us, and I looked up at Jed as he looked his sister over. They were complete strangers to each other, but in a second, I saw the scared little girl who leaned on her older brother for protection. She started crying, and I pushed Jed towards her, and he caught her seconds before she hit the ground.

My entire body broke into a cold sweat, watching them embrace, feeling the pain of their lives pulsating around them.

"Who is that?" Ryker asked, putting his jacket over my shoulders as I shook.

"His sister. She was taken from him when he was twelve, and she was sold into trafficking at some point." I swallowed, keeping my voice low. "She protected me today and got raped for it. Right in front of my eyes, Ryker." I said, shaking my head back and forth as it all weighed on me. "That piece of shit Titus was attacking me," My hands went to my throat where I could still feel his hands around my neck. "And she protected me."

His grip tightened on my shoulders as we watched Jed and Laila hold onto each other, "Jed killed Titus. It's all over now."

"Yeah, I guess so," I said and turned to watch as Shadeport crew and Reapers marched people outside of the building in lines with their hands over their heads. "What are you going to do to them?" I asked, noticing most of them were customers and girls. The Bloods had been all killed when they came outside to the attack.

"We'll help the girls the best we can, and we'll make sure the customers don't ever dare to buy a girl again for fear of what we'll do to them now that we know who they are."

I nodded, "Thank you." I looked up at him. "Thank you for helping me when I was stupid and got in over my head."

He gave me a one-sided grin and nodded back. "Yeah well, my wife would have killed me if I did anything less than the impossible for you."

I laughed, surprising myself as it bubbled up and broke out over my lips, and I covered my mouth. "I want to go home."

Jed turned towards me as Laila broke away from him and hugged me, wrapping her thin arms around my jacket-covered body and holding onto me. "Thank you, Carly." She whispered.

I shook my head, "I'm in your debt now, Laila. Not the other way around." I smiled at her as Jed came back to me and wrapped an arm around both of our shoulders. We watched as the Madam and the driver and Ogre were marched from the building too. The woman was outraged and screaming in fury as Zeke shoved her to the ground and looked over at me.

"What's the justice for these three?" He asked me, letting me decide what happened to them. I looked over at Laila, and she took a deep breath and held my stare. "Death for all," I said confidently. "How you choose to do it is your decision."

With that I turned away, walking away from the scene with Laila and Jed as gunshots rang out behind us.

Then there was silence.

CHAPTER 18 – JED

I stood in the doorway to our bedroom and watched Carly sleep in the center of our bed, the bedside table light casting a warm glowing light over her soft skin. She was curled in the fetal position, clutching the blankets in her hands tightly as her eyelids fluttered and the muscles in her face twitched.

She was having another nightmare.

It was four am, and this was the third one that had physically assaulted her tonight. I'd rescued her from the brothel that was trying to sell her last night, and my heart had broken over and over again in the last twenty-four hours, watching the weight her kidnapping had put on her soul. She'd insisted on taking Laila to the hospital last night, and we did, using Ryker's private wing with Dr. Boyd to care for her. A wave of overwhelming emotion crashed over me last night—joy, sorrow, relief—as I saw my baby sister after nearly twenty years, in that desolate place, knowing her pain.

I should have looked harder for her.

I let my self-doubt get in the way of searching for her, thinking she was better off without me, and instead, she'd been trafficked, getting raped and used repeatedly for years.

Carly didn't talk much after her rescue, and Laila said even less as she let Dr. Boyd give her sedation in the hospital to help her rest, and I was left reeling, with more questions than answers about what happened in that building. But I forced myself to just hold on to Carly as she clung to me and not berate her with my wants and needs right away. Elora promised Carly that she would look after Laila while Carly went home and rested, her best friend knew she wouldn't want to leave my sister alone after their rescue, and Carly had finally agreed to come home and sleep.

But it was killing me not knowing what happened to her.

When we got home as dawn kissed the sky this morning, she crawled into the shower and rubbed her skin raw, and sobbed as I held her upright until she could physically keep her eyes open no longer. Then I'd carried her off to bed and held her as her body gave out on her and she passed out. And she hadn't left the bed since.

Twenty-four hours of agony, laying in our bed as her body and her mind battled each other, and I was tormented by not being able to help her. I set my scotch down on the bedside table and took my shirt off, crawling into bed with just a pair of sweats on and sliding next to her curled-up frame.

"Carly," I whispered, gently pushing her honey-blonde hair back off her sweaty face. "Baby it's me, wake up," I said softly, not wanting to scare her. Her eyes snapped open, and she looked at me and then looked around the room with quick, panicky movements before her muscles relaxed into my touch.

"Jed." She whispered and slid forward, burying her face in my neck and taking a couple of deep breaths. Thank God she never shied away from my touch since rescuing her, it would have broken my heart to feel her cower from me, although I would have understood it. I couldn't do much to soothe her right now, but at least I could hold her. "What time is it?" She asked.

"Four am, you were dreaming again," I said, running my hand over the back of her head, smoothing her hair in a way I knew she loved.

She snuggled in closer to me and sighed. "I'm sorry."

"Don't." I snapped, and she flinched. I cursed under my breath and forced my body to relax and I felt hers ease in my arms as I did. "Don't apologize for something you have no control over," I said gently.

"I meant about leaving at all." She said softly and then pulled back to look at me. "I didn't think there was any other way to save Ellie from the pain of being exposed by him like that."

"I know," I whispered. Kissing her forehead and taking a deep calming breath of her scent. "I know you were just trying to fix it."

Her body shuddered against mine, and she crawled into me further. "I was so scared." She said with a breath. It was the first time she had said anything about it at all. I stayed quiet and held her as she worked it out in her head. "They didn't," She started and stopped. "He tried—but he didn't." I pulled her even tighter to me. "Laila saved me from being raped by Titus." My skin burned as I forced myself to lay still and calm as she spoke of her terror. "He raped her instead." She cried, and her shoulders shook as she let her pain out. "I asked her why she took my place, why she was so selfless for someone she didn't even know, and she told me it was because she owed you, her life. I couldn't figure it out at first, and then it just clicked. Like a lightbulb in my head, I recognized her features as similar to yours, and it all made sense."

"How did she know you were mine?" I asked.

"Earlier in the day, the Madam demanded to know who Frankie was running from, and I told her, trying to scare her into letting me go. I told her that not only was Frankie on the run from Ryker but that I was your girl and Ellie's best friend and that you'd burn her world to the ground to get me back. Laila was there during that conversation, but she never said anything. But then Titus came down to the basement and tried to—" She shook again. "He was so close, Jed." Her voice broke. "But once he attacked her, I fought to get to her. I tried, but they had chained me to the ground, and I couldn't get free. I tried." She hiccuped as she cried harder. "I tried to save her, I promise I did. If I'd known Jed, I would have traded places with her at that moment. I never would have let her intervene if I'd known what was going to happen to her."

"I know that, Carly." I said, pulling her head back and forcing her to look at me, "I don't blame you, baby."

"But I do." She cried. "He did it because he couldn't have me, because of the auction."

"I know Kitten." I soothed. "I know. But it's over now. He'll never touch you again."

"You killed him for me." She said, looking deep into my eyes. "You killed him for her."

"I killed them all for you, Carly," I said strongly. "They're never going to touch you again."

"I'll never be able to tell you how much you mean to me, Jed." She said, throwing her leg over my hip and rolling so she was on top of me. "I'll never be able to get used to how it feels in here," She grabbed my hand and put it flat on her chest over her heart, "every single second of every day since you first kissed me. I love you so much I ache from it."

Tears rolled down her cheeks as she stared down at me, and I lost myself in the bottomless depths of her blue eyes. I tangled my fingers in her hair and pulled her mouth down on mine, consuming her lips in a kiss that scared us both. It was raw and primal, and I had held back on it until now, afraid she would be scared by my lust after her attack, but she matched my intensity. Her tongue tangled with mine, and her nails dug into my chest as she rocked her hips.

"Jed, please." She whimpered, sliding her hand into her hair to tangle her fingers with mine that held her there. "I need your pain. I need to feel your brutality." She pulled our fingers, pulling her hair and tilting her head back as her eyes fluttered at the sensation.

"I should be gentle with you." I groaned, "I should be loving and tender, Carly."

She growled and bit my lip, drawing blood. "I need to know you still want me so badly that you can't control yourself, Jed." She licked the blood away from my lip and reached between our bodies to grab my cock. "I need to know that you still want me like you used to, that they didn't take that from me too."

"Kitten," I grunted as her tiny fist squeezed my bare cock inside the waistband of my sweats as she pumped me.

"Consume me, baby." She begged. "Make me forget everything else."

Any restraint I had or worries that she wasn't ready for me, broke away when she begged me like that. I flipped her over onto her back and crushed her body with mine as she spread her legs and arms, welcoming me against her. Our lips tangled and our hands were wild.

I grabbed the old shirt of mine that she was wearing and ripped it open, straight down the middle, and bared her naked body to me as she moaned.

"Yes." She panted, grabbing a fistful of my hair, and pulling my head down to her breast. I bit her nipple and then sucked it into my mouth hard as her hips bucked under me, rubbing her silky pussy against my stomach. I licked my way across her chest to her other nipple and attacked it the same way as she mewed and begged for more underneath me. "I want to suck your cock." She panted, "Please, Jed, fuck my mouth."

I growled and bit her neck, trying to contain my need for her as she clawed my back and arms.

"Yes!" She screamed, tilting her head to the side to give me more access to her flesh.

I popped my teeth off her skin and crawled up her body until my knees were on each side of her chest. I grabbed a fistful of her hair and pulled her head up, holding my cock in my hand. "This what you want, Kitten?" I asked.

She purred and licked the head of my cock, cleaning the bead of come off the tip, and moaned. "Give it to me, baby, fuck my mouth."

I pushed my cock into her mouth, all the way down her fucking throat, using the grip in her hair to pull her head up and down me. "Fuck!" I hissed as her nails dug into my ass, pulling me closer and down her throat even more.

She hummed and moaned, slurping up and down my cock as she sucked me like a fucking pro. My balls were tight, and my orgasm pushed forward, nearly making me come after only a few minutes of her sucking on me. "God, that feels so good." I moaned, throwing my head back. "You're going to make me come, Kitten." My hips jerked, and I pulled her head forward until her nose touched my stomach. She gagged and her eyes watered as she stared up my body at me, but not once did she try to get me off of her. She clung to me, demanding more, even as her body protested the invasion. I pulled her hair, pulling her off my cock as spit spilled from her lips onto her chest. "Do you have any fucking idea how incredibly sexy you are to me, Carly James?" I asked through clenched teeth.

I rubbed her spit into her chest with my hands, fondling her tits as she wrapped her fists around my cock and kept sucking on me.

"Come for me," She demanded. "I want you to come down my throat."

My balls tightened even more as she grabbed them, rolling them in her hand, and she let her fingers slide under them against my taint.

"Fuck." I roared and slapped my hands against the wall over the headboard, holding myself up. She sucked me deep again and used her dainty little fingers against my taint and then even further back, gently rubbing them over my ass. "Carly!"

She moaned and smirked at me as she popped my cock from her mouth, licking up the underside of it and then she sucked her fingers into her mouth and coated them with her saliva. "Tell me how it feels." She demanded as she slid her hand back under my balls and rubbed her slick fingers over my ass as she swirled her tongue over the head of my cock. I looked down at her through my arms and watched as her eyes lit on fire.

An inferno burned inside of them as she touched me in a place we'd never explored before.

"Tell me." she demanded again as I fought not to swallow my tongue altogether.

"It feels..." I growled as my eyes crossed, and my chest seized. "It feels amazing." With anyone else, I might have felt awkward or embarrassed, but as she pressed one tiny finger against my asshole and deep-throated my cock, I felt only bliss.

Blinding, golden bliss that took away my ability to even breathe. My entire body locked tight as my orgasm shot up my spine and through my balls. Come erupted out of my cock as she pushed her finger into my ass and hummed around me, swallowing me down her throat as the biggest orgasm of my life ripped out of me.

She never stopped her gentle touches, even as my orgasm faded and I came down from the high, she kissed and licked her way up and down my cock as she withdrew her finger and gently rolled my balls in her hand before laying back on the pillow and staring up at me with such wonder in her eyes.

I rolled off of her and collapsed on the bed, throwing my arm over my eyes as I tried to figure out what I ever did in life to deserve a woman like Carly Renee James. "I love you." I panted, reaching over, and grabbing her hand to hold onto my stomach. I turned my head and looked at her from under my arm and smirked at her, "How did I get so fucking lucky with you?"

She turned on her side and curled into my side, "I hope we never find out because then maybe the appeal will wear off and you'll leave me."

"Never." I bit out and lifted her, pulling her over my body until her knees rested on each side of my head. "Now ride my face to get that pretty pussy nice and creamy for me, because I'm going to fuck you so hard, even your womb will know who it belongs to."

Her eyes rolled as her hips involuntarily jerked, pushing her pussy closer to my mouth. Primal talk like that always turned Carly into an animal. Her body badly wanted me to knock her up, even if her head told her it was crazy.

I pulled her the last inch forward and directly onto my mouth and sucked on her swollen clit, flicking it with my tongue and nibbling it with my teeth as she held onto the headboard and rocked her hips.

"Fuck that feels good." She hissed. I held both of her ass cheeks in my hands, rocking her back and forth on my mouth and tongue fucked her pussy while using my whiskers to stimulate her clit.

She grabbed a handful of my hair and held onto my head like a handle and rode my face, exactly like I told her to. I ran two fingers through her wet folds, coating my fingers, and then pushed them into her ass. She moaned and leaned forward, exposing her ass more to my exploring and I fucked her with them.

"Don't stop." She panted. "Fuck me just like that baby."

"Hmm." I moaned around her clit and that did it. She came off like a box of fireworks, erupting in every direction as her arms and legs both twitched and convulsed around my head as her clit throbbed in my mouth.

She rode out each wave of pleasure until she collapsed forward and sagged against the wall.

"Turn around," I said, slapping her ass painfully and lifting her.

"I need a second." She whined, but I knew she was ready for me. The sooner after her orgasm, the better.

"No."

She slapped at my hand, but I didn't wait as I laid her back against my chest and brought her legs up to her chest, spreading her wide open for me. "Hold your legs back like this," I demanded. "Don't let them down."

She slid her hands under her knees and held her thighs against her chest as I grabbed the base of my rock-hard cock and lined it up with her soaking wet soft pussy and forced it in. I lifted my hips and slid in through her tense muscles and bottomed out.

"Baby!" She gasped.

"Be a good girl and take my cock." I ordered. But I had more in store for her than just that. I knew this angle was pushing the head of my cock right against her g-spot, and I knew what I could make her body do if I put my mind to it. I bit her ear and sucked on it as I pushed my palm flat against her lower stomach and rubbed her clit with my fingertips.

I used the palm of my hand and rubbed small circles against her stomach, and I could feel my cock through her soft flesh as I fucked her hard.

"Oh, my God!" She shrieked.

"That's it, baby," I growled in her ear.

Her hands let go of her legs as she clawed at my arms, holding on as I pushed harder with my palm and angled my hips even more, pushing my cock forward into her stomach more.

"Jed stop!" She panted, but I tightened my arms around her and held her exactly how I wanted her.

"Not a chance Kitten, I'm going to make that pussy squirt for the first time. You're so close, I can fucking taste it."

"No, no, no, no." She begged, but she rolled her hips, rubbing her clit against my hand even as her words tried to make me stop.

"Yes," I growled and slid towards the end of the bed, planting my feet flat on the floor and sitting up so she was spread open in my lap as I fucked her hard. Her head lolled as I fucked her wildly. I was so fucking deep inside of her I could feel her cervix against the head of my cock with each thrust.

She was clawing at my arms and thrashing around as I pushed her closer to her wet orgasm, and my body ached to feel her break around me like that.

I needed it.

"Give it to me, Kitten, squirt for me."

"Fuck!" She screamed, and her back arched as hot liquid branded my cock inside of her pussy. I pulled my cock out and rubbed my fingers over her pussy vigorously as she coated the hardwood floor between my legs and screamed violently. "Yes! More!" She demanded and I pushed my cock back into her and fucked her hard again, never letting up on the pressure on her stomach or her clit. "Fuck Jed, please! Please do it again!"

"You beg like such a good girl," I growled into her ear, and she threw her head back against my shoulder and bit my neck. "Yes." I bit out as my pain and pleasure mixed.

I fucked her like a man on the edge of a mental break, I didn't care about anything else past her pleasure and she quickly reached her peak again.

"I'm going to come again!" She gasped, shocked and delirious about it.

Within seconds the liquid heat branded my cock again and I pulled out, showering the floor with her vicious orgasm as she convulsed in my arms until I couldn't take it for another second. I stood up and threw her face down on the bed and slammed my cock back into her soaked pussy, pressing her shoulders down into the mattress as I fucked her madly. I wrapped both hands over the tops of her shoulders and pulled her back hard with every thrust, forcing her to take every inch of my cock. "Take it, baby," I demanded as she whimpered and moaned beneath me. "Take every fucking drop," I said and then roared as I came, filling her body with my orgasm, uncaring about anything else in the world as I emptied gush after gush into her.

"Oh. My. God." She panted, with a death grip on the bed sheets as I continued to stroke my cock in and out of her, unable to make myself stop. "Baby."

"I need to taste us." I panted into her ear as I pulled my body off of her and dropped to my knees behind her.

"Oh fuck." She said but spread her legs wide for me as I pulled her ass cheeks apart, opening her pussy for me. I ran my tongue up from her clit to her ass and then dipped it in, tasting every single thing we'd done in the last hour, mixing it into one indulgent treat. "I can't." She said and laughed lightly, crawling away from me up onto the bed and collapsing.

I wiped my mouth and climbed in after her, pulling the blankets up around us and pulling her into my arms.

"I need to get up and *mop* the mess up." She said, groaning and hiding her face behind her hands.

I chuckled and kissed her forehead. "It will be there when we wake up baby. We can clean it up then."

She settled into my arms and sighed against my neck. "How did you make me forget? That whole time, I didn't think about anything but you and me right here and now."

"Then I did my job well," I said, running my hands up and down her spine as silence fell over us. After a long time, she finally spoke.

"I want Laila to live here with us." She said, leaning up to look at me. "I want to help her, to take care of her." Her blue eyes were so serious and clear as she waited for me to reply.

"I love you for that, Carly. But we'll ask her what she wants. She hasn't gotten to decide for herself for a long time, and I think it's time we give her back that control."

"Okay." She said and laid her head back down on my shoulder. "I love you so much, Jed."

"I love you more," I whispered into her hair and finally felt a bit of peace in my soul for the first time in almost twenty years. I didn't know what the fuck I'd done to deserve her, or how I'd managed to save her from that brothel before something terrible happened to her. But I was going to take every single opportunity that I got from here out to prove to her that I was worthy of her love and that she deserved to be happy and taken care of.

I was going to take care of her because if something like this ever happened again to her, I'd never recover from it.

Even her sunshine wouldn't be able to warm up the darkness in my soul if I watched her suffer ever again.

EPILOGUE – CARLY

Months had passed, since my ordeal with the Youngblood MC. I found myself pausing some days, in the middle of some mundane task around the house, or halfway through a spreadsheet at work, and I'd be transported back to that day.

I'd remember different things each time, some days it was the smell of the mask the men had put over my head in the car. Other times it was the way the iron shackle around my ankle cut through the skin as I fought against it. The especially cruel days would bring back the feel of Titus' fingers around my neck, breaking off my ability to breathe, or the warm splatter of blood on my face as I shot Frankie over and over.

Those days were harder to shake off and move on from.

I killed a man.

A friend.

In a brutal way.

And that lived inside of me every single day. But I didn't always feel the darkness of that event like a bad thing. Some days it felt like a color of my character had been revealed in that moment. Maybe that darkness lived inside everyone somewhere, buried or repressed down deep in our souls, and only in extreme circumstances, does it come into play.

Jed had that darkness inside of him.

He unleashed it the day he killed his father. When he chose to run with the Shadeport Crew, he gave that darkness power in his life, and he used it often from then on. And that didn't make him weak, or bad.

It made him strong.

Powerful.

It gave him control.

And control was something I thrived on having in my life after that fateful day. It gave me peace and purpose.

I no longer hosted at Lux, but I still ran the marketing of both the strip club and Erotiq for Ryker. I enjoyed the behind-the-scenes gig, and it allowed me the flexibility to work when I wanted to.

Which came in handy, since little Gavin Lawson was born last month. Elora and I had been sitting around the kitchen island in the Mansion when her water broke, and I was by her side every minute after that until my best friend pushed my baby nephew into the world hours later.

And I soaked up as much time with him as possible, even still. And rocking him in the shade of our front porch was one of my favorite pastimes.

I looked down at the adorable baby boy in my arms, wrapped up in a black minky blanket with a matching black hat with his name written across the front, and couldn't help the smile that pulled my lips.

"You don't smile at me like that anymore." I looked up from sweet little Gavin's button nose and watched Jed walk towards the house.

God, he was sexy.

He had his hand in the pants pocket of his suit as he walked up the steps with a devilish grin on his face.

"I do too," I said and tilted my head back, offering my lips to him, which he greedily took and drank from.

"Hmm." he said, pressing his forehead against mine and breathing me in. "I missed you."

"Is that why you're stopping home in the middle of the day?" I asked as he walked around my chair and sat down in the one next to me, leaning over and putting his giant hand on Gavin's head and gently kissing it. Watching this dark and dangerous man of mine, gentle himself for this baby boy, did certain things to my insides.

My ovaries to be exact.

And he fucking knew it too.

"Yes, and no." He said, sitting back and crossing his ankles out in front of him, looking relaxed.

"Uh oh," I said, watching him.

"Ryker and I have to go away for the night, maybe two." He said, looking at me out of the corner of his eye as he sighed. "And I don't want to fucking do it."

"I'll be okay," I said quietly, but even I heard the lack of conviction in my voice.

He reached over and put his hand on the back of my neck and rubbed the tense muscles there as I looked down into Gavin's perfect face. He stretched and cooed in my arms, and I smiled at him.

"I know you'll be okay because you're staying in the mansion with Ellie and Gav while Ryker and I are gone." He said plainly.

"I can stay out here by myself–"

"I know you can, but that doesn't mean I want you to." He cut me off. "Zeke and Laila are staying in the mansion too. It will make it easier for Zeke to have you four all in one place to watch over."

"Zeke and Laila, huh?" I asked, raising my eyebrow at him, and fighting to keep the smile off my face.

"What the fuck is that supposed to mean?" he asked sharply, in full big brother mode.

I shrugged my shoulders and shook my head, "Nothing, Jed, just me being a girl." I said, looking back down as Gavin wrapped his tiny hand around my finger.

Laila moved into the barracks when she was released from the hospital, and I loved having her so close. She had grown to be not only a good friend to me and Ellie both, but a sister as well. The three of us girls were nearly inseparable these last few weeks, and it eased a part of my soul to know she was getting a family after all these years.

We all were.

"What did you mean by it?" he asked, not letting it go.

I chuckled at him and shook my head, "Have you really not seen how he's a completely different man around her?"

He watched me closely as he thought it over in his head before turning away and looking out over the yard. "Motherfucker." He spat out and shook his head.

"Sister fucker is more like it," I said, and he glared at me, and a giggle bubbled up. "Don't worry," I said, sighing and running my fingers through the hair at the back of his neck to relax him. "He hasn't done anything."

"Did she tell you that? That means she knows he wants to, and that's almost as bad, Carly! After what she's been through."

"Stop it." I said firmly, "She hasn't said anything to me about it, other than that she feels safe around him." I widened my eyes, trying to portray the importance of that to him. "You should be happy that someone has that influence on her right now."

He sighed again and cursed under his breath. "He's old."

"He's your age, and she's older than I am, so obviously that's not a valid argument." I deadpanned.

"Doesn't mean I have to like it."

"Doesn't mean there's anything there to like, Jed. Or that it's your place to even have an opinion, baby. She's just trying to figure out who she is now, she's comfortable here with all of us, and that's priceless. So don't you dare even hint to either of them that you disapprove, do you understand me?" I asked firmly.

"Hmm." He hummed, pursing his lips at me. "Give me my nephew." He said suddenly, standing up and lifting Gavin from my arms and then settling down in his chair while Gav cooed and snuggled into his favorite uncle.

"My ovaries are screaming." I mused as I watched them obsessively, and he looked over at me, smiling and winking, looking both heavenly and devilish at the same time.

"Say the word Kitten, and I'll put a baby in you, maybe even two."

"Two?" I asked, surprised.

"My mom was a twin." He said, smoothing his finger down the bridge of Gavin's nose affectionately. "They say it skips a generation, which means there's a good chance we'll have twins when you finally let me knock you up."

I scoffed at him and then jumped as Ryker and Ellie walked around the corner, laughing at him.

"That was romantic." Ryker snorted as Ellie climbed the stairs, holding her hands out for her baby.

Jed tightened his hold on Gav and turned away from her. "No way, I just got him!" He whined, and Ryker rolled his eyes as Ellie swatted him before leaning back against the railing, letting Jed have a minute with the baby. "Besides, he's keeping me from marching into the barracks and tearing Zeke to shreds."

"Why are we attacking Zeke?" Ellie asked, looking from Jed to me and back. I just rolled my eyes and shook my head.

"Laila," I answered, and her eyes rounded.

"Ooh." She said, rounding her lips in understanding.

"What's that supposed to mean?" Ryker asked, leaning on the post looking lost.

Ellie and I fell into a fit of giggles at how clueless men could be about certain things as Ryker looked even more lost.

This was my family.

And I was never letting them go.

The End

OTHER BOOKS

Did you know Ally writes across so many other types of tropes and themes?

Check out some of her other books here.

Looking for Series and Duets?

The Line Walkers Series:
https://a.co/d/bx376wq
Beauty In the Ink Series:
https://a.co/d/6tc8M7M
Bailey Dunn & Co Duet:

https://a.co/d/i9gwqL2

Shadeport Crew Series:

https://a.co/d/dVzGcyo

Kings of Hawthorn Series:

https://a.co/d/h1AITKM

How about some spicy standalones?

Sinister Vows:

https://a.co/d/gbe35fF

Guilty For You:

https://a.co/d/1ef3UPU

Secrets Within Us:

https://a.co/d/cTZ04XQ

AUDIOBOOKS

Did you know that the entire Line Walker Series is getting Audiobooks? EEK!!! I know, I'm so excited too!

Make sure to check out website- www.ammccoybooks.com, social media – Twisted After Dark: A.M. McCoy's Reader Group – on Facebook, and Audible for more details!

Also, did you know that my Beauty In The Ink Series got their very own audiobooks as well? Find those on Audible too!

STALK ME!

Want to stay up to date with all of my shenanigans and upcoming news? Pretty Please?

Check out my website: www.ammccoybooks.com

How about TikTok, are you there? https://www.tiktok.com/@amm ccoy_author?is_from_webapp=1&sender_device=pc

Facebook? I've got a readers group there! Twisted After Dark: A.M. McCoy's Reader Group is mostly unhinged and full of exclusive news! https://www.facebook.com/share/g/b41rkBMkSurWz43i/

IG? https://www.instagram.com/ammccoy_author/

Amazon?
https://www.amazon.com/stores/A.-M.-McCoy/author/B07QNRJ

MLB?ref=ap_rdr&isDramIntegrated=true&shoppingPortalEnabled
=true

I think that's all for now!